Bank of the Clown

Mark Luis Foster

Bloomington, IN   Milton Keynes, UK
authorHOUSE®

AuthorHouse™
1663 Liberty Drive, Suite 200
Bloomington, IN 47403
www.authorhouse.com
Phone: 1-800-839-8640

AuthorHouse™ UK Ltd.
500 Avebury Boulevard
Central Milton Keynes, MK9 2BE
www.authorhouse.co.uk
Phone: 08001974150

This book is a work of fiction. Places, events, and situations in this story are purely fictional. Any resemblance to actual persons, living or dead, is coincidental.

© 2007 Mark Luis Foster. All rights reserved.

No part of this book may be reproduced, stored in a retrieval system, or transmitted by any means without the written permission of the author.

First published by AuthorHouse 03/08/2007

ISBN: 978-1-4259-8595-0 (sc)
ISBN: 978-1-4259-8596-7 (dj)

Printed in the United States of America
Bloomington, Indiana

This book is printed on acid-free paper.

For my wife, Julie, my children, Cody and Annie, and for all corporate employees in America who have ever worked for a clown.

ONE

"The CEO must be eliminated."

The words came out strained and weak, but they were heard as loud as a rifle shot; the concussion was deafening, the implications were devastating.

As the old man spoke, his frail arms struggled to turn his wheelchair just enough to glimpse the last bit of sun as it sank into the Gulf of Mexico. Weak and tired, his confidant was finally with him, steadfastly at his side, a semblance of the old man's former self.

The confidant listened intently to the old man's words as seagulls noisily churned the tropical air above. Through a gravelly voice, dry from age but forced for clarity, the old man made it perfectly clear: The CEO's removal must be accomplished by the result of his own misdeeds, or at least the appearance of such. The maverick that saved the bank and married the old man's daughter must be taken out and summarily crushed under his own weight, with no apparent help from outside forces.

The CEO must be eliminated.

The gray-haired confidant nodded repeatedly to the feeble billionaire, in complete agreement that such a method was the only way in which he could achieve the coveted throne. He was silent, remaining at the old man's side like a sentry, watching him struggle to stay alert.

With eyes weighing heavy and drooping shut, the soft red glow of the sinking sun slowly faded from the old man's wrinkled, ashen, age-worn face.

November 1999

"I'm watching, I'm watching."

Wil Fischer's heart was trying to thump itself cleanly out of his chest, the aftereffect of his phone ringing before 5:30 a.m. Whenever it rang at such an odd hour, Wil always assumed the worst: that his mother's ailing condition had worsened. But on this chilly November morning, it wasn't news about his only surviving parent that had him upset. Instead, his blood pressure was elevated by a tip from a coworker that something was definitely amiss with his Minnesota employer.

Already dressed for the day at such an ungodly hour, Wil Fischer sat on his couch in a pool of discomfort, balancing a bowl of increasingly soggy cereal on his lap while pinching the phone's handset between his chin and shoulder.

"I don't see it," Wil said, hoping to keep milk from dripping from his spoon and onto his pants. His eyes stayed fixed on the words that scrolled just below the talking heads on the TV screen, but his body fidgeted from a ripening impatience. He stared at the computerized text that zipped by from left to right, the words blurring together with each electronically generated pass.

"I just don't see what you're seeing," Wil screeched again into the phone with frustration. "Are you absolutely sure?" He was profoundly irritated that the TV's text kept displaying numerous business headlines that had nothing to do with his employer of 11 years. Yet deep down, emanating from his usually dependable inner compass, he sensed something disturbing, an unstable feeling that convinced him that his coworker was right. He now had to prove to himself whether or not the words "merger" and "Union First Bancorporation" were actually listed together on the 24-hour news channel's business ticker at the bottom of his 19-inch TV set.

"I'm certain you misread it somehow," Wil said, his tone increasingly lacking any conviction. "After what Bob Harrington said, how could there possibly be a merger?"

He wanted to dismiss the thought entirely, remembering that just a few short weeks ago at the Annual Union First Bancorporation Stock Analysts' Meeting, that it was Robert Harrington, the charismatic and highly energetic CEO of the Minneapolis-based financial services company, who had stood in front of several hundred stock analysts and banking journalists to insist that the swirling merger rumors were unfounded. It was the first instance when Mr. Harrington had addressed the issue so directly, a bold attempt to squash a rumor that dogged the $45 billion financial services company during the preceding nine months.

Wil also remembered that Mr. Harrington was daring in his denial. The CEO had projected his repudiation onto a white screen behind the conference podium—words in big black letters—which read: *BIGGER IS NOT BETTER.*

Wil Fischer had felt oddly uncomfortable during that weeklong conference, held at the beautiful if not ostentatious Braemore Lodge and Resort outside of Denver. He had loved the luxurious surroundings, but given the company's recent stock slide, he felt embarrassed that so many Union First employees had been carted out from Minneapolis and Chicago, all at considerable expense, just to demonstrate new banking products and technologies that were barely off of the paper upon which they were originally proposed.

Yet he had also found himself swelling with pride. As a 39-year-old hunyuck from Minnesota, he had mingled among a variety of New York suits, rubbing shoulders with some of the top financial analysts in the country. Many of them stopped by his table in the exhibit hall—his table was one of 14 different demo stations set up for the conference—to ask him mostly repetitive questions about the ongoing development of his new online banking product.

As the product manager, Wil had worried at the time that his cutting-edge banking service wasn't ready for primetime. There was crushing tension from various Union First management groups to get the product out of development and into live production. It was expected to become a huge revenue generator for the bank, so the sales teams that were planning to sell it had been promising the service to existing Union First business customers for more than 18 months.

For the Colorado conference, Wil had to show off the product's potential, a risky way of proving that it would actually allow mid- to large-sized companies to manage their wire transfers and banking transactions via the simplicity of a computer desktop. To allow for his show-and-tell, Wil instructed the development team to use web-based programming, building hyperlinks and screen shots that could be used in a simple graphics presentation, all designed to resemble a product that was ready for the real world. In essence, it was the electronic version of a tall tale, because the product itself was nowhere near as complete as the demo implied. *If I'm forced to lie about this product, I'm going to lie about it well,* he had thought at the time.

BIGGER IS NOT BETTER. Wil had chuckled during the conference at the choice of words, yet the phrase had been comforting to him nonetheless. *It's proof enough for me,* he remembered thinking, *that a merger is nowhere in sight—and it's still game on.*

The information Wil so desperately wanted to dismiss came scrolling across the bottom of his TV screen in his Edina home. With a spoonful of cereal touching his lower lip, his body steadied itself as his blood seemed to solidify inside his veins. He was finally seeing the information with his own eyes, reading it as accurately as he could as the text flew by, his still-asleep brain absorbing each word. He felt a sudden but momentary paralysis, becoming a temporary stone likeness of himself, his deadweight pressing deeper and deeper into his dark leather couch. The phone felt frozen to his face. The only thing missing, it seemed, was a bird perched atop his head...

Union First Bancorporation of Minneapolis to merge with L.A.-based Continental-American Banking Group...

Wil jerked his body back as if hit by a bullet. Suddenly the milk-filled bowl pirouetted off of his lap and onto the expensive tan carpeting below.

"Damn it!" Wil shouted into the phone that was pinned to his ear. "I'll call you back."

He hung up on his coworker and ran to the kitchen to grab a towel. He quickly returned to the living room and tried his best to clean up the growing milk spill that was seeping into the carpet. As he sopped up the liquid and scrubbed the mess, he was drawn to the repeating text that was scrolling across the television.

...Union First to take Continental-American's name...

Given these events, Wil wondered whether that day's planned meetings would take place at all. It was an important day for his $21 million banking product, as he was scheduled to go in front of the U.F. Corporate Development Committee to ask for $2 million in additional funding. The new funds would bring the product into the testing stage where actual customers would stress-test it before the official rollout to Union First's corporate customers.

As he balanced on his knees, alternately sopping and scrubbing his spilled milk, his thoughts turned again to the conference in Colorado, and a feeling of tremendous betrayal welled up inside him. *Just like guys have always been taught,* he mused, *bigger really* IS *better.*

Wil stopped was he was doing. From his crouched position, he stared blankly at the TV. The talking heads finally went to commercial, and the annoying text went away. His brain throbbed.

It was at that very instant when Wil Fischer realized that Robert Harrington, the CEO of Union First Bancorporation, a man he so desperately wanted to trust, was just another big, fat, overpaid liar.

TWO

March 2000

The low rumble of the jet's engines was hypnotic to Wil. It lulled him into a half-comatose state, complete with a stare that locked his eyes in place on an indiscriminate part of the seat in front of him. He hadn't spent so much time in the air since he was a sales director for a regional TV network some years ago.

It was a Sunday night tradition over the past 12 weeks for Wil to pack up his suitcase with enough clothes and supplies to last for four days, and take a cab to the Minneapolis-Saint Paul International Airport for the four-hour flight to Los Angeles. Then, after a full load of merger-related meetings, he would return on Thursday night in time to unpack, wash clothes, and start the cycle all over again.

Union First Bancorporation was now officially in the midst of merger mania with Continental-American Banking Group. Even though months had passed since the original merger announcement, Wil was amazed at how things hadn't changed all that much. He wasn't sure if he felt relief—or frustration. It seemed to him that senior management was moving too slowly in their quest to merge two companies with completely different cultures seamlessly together. *Maybe they just don't know how to do it,* he thought.

As with any large merger, there was significant pressure from Wall Street and shareholders to combine two entities without disrupting customer service at any level. But employees and analysts alike knew that achieving such lofty expectations was always difficult. While the Union First name was synonymous in the banking industry with an outstanding sales culture and customer service, the same was not true for Continental-American Banks. The California holding company was a conglomeration of previous smaller bank mergers, which resulted in a fragmented sales organization and a disenfranchised workforce. Despite its problems, Continental-American alone boasted a total asset size of $145 billion, and operated from more than 900 retail bank branches in 19 mostly western states.

Wil sat back in his seat and looked out the window across the miles of vast Nebraska landscape that retreated some

35,000 feet below him. He knew this week was going to be especially tough; it wasn't going to be the normal round of rudderless meetings to which he had grown accustomed. This time, he had to demonstrate his online product in a live Internet environment at the Annual Nationwide Cash Management Trade Show near Los Angeles. This meeting symbolized the first attempt at combining the Union First and Continental-American business units into a single operating entity, even though the merger was not yet officially consummated.

He also knew his audience was to be especially difficult. Unlike the apathetic stock analysts who saw a smoke-and-mirrors demonstration of his product in Colorado some months earlier, this audience of cash management leaders from middle- and large-corporate businesses would be highly inquisitive and critical. Wil's product had to perform as advertised in a real-world environment on a show floor filled to the rafters with doubting Thomases.

Wil realized more than anyone on the team that despite additional funding and good development progress, his product was still plagued with technical glitches. It needed several hundred hours of development tweaks in order to make it battle-ready for the marketplace. But Union First management stayed on his back to ensure the product became viable, all in the hopes of becoming a showcase to Continental-

American's higher-ups in a kind of *look-what-our-team-can-do* boast. It was a bold approach that Union First's Information Technology management thought could somehow save its own Minneapolis teams from complete merger-related extinction.

I just need to get through this without a major system failure, Wil thought. *This thing cannot fail.*

The jet screeched to a halt at LAX and lumbered down the taxiway to the waiting gate. Once the lighted seatbelt signs were extinguished, Wil jumped into the cramped aisle that was filled with mostly tourists heading from Minneapolis's gray spring weather to the sunny shores of California's beaches.

Inside the gate, Wil was met by Lanny Taylor, a Continental-American Banking Group employee who had worked in the company's Cash Management Division in L.A. for the past 10 years. But Lanny wasn't a typical Californian. Fighting a constant weight problem and sporting pale skin, he might as well have been from Duluth, Minnesota, rather than from the warm, sun-baked streets of Alameda that he called home. At age 37, Lanny was only slightly younger than Wil, but he had been in banking all of his adult life. Since meeting Lanny during the early days of the merger meetings, Wil relied on his newfound friend for his sharp technical and programming skills—something Wil lacked.

Wil was always easy to spot in any crowd. His six-foot frame and brown hair towered above the mostly Minnesota crowd that spilled through the gate's jet way door. As soon as Lanny spotted him, he raced up to Wil as though he was about to execute a linebacker's tackle.

"You're on time for a change," Lanny said, thrusting out his big right hand for Wil to grab.

"Of all the weeks for that to happen," Wil shot back sarcastically, clasping his friend's hand. "You know how much I'm dreading this."

"Got a great parking spot," Lanny said, ignoring Wil's uneasiness. "Just a short walk from here and then I'll take you right to the hotel."

Lanny and Wil drove to the hotel convention center near Marina Del Rey with little trouble on that late Sunday afternoon. Soon Lanny's car was taking the turn into the roundabout in front of the massive complex, the car's brakes squeaking from overuse and slowing the vehicle to a halt. Bellmen were overrunning the place, and it wasn't long before a red-suited, twenty-something was opening up the passenger door.

Wil's right foot had swung out onto the colored concrete drive when Lanny's voice boomed. "I'll have them valet this thing and I'll warm up a beer for you while you check in." This was also a ritual during the past several weeks: Lanny would pick up Wil, then they would wile away their time together at the hotel bar. While Wil had no qualms about frequenting bars no matter what city he happened to be in, he often wondered how Lanny could justify spending so much time away from his wife and three young boys, especially on a Sunday afternoon, while Wil visited L.A.

Despite their differences in life, Lanny and Wil had become fast friends. Their friendship represented what was probably an idyllic partnership, a kind of Pollyannaish joint venture of cooperation between two different men from two entirely different companies who were caught up in the midst of absolute chaos.

"Can we rain check this one, Lanny?" Wil asked sheepishly. "I need some time to get ready for tomorrow. I've really got to get some rest."

Lanny frowned. "What? "You Minnesotans. You just can't handle your liquor."

Wil shook his head. "Go see your family. You and I are together through Thursday. Plenty of time for beer and such." Wil exited the car with purpose and opened the rear passenger door to grab his bags from the back seat. "I'll see you tomorrow," he said, stooping low enough to keep his head inside the car. "Thanks for the ride."

Lanny shot Wil a look of disappointment as the rear door slammed. He then sped off with a weak wave. Wil watched as the car rolled along the half-moon drive and bounced its way back onto the thoroughfare. To clear his guilty feelings for making Lanny pick him up—only to dump his bar date at the hotel's doors—Wil stopped to look skyward, letting the warm California sun heat up his solar-starved cheeks.

"May I get your bags, sir?" the crackly voice of the bellman asked, taking Wil out of his momentary bliss.

Wil let out a long sigh. "No thanks. I've got them." Wil was used to doing things himself. He joined the bank just as downsizing was in full swing and when the *do more with less* mantra permeated all levels of the company. He climbed the ranks of Union First in marketing, all without the help of many complementary personnel or real resources of any kind. The days of deep pockets and thick bank staff were a thing of the past, but Wil knew no differently. He made a name for himself by being a strong manager of major projects. Throughout his career, no mission or objective was too large for him. He was unflappable—and he was respected for it.

Lingering a moment in the California sun, the bellman still hovered, so Wil handed him a couple of bucks to make him go away. Wil turned sharply with bags in hand, walking between the clusters of palm trees that book-ended the hotel convention center's grand entrance. His latest mission to prove his product—and himself—had begun.

THREE

The legal consummation of the merger between L.A.-based Continental-American Banking Group and Minneapolis-based Union First Bancorporation was just weeks away, and newspapers in the Twin Cities began sporting display ads from area banks that were trying to make hay out of the current round of merger mania. Nearly every other page of the two metropolitan daily papers included ads that touted such archaic themes as *friendlier neighborhood service, the better choice for your banking* and the *anti-banking bank*.

There was one man who was paying especially close attention to all of the noise, smelling an opportunity. Richard Edmund "Dick" Cramer, the 59-year-old CEO of Midwest Federated Bank, had a penchant for wedging himself and his company into any fracas of the moment.

An ex-Marine and former steel worker, Mr. Cramer worked his way into banking when the industry was still asleep. Starting as a commercial banker at a small financial holding company in New Jersey, he was quickly promoted and was soon running its half-billion-dollar commercial banking division. Over the course of 15 years, he jumped to several banks located in other markets, serving as a vice president here, a bank president there, until he met Ms. Harriet Updike, the daughter of wealthy Minnesota real estate baron Randall K. Updike, who just happened to own a sleepy little bank in Saint Paul.

In the mid-1980s, Midwest Federated Bank had fallen on hard times and was on the brink of collapse. With the rich love of Harriet Updike on his side, Mr. Cramer and a tight band of close colleagues quit their cushy jobs at other institutions and swooped in to take charge. Before long they had completely reinvented the bank, converting it to a national charter. Within seven years of the turnaround, Midwest Federated went public with a stock price of $8. Several years later, the bank's stock had risen dramatically, and even with a subsequent stock split, it still commanded a $22 price. While some critics credited the turnaround to sheer luck, it was an unprecedented recovery for a company that, during its low point, had several analysts predicting its demise within a few short months. By 1999, Midwest

Federated Bank was a regional banking powerhouse, managing more than $10 billion in assets and 348 retail branches located in Minnesota, North and South Dakota, Missouri, and Nebraska.

To the common person, Dick Cramer projected an image of humble roots and established himself as the self-proclaimed "champion of the little guy." But despite his well-crafted public image, Mr. Cramer didn't make many friends during his meteoric banking rise. His brash, sandpaper approach to business dealings often left much wreckage behind, especially when working with outsiders who didn't understand his acerbic style. During the darker years of the company's turnaround, he often squeezed local service providers such as software and office supply companies so hard that they made no profit at all on Midwest Federated's business. Those providers often had such a bad experience that they vowed never to work with him again.

While Mr. Cramer's impetuous, ex-military style didn't mesh well with many people he encountered, those who were within the inner circle became loyal admirers of his no-nonsense, gut-following, times-a-wasting approach that was employed on every strategy and tactic he pursued. Throughout his life, wives also came and went every few years, but some observers thought he showed better judgment in

Harriet Updike Cramer, who was finally someone closer to his own age.

Sitting in his second-floor office in the opulent Midwest Federated headquarters building on Wabasha Street in downtown Saint Paul, Mr. Cramer paged through the morning's paper, reviewing the glut of banking ads that peppered the newsprint. Pages flew by faster and faster between his hands, and he got more agitated the deeper he delved into the paper's front section.

"Marci!" he yelled out the door to his assistant, his voice ricocheting down the Persian-rug-littered hallway just outside his office. "Get Barney on the phone, right now!"

Barney Jennings was the bank president of the Midwest Federated Bank locations in Minnesota, the oldest bank charter of the holding company. With regional headquarters based in downtown Minneapolis, Mr. Jennings had 75 branches in his operation, the majority of which were located within the seven-county metro area. Unlike the clan of executives who were brought in by Mr. Cramer in the 1980s to help right the ship, and placed in cushy jobs to reap the company's profits with little expended effort, Mr. Jennings was considered an inheritance—something of a rollover. While Mr. Cramer had dismissed the majority of the team he inherited back then, Mr. Cramer saw something in Barney W. Jennings that was worth saving. Soon after blowing into town and taking over the reins, Mr. Cramer asked Mr. Jennings to stay on—an offer that was gladly accepted. No matter the sources of his management team's talent, Mr. Cramer was known for rewarding his best cronies for having weathered the tough days that preceded this newfound period of prosperity.

"Barney!" Mr. Cramer barked over his speakerphone, both hands resting comfortably atop his thinning, dyed, jet-black hair. "What are you doing down there to take advantage of this Union First merger? Barney? You have thirty seconds." Mr. Cramer had an odd habit of calling out a response time when he was irritated. It was an intimidation tactic he normally reserved for much lesser subordinates who often crumbled under the pressure of a minute or less to explain some problem. But Mr. Jennings was used to this approach after all these years and simply viewed it as a timesaver. When impatient, Mr. Jennings didn't have to interpret the emotion in Cramer's voice or read his body language. Instead, he was provided with a convenient countdown.

"We're-we're-we're working on a few things, Dick," Mr. Jennings said in his trademark stutter, a kind of skipping start to sentences whenever he responded thoughtfully to someone.

"Like what?" Mr. Cramer bellowed.

"Direct-direct-direct mail. We're targeting non-Midwest Federated households around our branches asking them to consider us if they're tired of other banks merging."

"Damn it, Barney," Mr. Cramer snapped. "You're wasting money with that scheme. We ought to mail around Union First's branches, not our own. Those Union First customers are the ones who are vulnerable. If people live near our own branches and haven't switched their banking to us yet, then they likely never will."

Mr. Jennings was calm, but his stuttering always worked against his usually steady demeanor. "We-we-we considered that, Dick. But-but-but we felt that the overlap of Union First branches isn't that substantial, so most of those households would find us too inconvenient to come to bank with—"

"Bull!" Mr. Cramer said. "We need to grow households. We've got to expand our market share to stay viable here and hit our financial numbers, and strike when the iron's hot, Barney. The net's got to be cast wider. I'd like to see us advertise in the papers on this one. We've got to take advantage of this merger mess while people are ticked off. People will switch banks while they're ticked off, Barney, but we need to hit them while they're still ticked off!"

Mr. Jennings let the silence just hang there, an uncomfortable pause that kept stretching until he could focus and respond as thoughtfully as possible. "I-I-I agree," he replied softly. "We'll-we'll-we'll figure it out and get back to you."

"Good." Conversations with Mr. Cramer's cronies were often brief and clipped when he was on the warpath. At the end of his lashings, he usually didn't bother to say goodbye, opting instead to punch off the speakerphone button as though he was launching a missile. After doing just that to Barney W. Jennings, Mr. Cramer picked up the newspaper again and started in on the Sports Section, his blood pressure returning to its normal, icy state.

FOUR

The hotel's convention center was filling up with attendees early, and Wil couldn't understand why. The L.A. weather was warm, bright, and smog-less. *Why aren't these people out walking along the beach?* he wondered.

He felt uncomfortable being inside of Continental-American Bank's excessively large display exhibit that was sprawled out on the show floor. Since Continental-American and Union First were going to be one big, happy family soon, Wil knew that a message of unification would be conveyed to the attendees if both organizations cooperated under one display roof. Despite the reasoning, he still felt like he was inside of enemy territory.

He was delicately balanced on his tiptoes, busily positioning the oversized presentation monitor that was bolted to one corner of the exhibit, when Lanny patted him on the back.

"You okay, Wil?" Lanny asked. "Get your beauty rest last night?"

"I did," Wil said. "I hope you didn't mind."

"Yes, I did mind, but I can forgive you under one condition," Lanny said. "Tonight, we head down the street to that outdoor bar where we ended up last week. Of course, you're picking up the tab."

"Got it all figured out, I see." Wil cracked a smile while nudging the monitor to eliminate a distracting glare caused by the massive candelabras that studded the ceiling above him. Once accomplished, all that was left for him to do was to plug it in and power up the system. With a snap of electricity, the monitor hummed to life, and Continental-American Bank's red, white and blue logo slowly appeared in sharp resolution at the center of the screen.

"I'm impressed," shot Lanny. "You've finally gotten religion."

"Jury's out for me, man," Wil said, shaking his head in mock disgust. "But if we have to call ourselves Continental-American, then we'll call ourselves Continental-American."

A crackling sound interrupted from the public address system overhead. "The exhibit hall is now open," the female voice announced. "All exhibits are to be up and operating."

The din inside the great hall increased dramatically as conventioneers broke away from private conversations and began roaming the exhibits in large groups. There were more than 200 exhibits from a variety of U.S. banks and service providers that were scattered throughout the large space. This convention was a well-attended banking event every year, attracting several thousand people from the financial services industry who were either selling their own products and services, or looking to buy them from someone else. Most of the conventioneers were product managers and tech people who trolled the various vendors and their own competition for the latest gizmos and technology applications. Some participants were from major companies who were looking for more efficient ways to manage their banking resources. But there was also an under-the-radar job recruitment industry at work, with middle managers pressing the flesh with competitors in the hopes of landing the next big corporate banking job. The whole thing was an industrial incest-fest, with banks, vendors and commercial prospects all learning—and stealing—from one another.

As he leaned against a black metal support pole at one corner of the Continental-American display booth, Wil suddenly found himself facing his first customer—a slim, middle-aged man with brown hair who worked for a regional bank in Florida. "That's a nice screen up there," the man said.

"Thanks," Wil answered, a smile allowing for a flash of white teeth. "Our project team worked hard to make sure the user interface was not only easy to navigate, but also pleasing to the eye."

The smile on the face of the man from Florida suddenly disappeared. "Actually, I was talking about the screen. She's a beauty."

Wil raised his eyebrows, realizing with irritation that his prospect was duly impressed with the 45-inch boat anchor that resembled a monitor and sported crystal clarity, and not with the user interface that it was displaying. Wil figured that the man would ask next to have *Wheel of Fortune* put up on the thing. "Yeah, she's a beauty all right," he answered. Wil's posture went limp.

Over the next few hours, things gradually improved for Wil. Although he was on his feet all morning, he found a good rhythm and comfortable zone as he repeated his product demonstrations for anyone who listened. His fears of embarrassment due to some unforeseen failure had quickly diminished. While he did encounter a few minor technical glitches, overall he felt the live product performed very well.

Wil enjoyed it most when he got the right prospects in front of his screen, such as commercial banking customers from California or Minneapolis. It was then that he was in his game, using a good balance of humor and technical prowess to show off his electronic banking marvel to a genuinely interested audience.

Lunchtime came up on him quickly, and he was surprised at how time had flown by. With his feet and back hurting, he limped down the hall toward the ballroom where the demonstrators' luncheon was to be served. He was intercepted by an uncharacteristically rattled Lanny Taylor.

"Steve Korbit wants us up in the hotel restaurant," Lanny said through heavy breaths, sweat beading up on his forehead. "Right now."

"Korbit? What's it about?"

Lanny shrugged. "Dunno. It came up quick. All the presenters were asked to attend."

"Probably has a hangnail," Wil mumbled. He was no fan of his current boss, and he was letting his opinion of the man slip out more and more.

The Hotel Grille was two floors above the hotel's main lobby. As soon as he entered the restaurant, Wil noticed immediately that it faced west with a relatively unobstructed view of the Pacific Ocean, a breathtaking view through six large windows. But despite the gorgeous angle, the place was annoyingly dark, especially for 12:30 in the afternoon. By the time Lanny and Wil arrived at the long table in the center of the restaurant, Steve Korbit and the other five presenters were already seated.

"Gentlemen, I'm so glad you're here," Mr. Korbit said, guiding his disheveled, salt-and-pepper-colored hair off his forehead with his right hand.

Wil felt a sudden chill go through his body. Steve Korbit was in charge of product development for Union First in Minneapolis, but never once in 12 months had he ever told Wil or anyone on his team that he was glad to see them. Steve Korbit's usual motivation was to look out for Steve Korbit, and no one else.

"Thanks for breaking away from the group to meet with me," he said to the group. "I wanted to convey some new information that is merger-related. This is highly confidential, and I need to ask you to keep it that way—at least for now."

Mr. Korbit went silent as the waiter interrupted to take Lanny's and Wil's drink orders. Once the waiter received their requests and moved away, Korbit leaned in, his pointy chin hovering above his empty bread plate. "I just had a joint phone conference between the Union First Senior Development Committee and the Continental-American I.T. management team," he said, sounding boastful and self-important with every word. "They just announced a restructuring. Effective immediately, we are all reporting into L.A. All Minneapolis product staff will be accountable to the Continental-American Information Management Division, which is centered here in California."

There was a mass exhale of frustration from the seated group, but Wil felt remarkably unfazed. "Don't panic, guys," Wil said. "This kind of thing happened all the time in the television industry. One thing I learned is that no merger is going to occur without structural and organizational changes. To think that everything's going to stay the same is just pie in the sky."

"Yes, that's right, Wil," Mr. Korbit said. "Thank you for saying that." He looked away and down at the table. "Wil, I'm afraid there's more."

The optimism on Wil's face dissipated as another shudder ripped through his body. If what Steve Korbit was about to say concerned a mass layoff, Wil didn't know how he'd react. He had on occasion thought about what he would do if the pink slips were handed out. Part of him had hoped for such an event in his life, which would force him to look for other, perhaps brighter, opportunities. Maybe, he had figured, there was a chance to get back into television. But there was pride at stake, too. While he had experienced many failed and broken relationships with women over the years, one thing kept his ego fueled: They were all impressed with his money. His nice cars, high-end furniture, fashionable artwork and a beautiful home in snobby Edina, Minnesota, were trappings that could not be afforded on a TV industry salary. He was definitely hooked on his comfortable lifestyle, and going backward would not be easy.

Mr. Korbit's voice lowered. He was now leaning in so close that his long, pointy chin was nearly touching the white plate. "They're shutting it down," he said, casting his eyes downward again. "Effective immediately, the Union First online product suite is eliminated from the development agenda."

Wil tilted his head toward Lanny. Wil's eyes grew wide as saucers.

"What the—?" Wil said. "They're shutting it down?" His voice got louder, which caused patrons at nearby tables to take notice. "What do they think they're doing?" Wil asked. "Why my product, after all the progress we've made?"

"Doesn't make sense," Lanny calmly chimed in, defending his friend.

Mr. Korbit straightened up. "Continental-American has its own similar product under development, and their management decided that it was more robust than ours. All of our funding will be shifted to their team to help make it market ready."

Similar product? More robust? Who in the hell made that call? Wil wondered.

"There has to be some mistake," Lanny said defensively. "I've seen the specs on the Continental-American system. It's nowhere close to what Union First built. Wil and his team are nearly ready for rollout, while Continental still has months of work, maybe longer, to get it going."

"It's a done deal," Mr. Korbit shot back. "No sense in fighting it. You'd be wasting your time. And whatever you do, do not contact your team members about this yet. This is to remain under wraps until Continental-American can get their act together over this thing."

Wil fumed, but he fought hard to keep his voice even and emotionless. "Steve, no offense, but this doesn't add up," Wil said. "We've spent twenty-three-million dollars. Our product is nearly ready to go. Why shut us down now if they're not ready themselves?"

He ignored Wil's question and narrowed his eyes. "Wil, I'm going to have to ask you to continue demonstrating the product like all is well," he said. "We don't want to tip off anyone back home about all this just yet."

In the wake of the shocked silence, Mr. Korbit made a nervous glance at his watch and stood. "I've got another meeting, so enjoy the rest of your meal, guys," he said. "Sorry I don't have better news. Wil, pick up the check, will you?"

Wil barely registered a nod and pushed himself back from the table, crossing his arms in disgust. As he watched his boss leave, Wil realized that in an instant, his entire career had hit an impenetrable wall.

FIVE

Ari Weizmann was used to being alone at a table during the first 10 minutes of a scheduled business lunch. As one of the best executive-level recruiters in the Twin Cities, Mr. Weizmann often met at lunchtime with busy company executives who needed his services in order to plug a hole vacated by some departing or fired colleague. It was an axiom of Mr. Weizmann's that while candidates with whom he interviewed or counseled were either always on time and often early, his retained clients and their representatives always seemed to run late.

Today was no exception, and Mr. Weizmann wasn't worried. He had done a lot of searches for Midwest Federated Bank, mostly under the direction of Barney Jennings, who was often late to both business and social functions. The waiter had just refilled Mr. Weizmann's water glass at his table that overlooked the busy Crystal Court area in the IDS Center when Mr. Jennings finally rushed up.

"Sorry, Ari," he said, pulling out the chair directly opposite of his luncheon guest. "I-I-I hope you ordered."

"I figured you wanted your usual." Mr. Weizmann sometimes became personal friends with his clients. He and Mr. Jennings had known each other since Mr. Jennings came to the Twin Cities in the 1980s. After many successful executive searches for Midwest Federated, the two had become fast friends, spending time at off-Broadway plays with their wives or playing golf at various upscale clubs in the area.

"What's going on over there?" Mr. Weizmann asked. "Victoria said you seemed a little anxious to meet with me."

Mr. Jennings frowned. He didn't like it when his administrative assistant conveyed more information to people—even friends—than they needed to know. "I-I have a search that I need to give you, Ari. I-I-I need a good marketer, someone who can take this bank out of its sleepy state and onto the showcase floor."

"Really?" Mr. Weizmann asked. "Marketing? So unusual for you guys. I haven't done a marketing search for you in quite some time."

Mr. Jennings nodded his head. "Do you know anybody you can pick up? There-there-there are a lot of banks in town doing a good job with advertising and promotion. There must be good people out there. If-if-if I don't get somebody on board soon, we're in danger of stagnation."

The waiter set salads in front of both men and sloppily refilled their water glasses. "I have a few people under me who know the marketing world in town fairly well," Mr. Weizmann said. "What exactly are you looking for?"

"I-I-I need someone with solid marketing and banking experience, someone who knows this marketplace," Mr. Jennings stammered. "We-we-we need to get this bank to the next level, and I don't want to waste time training anyone. They-they need to hit the ground running."

Mr. Weizmann knew that it was a matter of time before the floodgates opened across the street at Union First. With the thousands of people employed there, it wouldn't be long before merger-related job duplications began to create attrition among the employee base. And that created an opportunity.

"I'll get right on it, Barney," Mr. Weizmann said, digging into his salad. "You can count on it."

SIX

The rattling of the drink cart startled Wil. It was 3 a.m. on Tuesday morning, and he realized he must have fallen asleep before takeoff from LAX. With one eye open, he noticed that the aircraft's cabin lighting was on its dimmest setting, and he wondered who wanted coffee, soft drinks or beer at this hour.

He was on the redeye bound for Minneapolis, cutting his California trip short by three days. After the dreadful lunch on Monday where Steve Korbit had dropped the equivalent of an A-bomb on his project, Wil had returned to his post on the convention floor to continue his demos. But the energy was sapped from him for the rest of the day, and he often found himself propped against one of the corner poles of the Continental-American exhibit display, purposefully avoiding any engagement of his prospects in any kind of sales talk.

Then even worse news came. At 2:30 during that long afternoon, he learned that Steve Korbit was overruled by L.A.

The demos of his now defunct product were to be shut down immediately. Within an hour of that decision, Wil had contacted UFBC Travel Services and was booked on the 12:15 a.m. flight to Minneapolis. Most of the other Continental-American and Union First employees at the conference were unaffected by his product's shutdown, so they stayed behind to man the other demonstrations. The only evidence of Wil having been there at all was the gargantuan TV monitor, which was left running with the Continental-American logo prominently displayed, its multicolored swirls dancing innocently across the screen.

    The 757 touched down in Minneapolis at 6:30 a.m. local time. Light snow was falling, which was an unwelcome sight to Minnesotans when spring should be bringing warmer temperatures instead. Wil found he was feeling fairly refreshed, except for the kink in his neck caused by sleeping against the fuselage for four straight hours. Rather than driving home to Edina, he decided it was more efficient to go directly to downtown Minneapolis to freshen up at the YMCA where he was a member. With some fresh clothes still packed in his suitcase, he knew he could shower, shave, change and still make it to the office in time to catch a cup of coffee and contact Ben Johnson, the head of the Union First Commercial Banking Group. Ben was a big fan of Wil's, and he was always interested in hearing the status of the online product; Ben knew it was sure to help increase sales to his own client base.

Wil thought that if anyone could talk some sense into management about the decision to kill his product, it was Ben Johnson. Normally Ben himself attended the convention in L.A., but this year, with the final merger between Union First and Continental-American looming, he decided to send only key sales people for the week. It was an expense-control decision that Wil admired.

Wil left the Y in plenty of time and arrived at his own office on the eighth floor of the Union First Bancorporation Tower in Minneapolis shortly after 8 a.m. He threw his keys onto his desk and noticed the voicemail light of his phone was blinking. The display indicated there were only two messages waiting, an unusually small number after being gone a whole day, but a pleasant surprise to Wil nonetheless.

Those will have to wait.

Will picked up the phone and punched in Ben's five-digit extension. Casey, Ben's assistant, saw Wil's name on the caller I.D. screen and answered with instant familiarity.

"Hi Wil," she said. "He's not in yet. Would you like me to have him call you?"

"Yes, Casey. Please. Tell him it's urgent. Do you know where he is?"

"I'm not sure," she said. "He might have had a meeting this morning that he didn't tell me about before he left yesterday evening. But I'm certain I'll hear from him shortly. I'll have him call."

Wil knew that Ben was difficult to reach on the first try, as he was one of the hardest working and busiest executives Wil had ever met. Wil had plenty of work to do in the meantime, so he replaced the receiver and powered up his computer.

As he logged into the computer system, he was distracted again by the incessant blinking of his voicemail light. He wondered who had called him when most of the people with whom he worked didn't know he had returned to Minnesota so soon. Wil also figured that the news of his project's demise could not have made it to Minneapolis—at least not yet.

Wil dialed up the voicemail number and punched in his access code. "You have two messages," the automated female voice droned. He punched another key, and out came the voice of Lanny.

"Wil, call me. Things got worse after you left. You have my cell number." Lanny's voice sounded concerned— almost depressed. It was unusual for his friend to sound so low, but nothing could be considered business-as-usual during merger mania. Wil quickly hit the delete key, and before the next message came up, he punched another line and called Lanny's cell. It was only 6:15 a.m. in L.A., but he knew Lanny was up and dressed by now.

"Wil!" Lanny shouted as soon as he answered. "Where are you? Are you home yet?"

"I came into the office a little while ago," Wil said. "What's the matter? You didn't sound so good on your message."

"They're all idiots," Lanny snapped.

"Who?" Wil asked.

"The execs just cut half the product group here. They're handing out severance packages left and right. They're only giving me ten weeks, one week for every year I've been here. Ten rotten weeks!"

Wil was alarmed. He never heard his friend sound so upset. "They can't do that," Wil said. "The merger hasn't even happened yet. How can they—"

"It has to do with that announcement yesterday," Lanny interrupted. "There's going to be a big realignment of staff. I think there's a lot of pressure to get expenses down. Both companies have been spending like drunken sailors the past three months."

"My God, Lanny," Wil said, dismayed. "I'm so sorry."

"Do you think Korbit knew about this when he gave that speech to us?" Lanny asked.

"I don't know. I certainly hope not." There was an uncomfortable silence. Wil could sense Lanny's blood boiling. Wil cleared his throat. "Lanny, I just don't know what to say." Wil was having trouble grasping what was being thrown at him; it seemed that the company was literally crumbling around him. "I'm sure you'll find something else. Ask Human Resources about outplacement." Wil was trying his best to sound sympathetic, but the jetlag was finally catching up to him, and his tone sounded less than convincing.

"Those bastards," Lanny said. "This is unbelievable."

They chatted for a few more minutes and exchanged personal contact numbers to ensure they could stay in touch. Wil found himself choked with emotion as he said goodbye to his friend. He felt shameful for not having that drink at the bar on Sunday afternoon. He felt worried about Lanny and his wife and kids. He had never met Jill Taylor, but he imagined that she was bound to be devastated by her husband's news.

After they hung up, Wil sat in silence at his desk, staring straight ahead at the wall. His head throbbed. His heart sank. *This was turning out to be one hell of a week,* he thought, *and it's only Tuesday.*

Wil was suddenly thrust back to reality by the continued blinking of his voicemail light. Hoping he could get distracted by a call from Jessica, his latest love interest, he lifted the receiver and retrieved the second message.

"Hi, Mister Fischer, this is Kelly Iverson from Weizmann and Associates," the cheery recorded voice said. "We're an executive search firm in Minneapolis and we'd like to get your thoughts about a highly confidential search that we're conducting for a client in this market. If you have a moment, please contact me."

At least someone is looking out for me this day. Wil jotted down the number and allowed himself a grin. Wil knew of several people who joined Union First in various capacities over the years who were represented by Ari Weizmann.

Wil got up and softly shut the door to his office. He reseated himself, picked up the phone, and dialed the number.

SEVEN

Most advertising campaigns took a while to develop. Even small campaigns that had only a few media mixes—such as newspaper, direct mail, and radio—took several weeks, even months before they could be effectively launched in the marketplace. Such ramp-up was required prep time for most companies to conduct research, define their target audience, and test materials to determine audience reaction.

Midwest Federated's approach was different. Dick Cramer's get-it-done style permeated the organization at all levels, and the "shoot-now, ask-questions-later" mentality was officially baked into the culture. Management always prided itself on being able to spin on a dime, launching products, changing branch hours or rolling out a promotion in the fraction of the time that it took other banks.

It was only a few days since Mr. Cramer had spoken to Mr. Jennings about the anti-merger advertising promotion, yet the Marketing Department had already produced two newspaper ads and a direct mail piece that were under review. Midwest Federated wasn't known for quality, award-winning advertising. They were simply trying to attract every second- and third-shift workman, every mom who was single, and every moderate income family in the area who didn't have much time for banking, and who certainly didn't need any sophistication when it came to financial services. Midwest Federated Bank was about simplicity—checking accounts and loans were its primary offerings—and the bank promoted its services to its base of customers and prospects at the plainest, most basic level possible.

Barney Jennings had driven east to the Midwest Federated headquarters building in Saint Paul to ensure that he had time with Mr. Cramer to personally present him with the latest advertising materials. Mr. Jennings was keenly aware that when Mr. Cramer wanted something done, it was protocol to get the CEO's input first before anything reached a final production stage.

Mr. Jennings ascended the steps to the second floor and into Mr. Cramer's office. To outsiders, the CEO's office seemed excessively large, taking up nearly a quarter of the total space on the second floor of the building. While many of the operational divisions of the bank were located in the regional building in downtown Minneapolis, the more opulent Saint Paul location was built a few years earlier to specifically house the executive management team of Midwest Federated—and its fleet of lawyers and accountants.

To Barney Jennings, the office's surroundings were a living testament to the man who built—or rather, rebuilt—the company. Mounted deer heads adorned one entire wall of the massive office, the trophies of past hunts that Mr. Jennings also reluctantly (and not so successfully) attended. Numerous framed photos taken during Mr. Cramer's days in the Marine Corp were proudly displayed behind his large oak desk, a piece of furniture so large that someone had once joked that a helicopter could safely land on it. A three-foot-long I-beam of steel, professionally mounted and polished to a high sheen, sat proudly displayed on a table near the door. It was a not-so-subtle reminder to those who entered that Mr. Cramer came from humbler roots.

The office also boasted a large conference table, the central location for many upper-management meetings. Mr. Cramer didn't like to leave his office if he didn't have to; he preferred it when everyone came to see him.

"Dick," Mr. Jennings said as he bounded across the double-door threshold of the office, "I've got great things to show you."

"Terrific!" Mr. Cramer exclaimed. He stood from his desk and moved to the conference table, removing his suit coat to reveal his trademark canary-yellow shirt.

Mr. Jennings deposited an array of papers on the table that showed two versions of the proposed newspaper ad and a mockup of the direct mail piece. All the materials were designed to indirectly criticize Union First Bank, its major competitor in the marketplace, for selling out to a California company.

"How are you going to do the direct mail?" Mr. Cramer barked. "What did you decide?"

"We're-we're going to mail around Union First's branches, just like you suggested," Mr. Jennings stammered. "Our-our goal is to get a lot of people to think about switching to Midwest Federated. Our message to readers is to try us out. Come to one of our seventy-five branches in the Twin Cities area, and customers won't be disappointed." Mr. Jennings was so proud. He had written much of the ad's copy himself, something that would make most advertising executives cringe.

Mr. Cramer examined the piece, and then nodded enthusiastically. "Good, Barney. That's real good. Are we just doing this in Minnesota?"

"Yes," Mr. Jennings answered with a smile. "Union First doesn't have much overlap at all in our other states."

Mr. Cramer picked up another piece of paper from the table. "Newspaper ad?"

"Right," Mr. Jennings said. "We-we-we think this will get us some attention."

The format was a third-of-a-page-sized display ad that was scheduled to run in the daily newspapers. Mr. Cramer read the headline aloud: "Bank changing its name? Midwest Federated is waiting for you. Established in nineteen forty-five." A smile erupted on his face. "I like it," Mr. Cramer said. "But don't buy any ad space in that weekly conservative piece-of-garbage newspaper. I want this in the dailies. Call Gene at the Daily Post. He'll give you a good rate." Mr. Cramer was known in town for his liberal views. He often sparred with conservative leaders at the state and federal level over budgets for welfare programs or government assistance. For a man who worked in an overly regulated industry, it was puzzling to some that Mr. Cramer wanted even more government intervention in society. Perhaps it was because his liberal nature was so deeply rooted in his background. His father was a coal miner who helped him get his first steel mill job, where unions ruled the roost. Liberalism simply ran in his blood.

"I want you to present this at the board meeting on Thursday," Mr. Cramer said. "Make sure the board members all know about this before we roll with it."

Mr. Jennings nodded, secure in the knowledge that the board meeting was going to be an important one already. Thanks to Mr. Cramer, a major proposal was on the docket to grant 2.5 million shares of stock to the top nine executives in the company as soon as Midwest Federated hit certain financial targets. The majority of shares were to be divided equally among Mr. Cramer's executive staff, with nearly a third of the vested shares being delivered directly to Mr. Cramer himself.

Also up for vote was a proposal to update the golden parachute for Mr. Cramer and his senior executives. Should Midwest Federated Bank ever get purchased by another entity, each of Mr. Cramer's staff was to receive four times their annual salary in a lump sum payment, as well as a one-time bonus comparable to an average of the previous five years in bonus payouts. Mr. Cramer himself was to receive the same deal, with an additional entitlement of a gross-up—a provision of cash to pay the taxes on his windfall, as well as the taxes on the gross-up itself. Once board approval occurred, the proposal was to be put in front of the shareholders at the annual meeting, scheduled for just a few weeks away. No resistance was expected, granting a sweet deal for the inner circle, with the sweetest deal of all reserved for Richard Edmund Cramer.

"We'll have an easy time of it at this meeting," Mr. Cramer said, smiling broadly. "Old man Updike won't be there."

Mr. Jennings tried to mask his frown. Where Randall Updike was concerned, Mr. Jennings never appreciated his boss's lack of respect for the bank's founder.

Mr. Jennings stared down at the floor for a time. "All right," he softly replied, finally casting his eyes up at the CEO. "I'll put it on the agenda."

EIGHT

Four days had gone by and Wil still had not heard from or seen Ben Johnson. His admin called late on Monday afternoon to tell him that Ben was called unexpectedly to L.A., which wasn't all that surprising to Wil. With the actual merger being completed in just a few weeks, the major divisional leaders of the bank were also being dragged through some serious reshuffling, which was resulting in many unplanned meetings. But now it was Friday morning, and Wil found himself wondering why Ben hadn't at least tried to return his call via cell phone.

Wil went about his other business, glancing at his watch often. He had a meeting scheduled several buildings away with a senior executive of Midwest Federated about an opportunity that could lead to a job safety net, should the ax finally fall at Union First.

But Wil wasn't a fan of Midwest Federated Bank. The institution was viewed by the industry as a "bottom feeder" bank, a label it earned from its renowned focus on acquiring low-end customers who were largely ignored by other banks, and a technological infrastructure that was woefully behind the times.

Wil finished returning several emails before he logged off and headed out the door for his interview. Despite a light drizzle, he decided to take the street route rather than the skyway system, an interconnection of enclosed and heated bridges that allowed Minneapolis workers the luxury of walking all over downtown without ever going outside. With the winters and cold springs lasting so long in Minnesota, the skyway was a necessity for the sake of commerce as much as it was a privilege. Wil wanted to make a beeline straight to the regional MFB offices, and rushing the street would get him there the fastest.

He paused briefly when he reached the automatic glass doors at the Midwest Federated Bank entryway, pausing momentarily while the motors squealed in pain to draw open the doors. He noticed the building was showing its age in contrast to the newer, more cosmopolitan structures that got built up around it during the past 15 years. The building's dark brick motif and shabby condition made for a bad first impression. It certainly paled in comparison to the more modern, posh surroundings of the Union First Bancorp Tower, which was added to the Minneapolis skyline in 1991.

Wil stomped his feet on the worn commercial-grade floor mat inside the foyer to get the last droplets of water off his shiny black shoes. He removed his overcoat and swung it around his left arm, then followed a long hallway that spilled into the spacious but dim retail lobby of Midwest Federated Bank. As he understood it, this location was the flagship of their entire fleet of retail branches.

Dark, he thought. *What a tomb.*

He remembered reading that Midwest Fed had retrofitted its bank locations in the early 1980s to reflect Roman architecture style—high arches, columns, marble, and inlaid ornamentation. Even under Dick Cramer's control, new branches that were recently built were designed to emulate the look.

Wil, however, felt that it all appeared incredibly outdated. He paused a bit and scanned his surroundings, taking it all in, knowing that even brief familiarity with the branch layout may help him in the interview that was just minutes away.

He noticed a large teller counter directly in front of him that contained numerous teller stations. The long counter curved gently around a wall that contained an embedded, round, silver vault door in its center. *Funny, you never see vaults anymore,* he thought.

He counted a total of seven teller stations, with only two of them manned and open for business. The other five were closed and marked with small black signs and white lettering that read: *NEXT STATION PLEASE.* He counted eight customers standing in line to be received by the next available teller. He then noticed that the majority of the customers in line were male. He also recognized that none looked happy, a sure sign that each had been standing there a while. *If this was a Union First branch, they would have open three more lines by now,* he thought.

Toward the back of the massive lobby was a sea of wooden desks, half of which were occupied by male bankers dressed in shirts and ties, while the rest of the furniture sat unoccupied. He noticed that only two of the bankers were actually helping customers, while the others sat either staring at their desktop computer screens or chatting quietly among themselves.

Wil located the elevator that took him up to the fifteenth floor of the Midwest Federated building, where he was to meet with Mr. Barney W. Jennings. He knew little about the man, and had never even heard of him prior to being contacted about the job. Wil had tried a quick Internet search on Mr. Jennings several days before, but he came up with only a few stray quotes attributed to the man in archived company news releases.

The little that Wil did learn about him came from Mr. Weizmann during his screening interview on Wednesday. As the elevator slowly ascended, Wil remembered the descriptions provided by the recruiter:

An affable man.
Runs a good bank.
Knows the founder.
Great friend of mine.

Wil felt energized by all those things. His boss, Steve Korbit, could never generate anything close to those types of descriptions.

The elevator doors slid open and Wil immediately walked up to the main receptionist. "Hi, I'm Wil Fischer. I have an interview with Mr. Jennings."

"Oh, yes, Mister Fischer," said Victoria, the middle-aged receptionist with yellow hair, her earrings flopping against her cheeks as she talked. "He is expecting you. Please have a seat. Can I get you anything?"

Wil had recently scanned a book about interview etiquette to ensure he would do everything right, and he instantly recalled that one of the tips was to never accept anything to drink—even water—at a formal interview; the risk of spilling or choking was simply too great. *Best to just get through the cotton mouth and avoid spilling something all over myself.* "No, thank you," he said with a smile, sitting in one of two gray reception chairs that book-ended a small table.

Within moments, a man who fit the description of Mr. Jennings appeared at the door that was to the left of the reception area. The man's eyes were cast downward, as though consciously trying to avoid catching Wil's glance. He was a tall, thin man with gray swept-back hair, wearing a crisp white shirt, a bold red tie, and tan dress slacks that were far too tight-fitting for a man in his late 50s. The man grabbed the stack of phone messages that were written on salmon-colored slips and quickly flipped through them.

"Mr. Jennings," Victoria softly prodded, "this is Mr. Fischer for you." She nodded toward Wil.

Mr. Jennings looked up and turned his head toward his guest, cracking what Wil thought was an artificial smile. "Good morning," Mr. Jennings said. "Come-come-come on in."

Wil obediently stood and walked the few feet that separated him and Mr. Jennings. "Nice to meet you," Wil said. The handshake delivered by Wil was firm, but Mr. Jennings' hand seemed cool and damp.

The men entered Mr. Jennings' office, which was nicely appointed and uncluttered. Wil noticed the generic artwork that adorned the walls, the type of warehouse-stocked paintings he had seen countless times in other offices throughout downtown. His desk was of modest girth with a large wall-sized bookcase credenza dwarfing the space behind it. A couch and chair were arranged in one corner of the office, with a coffee table nearby that sported a small but thriving green plant.

Mr. Jennings gestured for Wil to sit on the couch while he planted himself in the chair. "I-I-I was impressed with your resume," Mr. Jennings stammered. "You've-you've done quite a bit in your career in a short period of time."

Wil paused a moment after realizing that the man had a gentle stuttering cadence. "Eleven years went by quickly," Wil finally said with a smile on his face.

"There-there-there are a few of us around here who have been in the industry a lot longer than that," Mr. Jennings said.

Wil imagined that this bank was full of people who had worked in banking all of their lives. Midwest Federated seemed like the kind of institution that coveted accountants and traditional bankers, a more old-fashioned approach to banking than the one to which he was accustomed.

"I-I-I started in banking as a teller, right out of college."

Wil was having trouble envisioning this skinny gray-haired man in too-tight pants as ever working in any kind of a customer service role. "The passage of time is one thing in life you can always rely on," Wil said lamely.

After the small talk, Mr. Jennings turned more serious. Wil quickly discovered that Mr. Jennings was not the best interviewer, seeming to spend more time talking about the bank and its goals than asking questions of Wil.

More than an hour of Mr. Jennings' soliloquy had elapsed when the front receptionist interrupted with a knock, partially opening the office door.

"Your next appointment is here, Mr. Jennings," Victoria said, her head just peeking through the door's crack.

Mr. Jennings frowned. "I'll be right out."

"That went by fast," Wil said, looking at his watch.

"Yes, but I enjoyed it very much. Let-let-let me ask you something, Wil. When could you start?"

Wil wasn't ready for that question. *I just spent an hour listening to this guy do nothing but talk, and now he wants to hire me?* "Any time, I guess," Wil managed with a shrug.

"Good. Let-let me talk to a few people here, and I'll get back to you about next steps."

Both men stood and shook hands, and Mr. Jennings led Wil out the door. Wil then entered the elevator door and hit the lobby button. *I might have just knitted myself a security blanket,* he thought to himself, a grin cracking across his face as the elevator doors snapped shut in front of him.

NINE

The weekend flew by and was just about over when Wil pulled into the driveway of his Edina home, having spent Saturday and Sunday with his mom in Sioux Falls. The sun was falling just below the horizon, and he was looking forward to vegetating in front of the TV for the rest of the evening. He bent over to gather the weekend newspapers that were stacked on his front porch, and he entered his house.

Wil started a load of laundry and put the things away he had taken on his brief trip to South Dakota. He eventually finished his chores and turned on the TV, simultaneously paging through the Sunday edition of the *Minneapolis Daily Post*. He alternately turned pages and TV channels, scanning headlines and video images, multitasking like he had learned to do long ago while working in the television industry.

When he got to page seven of the newspaper, he stopped. In the upper right-hand corner of the page was a large display ad from Midwest Federated Bank. Out of all the ads on the page, the Midwest Federated ad jumped out at him, taking him by surprise. He really hadn't thought much about his interview since Friday, given all the distractions that came while visiting his ailing, high-maintenance mother. He closely examined the ad, and found himself rereading it several times. *What in the world are they trying to sell?*

"Bank changing its name?" he read aloud. "Midwest Federated is waiting for you." *What a lame headline.* He looked at the old-fashioned typeface, and then read to himself the paragraph positioned below the headline:

> *If you're tired of banks merging, come to Midwest Federated. We're committed to the neighborhoods we serve, and we'll never sell out to an out-of-state company. That's our pledge to you, our customer.*

Wil shook his head. *How incredibly, embarrassingly bad,* he thought. *This is their way of growing market share?* The ad seemed so amateur to Wil, and he felt mildly ashamed for thinking that jumping to such a backwards institution was ever a good idea. *If this is my only choice, then I'm in deep trouble.*

He carefully examined the bank's logo at the bottom center. It was constructed in simple black Arial letters with the *M.F.B.* centered above smaller type that read *Midwest Federated Bank.* Positioned under that were the words *Established 1945.* The entire design seemed substandard to Wil. It looked to him as though someone without a design background had whipped this out on a low-end computer somewhere. He then remembered that Barney Jennings told him that the Marketing Department needed some revitalization and updating, and that some of the staff should probably be let go once a new marketing director was hired who could rebuild it from scratch. *Am I really willing to give up my eleven-year career at Union First Bank to do that?*

Monday morning came quickly, and Wil found himself at his desk by 7:30. He had already made his decision: He was going to stick it out at Union First, no matter what. He was convinced that he was far too valuable to be let go. It was too bad that they severed Lanny Taylor, but he reasoned that it was probably just the unfortunate luck of the draw.

He was about to step out of his office to fill his coffee cup when Ben Johnson showed up at his door. Snappily dressed in an expensive black suit and a blue power tie, Ben Johnson had a habit of just barging into people's offices when he had something to say.

Ben closed the door and sat down in the chair in front of Wil's desk. "I wanted to catch you right away this morning," Ben started in. Wil always admired the way he cut right to the chase in his conversations.

"I've been trying to reach you," Wil said.

"I know. I had to fly out to Los Angeles unexpectedly last week. I just got through a series of meetings that decided the fate of a lot of things."

Wil nodded weakly. "So you heard about the online product?"

"Yes, and I was very disappointed. I know what it meant to you and the product team, Wil. It had to come as a major blow."

"They shut the thing down while I was demonstrating it on the convention floor."

Ben shook his head and rolled his eyes in disgust. "Not exactly the most professional thing to do."

Wil leaned toward Ben. "You know as well as I do that Continental-American's commercial online system is nowhere near as good as our own architecture," Wil said, clasping his hands rigidly in front of him. "It's going to set their product's delivery back months, if not longer. Your sales people are going to be without a computer interface for your commercial clients, and I doubt they're going stay silent about it."

Ben adjusted his body in the chair. "I agree," he said. "I took it up with Clyde Mulder himself last week, the top operations guy for Continental-American. But that was before I found out he was the one who made the original decision to shut us down."

Wil kept his eyes fixed like lasers on Ben. "Then take it up with Harrington."

Ben shook his head. "He's too far removed, Wil. The CEO is not worrying about whether a product gets launched or not, with the merger and all."

Wil rapidly blinked his eyes. "I'm sure he'd wonder why we spent twenty-three million dollars on a product that was shut down as soon as it was completed." Wil could feel himself getting more heated. "I just don't get it. What's motivating this decision?"

Ben looked down at the floor. "Mergers sometimes net crazy decisions. There are all kinds of things that happen when so much is at stake, like development dollars…ego…hell, even who's sleeping with who, for all I know."

Wil let the explanation hang for a moment. "It's B.S.," he said.

Ben leaned in and positioned his elbows on the edge of the desk, studying Wil. "Want two pieces of advice that I got from someone a long time ago, when the very first bank I worked for got purchased?"

"Okay."

"First, during a merger, never, ever, believe anything anyone tells you."

Wil didn't blink. "And second?"

"Never trust management. Period."

Wil maintained his stare. "You're management."

Ben smiled. "Believe me...I feel more like an outsider these days. And you're not going to like what I have to tell you next."

Here it comes, Wil thought.

Ben let out a long sigh. "I didn't know how to tell you this. All of product management is not only going to report to L.A., but also relocate there. No more presence here in Minneapolis."

Wil's mouth fell open. "What?"

"Turns out that Clyde Mulder is a freak about having people located too far from him. Doesn't like telecommuting or geographically-scattered teams. Must be a control thing."

"Then why did he let Lanny Taylor go?" Wil asked. "He was already in L.A."

Ben nodded. "That's strike number two. There are only so many chairs that are going to be filled. I wanted you to know so that you can keep your eyes and options open once they decide to start the shredding here."

Wil forced air from his mouth through his tightly pursed lips. "I'm going to level with you. I may have an opportunity to work across the street."

Ben raised an eyebrow. "At Midwest Federated?"

Wil nodded.

Ben stood, rattling the keys in his pocket. "My advice? Don't jump now. Ride it out. If they eliminate your position here, there may be other opportunities that open up. You've got a great marketing background. At the end of it all, you still might get a re-lo to L.A. For a single guy like you, that should be a great thing."

The thought of moving to California was not something Wil relished. He was already too far away from his ailing mother, who was some four hours away by car, but still close enough for an occasional visit. She was in the depths of depression since his step dad died two years ago, and he didn't dare move halfway across the country now. "Things seem to be happening too fast, Ben. I've got to look out for myself."

"Keep your chin up," he said, opening the door and standing on the threshold. "Good things come to good people."

As Ben Johnson left, Wil turned to stare out of the window of his eighth-floor office. *Good things come to good people,* Wil thought, *except for the likes of Lanny Taylor and Wil Fischer.*

TEN

Dick Cramer began his weekly conference call with all the regional Midwest Federated presidents the same way he always started them: with a countdown. "You all have two minutes apiece to tell me what's going on in your market. Kansas City? You go first."

Randy Neymeier, the president from Missouri, cleared his throat and went into a two-minute rehearsed speech about deposit growth, checking account acquisition, net margin and loan volume. His voice was nasally and high-pitched, the kind of voice that sounded helium-induced. He went on for two full minutes, and then pressed ahead for three more, then five. It was an allowable infraction in Mr. Cramer's world of preset limits, as long as the CEO's interest stayed piqued. At the conclusion of Mr. Neymeier's rosy report from the Missouri region, other updates followed with similar discourses from the presidents in Omaha, Fargo, and Sioux Falls.

Mr. Cramer left the Minnesota update for the end, and as soon as Mr. Jennings started his report, Mr. Cramer interrupted with a question. "Barney, I saw the ad in the paper yesterday. Loved it! Any reaction yet?"

"Probably too-too-too early, Dick," Mr. Jennings said, his voice crackling across the speakerphone. It was normal for him to participate via phone each Monday from his downtown Minneapolis office to avoid fighting the morning traffic to get to the main headquarters building, located 10 miles to the east in Saint Paul. "But I was pleased with the placement in both papers," he continued. "Direct-direct mail will drop this week."

The long pause that followed meant Mr. Cramer was deep in thought. Cramer's voice boomed in again. "We should put a starburst on that ad in this Sunday's paper. Add a C.D. rate. Big and bold. And how about a picture of our credit card? Add a picture. People respond to pictures. Give the reader something to choose from."

Mr. Jennings winced. While he largely respected Mr. Cramer for everything he did for the company in the early going, he hated it whenever the man tried to wear a marketing hat. It sometimes took a lot of convincing and arguing to talk him out of a stupid idea, and Mr. Jennings didn't look forward to such exchanges.

"We-we-we can talk about adding a rate," Mr. Jennings said. "I'll talk to the marketing folks and see what they think." Delay was his only form of defense.

Another pause followed, which was filled with crackly static from the speakerphone. "Have you hired your marketing director yet?" Mr. Cramer finally asked.

Mr. Jennings managed a smile in his voice. "Not-not-not yet, Dick. But I'm making the offer today."

Steve Korbit was on his way to see Wil in a hastily arranged meeting. In the past 12 months, Wil had engaged in meaningful, pre-scheduled conversations with his boss less than six times, so Wil sensed that this last-minute conference, coupled with the insider info he received from Ben Johnson, meant that his boss was going to share some bad news.

Wil sat at his desk, staring at the email window on his computer screen. His email volume had slowed to a crawl since all product development was halted, and it was unnerving to him. Just a week ago, it was common to have so many emails by late morning that he couldn't possibly read or respond timely to all of them. This new decompression seemed too sudden. And so did the mysterious meeting with Steve Korbit.

A few minutes went by, and Mr. Korbit called Wil to say that he was still across town at the bank's Operations Center. Factoring travel time and parking in the massive Union First underground ramp, Wil figured it was another 10 minutes or so before Korbit would arrive.

After hanging up, Wil stared at his nearly empty email window, and his phone rang again. He glanced at the caller I.D. screen, but he didn't immediately recognize the number.

"This is Wil Fischer," he said with the phone to his ear.

"Wil, it's-it's Barney Jennings from Midwest Federated Bank. I'm prepared to make you a job offer today. Are you able to talk?"

Wil was stunned. He wasn't ready for a job offer so soon. When he came to work this morning, he had put the Midwest Federated opportunity out of his mind. But now, a warm wave washed over him. He suddenly felt needed again—and important.

"Sure," Wil responded after a short beat. "Now is just fine." Wil didn't even bother to get up and shut his office door. If Steve Korbit came in while he was on the phone getting an offer from another bank, then so be it.

"There-there-there is a courier on his way to you with the details," Mr. Jennings said. "He should be there any moment.

When you get it, call me back with your answer. I want you to come and work for us, Wil. You'll-you'll be a great addition to the team here."

Wil smiled broadly. He hadn't felt this good in a long time. "Thanks, Mister Jennings. I appreciate it very much. I'll get back to you."

They said their goodbyes and just as the receiver was being cradled, a delivery man in a bright orange jacket stood at his door. "Wil Fischer?"

"Yes."

The orange-clad man handed Wil the envelope and swiftly exited. Wil wasted no time and ripped it open. He read the first sentence aloud softly.

"Dear Mister Fischer, we are pleased to make this confidential offer of employment to you." A quick glance below the first paragraph caught his eye next. There were numerous bullet points detailing salary, bonus, benefits, pension, 401K, and, *what's this? A company car!* Such a luxury was only reserved for the highest of executives at Union First. With all payments, gas, oil and maintenance to be covered by Midwest Federated, Wil quickly calculated in his head that a company car was a $10,000 annual benefit.

Wil was lost in the glow of the moment. In a way, he couldn't believe it was true. The salary offer was huge, much larger than what he had expected, *and the car!*

He was in the midst of rereading the letter for the second time when Steve Korbit blew in, shut the door and sat down. "Wil," he began with a forced empathetic tone, "I have some hard, tough news. You know that there are many changes in the works. With the product team now reporting to L.A., there needs to be some shifts in personnel and work responsibilities."

Wil couldn't bring himself to look at his boss, opting instead to stare down at the offer letter from Barney Jennings that was positioned between his hands.

"Frankly, Wil, with your expertise in marketing, we just don't see a fit in the product group anymore. You have great skills, but it's just not the right set of skills for the continuing operation."

Salary, bonus, pension...

"So I'm prepared to offer you a severance package of eleven weeks."

...company car...

Wil's eyes didn't leave the page. He thought of his mother in Sioux Falls.

...We are pleased to make this confidential offer of employment to you...

"I accept," he blurted aloud, a smile lighting up his face.

Mr. Korbit furrowed his brow; this wasn't the reaction he was expecting. He looked down and picked at his fingernails.

"Fine, then. I'll get the paperwork to you this afternoon." After some awkward silence, Mr. Korbit rose from the chair and extended his hand toward Wil. "I enjoyed having you work for me. You'll be missed."

Wil let his smile dissipate and looked up slowly from the offer letter. Sensing he had the edge, he opted not to return the handshake, and just glared at his now former boss with a piercing, uncomfortable stare. There was so much he wanted to say about Steve Korbit's lack of backbone, his poor management skills, and his penchant for upward ass-kissing. But Wil wasn't that way. He didn't want to burn any bridges, no matter how tempting it was to unload his feelings.

"Thanks," Wil said, holding his gaze on Mr. Korbit's eyes. "I'll wait for the paperwork."

As Mr. Korbit's extended gesture went unanswered, his arm limply returned to his right side. He gave Wil a departing frown, then turned and left.

Wil never saw him again.

ELEVEN

May 2000

Lanny Taylor had sent more than 100 emails to people in the L.A. area informing them that he was now unemployed. He had solid contacts in the area, most of them generated during his years at Continental-American. The banking group worked with hundreds of service providers all over the country, especially in California where the headquarters was located. As one of the now former senior product managers who had worked closely with many of those providers, Lanny had developed a solid contact list of technical and financial services support associates with whom he could network. Given his strong working relationship with many of them, and the numerous lucrative bank contracts that resulted from his dealings, Lanny felt that many of them owed him a job.

Despite his large prospect list, he was beginning to feel isolated as time wore on. Several weeks had elapsed since the curtain fell on his Continental-American career, yet only a handful of people in his network had acknowledged his plight via a returned email or phone call. Lanny knew that the shoe was now firmly on the other foot. He got wined and dined over the years by contractors whenever he had a big budget to back him up. But unemployment held a different stigma: rejection.

The heat was also on at home. Jill Taylor, his wife of 15 years, was a stay-at-home mom and responsible for watching three young boys—a full-time career in itself. The Taylors had lived well during their marriage, buying a nice home in Anaheim. They were fulfilling the American dream with the latest model cars, great vacations, and plentiful food on the table.

Jill was becoming a little more than anxious. She could see that Lanny was slowly losing momentum in his employment search. She noticed that while he started out of the gate strong on his searches, his spirits dimmed as time dragged and prospects dried up. Jill did what she could to keep him motivated, but with the clock ticking on his short severance agreement, tensions in the household were running at an all-time high. She had even connected her husband with an L.A.-based executive recruiter, a referral she had received from a close friend of hers. But that effort had also proved fruitless.

The Taylors' style of living had worked against any financial cushion for emergencies. Their high-on-the-hog lifestyle diverted funds into everything but savings and investments over the years. When the severance ran out, the mortgage, car and insurance payments would become impossible to service. Lanny and Jill knew all too well that time was of the essence in landing a new job.

Lanny was darting down the freeway on his return trip home after meeting a friend in downtown L.A. It was a pleasant break from the grind of job-hunting, with Lanny choosing instead to spend a relaxing hour with a buddy over lunch. The sun was shining brightly on the late spring day and L.A. traffic seemed lighter than normal for a Thursday afternoon. His cell interrupted the bliss.

"We need to talk," Jill's voice cracked. She skipped saying hello.

"About?" Lanny asked, knowing full well what was on her mind. She sounded like she was crying.

There was tense silence. "We have to decide what we need to do next, Lan. I'm not...it's just that..." Her voice trailed.

Lanny's heart sank. He never anticipated that he'd be in such a bad situation. His entire career was filled with advancement and success. He had never once been fired or laid off. It was becoming too much to bear.

With the phone still pressed to his ear, the road noise around him got louder, but it was unmatched by their mutual, deafening silence. All at once, it hit him: His entire world was completely falling apart.

TWELVE

Andy Gerhardt was stretched out on his bed when there was a soft knock at the hotel room door. The flight to Miami took longer than he anticipated due to morning thunderstorms parked over the Ohio Valley, which forced him and the Midwest Federated corporate jet he was piloting to take a long, circuitous route out of the way. Now he was bushed. He was hoping for a few hours of relaxation before wandering downstairs to find some lunch.

As the company's primary pilot, Andy often found himself sequestered in hotel rooms or wandering the grounds of various venues while Midwest Federated executives attended functions at sites all over the country. He wasn't paid much, but the thrill of flying a Gulfstream IV business jet and visiting cities that he only dreamed of seeing as a kid were compensation enough. While he had to be on call like some over-trained taxi driver, he never thought he'd be flying so much this late in his lifetime.

He slowly eased off the bed, his 61-year-old body creaking as he strode to get the door. Through the peephole, Andy saw the youthful face of Ron Mayville, his new 35-year-old company copilot.

"It's Mister Cramer," Ron said with some concern in a hushed voice, quickly entering the hotel room and closing the door. "He's pissed." Ron nervously rubbed the back of his short brown hair.

Andy knew that it was standard operating procedure for Mr. Cramer to be mad about something. Cramer was a very particular and selfish traveler, normally reserving the corporate jet for just him and three or four other close executives; anyone else who needed to travel was forced to fly commercially. God forbid if something was out of place or not up to expectations during one of these trips; that's when the fur flew.

Mr. Cramer got very involved in the planning details of the latest annual bank outing, which was being held at the expensive and fashionable Beachside Resort and Hotel along Florida's eastern coast. Andy remembered hearing all the chatter during recent trips about how the meeting was to be so much more fun and relaxing than previous trips, especially since the board and shareholders had recently approved the millions of shares of stock and the new golden parachutes for company executives. The event was an entire week in Florida for the board members, the bank's regional presidents, wives, guests, and the CEO himself to enjoy golf, tennis, shopping, cigars, and people-watching, all written off under the auspices of a business meeting.

"Why is he pissed?" Andy asked.

"It's the beer," Ron said. "Turns out we were supposed to load several cases of Maylard's brand beer onto the jet, but that instruction didn't reach the hangar in Saint Paul before we took off."

Andy knew that Maylard's Beer was a rare and expensive ale that became Mr. Cramer's favorite after a brief trip to Wisconsin during the previous year. As gratitude for the long hours of flying at the time, Mr. Cramer had awarded him a case of the concoction, made at a microbrewery near Milwaukee. Andy thought the beer packed a wallop and clouded his cognitive abilities more than any other beverage he had ever consumed. The aftertaste was bitter, almost acidic, and he only recently discarded his remaining supply.

Andy rubbed his eyes, causing his glasses to bounce up and down on his nose. "I suppose you're about to tell me," he said, exhaling in frustration, "that they can't substitute a different brand for something more...local."

"Correct."

Andy tilted his head down to look at Ron over the top of his glasses. "How many seconds did he give you to explain?"

"Thirty."

"He *is* pissed." Andy rubbed his eyes again. "Then, let me guess," he said with a frown on his face. "We're instructed to return to Saint Paul."

Ron nodded slowly. "Immediately."

"Of course," Andy sighed. "Immediately it is, then."

Within 40 minutes, the two pilots were wheels-up and headed back to Minnesota at 32,000 feet, all alone in their Gulfstream IV business jet, on what was sure to be the most expensive beer run in history.

THIRTEEN

The phone rang at least three times before Wil could even force an eye open to look at the caller I.D. screen. He had become quite used to sleeping in, having negotiated a June start date for his new job as the marketing director of Midwest Federated Bank in downtown Minneapolis. He had a few more days of break left, and he intended on catching up on as much rest as possible.

When it rang again, he squinted through sleepy eyes at the phone. UNKNOWN CALLER filled the phone's display screen, so he just ignored it. He had answered several repeated anonymous calls during the week, but each time, he was met with silence.

"You sure are popular this time of day," the groggy-sounding female voice said, coming from underneath the covers. Jessica Tolkin had frequented Wil's bed on and off during the previous six months, representing one of the longest, if not most inconsistent, relationships he had had in quite some time. She was different from the other women who drifted into and out of his life. The other women were usually corporate professionals who worked in the banking or investment industries, caught up in their own careers—and themselves. What made this former Chicago native different was the fact that Jessica was not only smart, but also grounded, funny, and genuinely engaged in Wil's interests. Most of all, she wasn't hell-bent on a professional career. She had worked in the restaurant industry as a waitress and hostess for most of her adult life. That meant lousy hours and even worse pay, but those things didn't bother Wil. He was falling in love.

"It's these damn telemarketers," Wil said, yawning as the phone finally quit ringing. He rolled away from the phone and pulled down the covers, kissing her exposed bare shoulder. "I suppose we have to get this day started eventually." He gazed into her eyes as though he was going to kiss her intensely on her lips. But he decided instead to tickle her to the point that she gyrated wildly, laughing and kicking the covers completely off of her beautiful, artificially tanned body.

"I need to get going too," she yawned, stretching her arms above her head and looking at the clock on the nightstand. "I've got to be at work by noon today." As a restaurant employee, Jessica's erratic hours only added to the chaos of their ongoing relationship. "I'll make a quick pot of coffee."

Wil rose from his bed and headed naked into the bathroom. "Make it a strong batch," he said, shutting the door behind him.

"I always make it good and rich," she answered, her voice loud enough to project her morning hoarseness through the bathroom door. Jessica retrieved her clothes that were scattered on the floor and quickly dressed.

As he gazed at his stubbly face in the bathroom mirror, Wil felt confident that he could hit the ground running on his new job at Midwest Federated Bank. Despite his lack of respect for the company, he had no regrets about accepting the role, and the fact that he was to be paid a severance by Union First Bancorporation for a few more weeks, while collecting a sizable paycheck from his new employer, made the thought of his transition all the more palatable.

He splashed cold water onto his face and realized for the first time that he was getting anxious to start his new job. Waiting for him on his first day would be the results of some consumer research he had asked Barney Jennings to commission as a way of quickly understanding the Midwest Federated brand attributes. Mr. Jennings wanted Wil to bring the bank's image out of the 1970s, but brand research was not something that Dick Cramer or even Mr. Jennings had in mind. Wil was good at the power of persuasion, and he got Mr. Jennings to agree to the research project as a kind of condition of employment.

Wil had hired Cox Research Group, a well-respected consumer research company in Minneapolis, to conduct the study. The bank's budget for such things was small compared to the bottomless money troughs that Wil was used to managing at Union First, but he was able to convince the people at Cox that more business might be in the offing if they did a good job on a shoestring budget. Cox was hired to interview 1,000 random consumers in the metro about their banking habits, their perceptions of banks in the area, and brand-related information, all of which should prove interesting to Wil and Midwest Federated management. He also hoped that the results would make a strong statement about his abilities as a strategic marketer; he wasn't just going to shoot from the hip on his new job. Wil liked data and information to guide and support his decision-making, especially as it related to marketing and advertising. The conclusions of the survey were expected to be on his desk on his very first day.

He examined his face in the mirror, rubbing the stubble that had formed overnight on his chin. *It's going to be good to be back doing what I do best,* Wil thought, bringing another handful of cold water to his face.

The phone rang again. "Do you want me to get that?" Jessica shouted from the kitchen.

"I've got it." Wil emerged from the bathroom and dashed to reach the phone on the other side of his king-sized bed. "Hello? Hello?" Still nothing but silence from the other end.

Sheesh, he thought. *Relentless telemarketers.*

FOURTEEN

Lanny Taylor sat in the driver's seat of his parked car staring blankly out the windshield at Temescal Park in Los Angeles. It was early morning in L.A., and the area was largely deserted. It was at that moment in the silence and isolation of his vehicle that Lanny knew he had hit bottom. His former business contacts had not yielded any meaningful leads for quite some time. Worse, his wife had completely withdrawn from him. His friends seemed to avoid him as though he had a contagious disease. And the pitiful 10-week severance agreement was ending. With nothing to hope for and without a backup plan in place, the Taylors were in deep, deep trouble.

    He sat motionless, looking into the fog that was just beginning to lift above the park. He thought of his boys. He thought of Jill. He thought of the life of comfort and indulgence that he naively believed would last forever, but was now becoming a memory.

The vintage British Enfield revolver was in his family since the 1930s, handed down from his World War II veteran grandfather to Lanny's own father some years ago. Lanny was ashamed to have taken it without permission from his dad's home in San Francisco. But he was careful to keep it well hidden in a rarely-used wooden storage box in his basement, locked away where Jill and his kids had no knowledge or access to it.

The revolver looked particularly shiny and polished, Lanny observed, even when illuminated with just the dull, diffused light of a foggy morning. He held it in his hand, admiring its weight and feel. With just one bullet in the six-round chamber, he knew it could unleash more than enough power to accomplish the deed that he now contemplated.

He picked up his cell phone from the seat beside him and punched the redial button once more. This time, he vowed that he'd finally identify himself when the call was answered. Today was the day—the hour and minute crashing down upon him—and Lanny knew that the only person in this world who could stop his next despicable act from happening was a man who lived 2,000 miles away. It was a cry for help that, up until now, he was too shy to verbalize. His life was now literally in the hands of a friend who lived in the middle of the country: a friend named Wil Fischer.

FIFTEEN

Jessica finally emerged from the bathroom looking refreshed, having just applied some lipstick and arranging her hair into a neat ponytail. She didn't have clean clothes into which she could change, so she would do what she always did when she stayed at Wil's house: race home, shower and dress into her uniform in time for her shift at Currell's Restaurant in Richfield.

She joined him by sitting at the breakfast nook in the kitchen, which overlooked a large pond across the street. The weather was finally warming in Minnesota, and the geese had returned in full force, nearly covering the water's surface for what was certain to become a mid-morning honk fest.

Wil sprawled the *Minneapolis Daily Post* onto the table in front of him, positioning his coffee cup far enough away to avoid spilling it during his page-turning session.

"Anything new in there?" Jessica asked, bringing a cup of steaming coffee to her lips.

"Politics, politics and more politics," Wil said. He unfolded the Business Section and found a brief article about the Union First and Continental-American merger. He quickly scanned the article, reading that federal regulators had finally approved the transaction between the two companies. He slowed long enough to read a quote from CEO Robert Harrington, who was attributed as saying that Union First locations across the country were to be renamed "Continental-American Bank" in the coming months. *With all those branches, that'll make some sign company very happy...and rich*, he thought.

He read further and shook his head when he reached the paragraph in which Mr. Harrington was quoted as saying that there would be "few layoffs at this time due to the acquisition." *Right*, Wil thought. *Most of the layoffs had come before it.* He didn't finish the article and quickly turned the page, stopping on the Midwest Federated anti-merger ad that had been running for several weeks. He allowed himself a snicker.

"What's funny?" Jessica asked.

He turned the paper around to show it to her. "What do you think of this ad?"

She squinted at the headline. "Bank changing its name?" she read. "Midwest Federated is waiting for you." She snickered back. "Wow. Makes me want to just run over there and open an account." A louder laugh followed.

"I hope I know what I'm doing, joining up with this bank." Wil said, shaking his head. "This is just embarrassing."

"You'll be able to make a difference there right away, I'm sure," Jessica said. "I don't even have an advertising background, and I could make an ad better than this."

He smiled. "Maybe I should hire you."

"Think again." She glanced at her watch. "Speaking of which, if I don't get going, you may be forced to hire me, because I'll be fired if I'm late again." She got up from the table and kissed Wil goodbye. "Thanks for everything."

He returned the kiss, holding her lips to his own even longer. He pulled away sharply and looked into her eyes. "My pleasure."

Jessica winked and left the house. Just as the front door shut behind her, Wil's phone rang.

"Damn unknown number," Wil said aloud in the now empty house. "Leave me alone!" After the fourth ring, Wil masterfully snagged the receiver with the tips of his fingers in a quick, single motion.

"What do you want?" he shouted, pressing the handset firmly and uncomfortably to his right ear and cheek. "Speak!"

He fully expected that some robotic voice was about to inform him of the benefits of aluminum siding.

"Wil?"

The voice was weak and sounded as far away as the lunar surface. Wil paused, straining to hear the distant sound.

"Yes?" There was static on the line, and it crackled in a spiking pattern that told Wil there was a lightening storm dancing on a cell tower somewhere.

"Hello?" the weak and distant voice asked.

"Lanny?" Wil answered. "Is that you?"

SIXTEEN

The Gulfstream corporate jet had made its appointed beer run to Saint Paul and was back on the ground in Miami by 7 p.m. eastern time that night. Andy and Ron had arranged for a large SUV to greet them at the airport so that they could transport their bulky cargo of expensive liquor back to the resort hotel.

    Andy was used to not only serving as the corporate jet pilot, but also as a waiter, maintenance worker, concierge assistant, taxi driver, and now, beer distributor. A Hispanic hotel staff member met the black-colored SUV as it drove up to the main doors. Andy signaled Ron to jump out to help unload a dozen cases of Maylard's Beer onto a flatbed cart. The hotel's staffer guided them into the plush surroundings of the Beachside Resort and Hotel, which was located alongside the beautiful Atlantic coast.

The cart was heavy, so the only way up to Mr. Cramer's presidential suite was the service elevator. The three men wrestled the unwieldy cart into the carriage and pressed the button marked *VIP*.

Once arriving on the twelfth floor, they all noticed a dull but heavy bass sound thudding its way down the hallway, growing louder as they neared the suite's doors.

"This is where President Clinton once stayed when he visited," the staffer shouted above the noise in a thick Hispanic accent.

"Really?" Andy asked. "How much?" Andy grunted as he talked, struggling to push the cart full of beer down the carpeted hall.

"Tres mil dólares," the man answered with a grin.

"A night?"

The man nodded. Andy shook his head.

They all stopped at the door and knocked. Once opened, it became instantly obvious to Andy and Ron why the price was three grand a night. The presidential suite sported two baby grand pianos, three bathrooms, a bar, a large kitchen and enough living space to accommodate a small army if necessary. Tonight, however, it was filled with bank executives, board members, girlfriends, guests—plus a lot of other people who Andy did not recognize.

"Well, hell's bell's, there you guys are," said Mr. Neymeier, the president of Midwest Federated Bank in Kansas City, shouting above the loud music in his nasally voice. He rushed up wearing a garish Hawaiian shirt, a broad smile lighting up his face, and a drink balancing in his right hand. Mr. Neymeier always thought he was the funniest person in the room. "You guys are the most popular people here who aren't in attendance."

Andy and Ron just nodded at him and wheeled the heavy cart into the suite's main foyer.

"Did you keep 'em refrigerated?" Mr. Neymeier asked, hovering over the beer load.

"Oh yes," Ron answered in an assuring tone. "They're still good and cold."

"Where's Mister Cramer?" Andy asked tersely. Andy wanted to tell the man personally that the precious cargo of alcohol had finally arrived.

"He's doing a 'see-see-see' in the biffy," Mr. Neymeier said.

"A what?" Andy asked flatly. He dreaded the answer.

"You know. A see-see-see. Right in there." Mr. Neymeier pointed toward the bathroom door.

Andy and Ron gave each other a puzzled look. They had noticed several unidentifiable but attractive and seductively dressed women going in and out of that particular door from the very moment they had entered the suite. But Andy couldn't begin to imagine what was going on in there—much less what a "see-see-see" was. He was certain that he didn't want to know.

Andy suddenly felt claustrophobic, so he decided it was time to cut and run. "Could you just let Mister Cramer know that his beer order is here?"

"No, no!" Mr. Neymeier shot back in his hyper-high voice, sloshing a portion of his drink over the side of his glass. "Go on in. You tell 'em yourself, right in there!"

Ron looked Andy square in the eyes and fought hard not to blurt out a laugh, for he knew that Andy hated this kind of scene. It was a kind of *Bankers Gone Wild* underworld that Andy always tried to avoid.

Ron attempted to bale out his fellow pilot. "You, uh, want me to take care of this?"

Andy raised his eyebrows and took on a mischievous grin. "No. You're too young." They both smiled and Andy took several steps toward the bathroom door. His steps quickened as he trailed behind a tall, young woman wearing an incredibly tight blue cocktail dress and carrying a razor-thin purse. As he followed her, Andy also noticed a small and delicate tattoo in the shape of a rose that was visible on her long, gorgeous neck, positioned just above the collar bone.

As he entered the bathroom, Andy was relieved at the temporary protection it provided from the loud music that permeated the rest of the suite. The lighting was dim in the room, and once his eyes adjusted he couldn't believe the enormity of the space; it was as large as some hotel rooms alone. He also noticed how easily the bathroom handled the all-female crowd.

There was abundant laughter and giggling coming from the thick mass of tall and tanned women who mingled near the vanity on the opposite wall. Andy still couldn't spot Mr. Cramer.

He decided to step in a little farther, trying hard to remain unnoticed. As he got closer to the throng, he finally saw Mr. Cramer near the full-length mirror at the far end of the room. He was seated in a chair wearing tan pants and his usual canary-yellow shirt, and he was facing the long mirror.

Andy stood there a moment, observing, attempting to get a grasp on what was going on. Above all, he wanted to ensure he didn't interrupt the proceedings just to tell Mr. Cramer that his beer had landed. He reasoned that such ill-timed interruptions would undoubtedly generate negative repercussions.

Several women were standing in a semicircle behind Mr. Cramer's chair. Andy soon focused again on the tall, attractive one who was wearing the tight blue cocktail dress—the woman he had followed into the room. He watched as she looked in the smaller mirror above the sink, and he marveled when she removed a comb, brush, lipstick container, and several other unidentifiable items that he thought couldn't possibly fit in a purse that small. He also thought it was strange that she was emptying the purse's contents onto the vanity—but then the whole scene in the room was odd.

He turned his attention back to the larger group just as one of the women in the semicircle broke ranks and sauntered up to the full-length mirror. She pranced in front of the mirror seductively, wiggling her hips and tossing her long hair, acting like she was parading in front of a camera. The woman shot herself a sexy look in the mirror and turned her head toward Mr. Cramer, a move that got the entire group of women behind him cooing and applauding. Mr. Cramer sported an expression of great pleasure and approval.

Andy was still unnoticed by the crowd, free to observe the entire event from just a few feet away. But because he didn't understand what he had just walked in on, he was beginning to feel more than a little uncomfortable.

The woman who was parading in front of the mirror quickly turned back to face the glass, placing both of her hands on each side of her breasts. Andy could see that she had carefully positioned herself in the mirror just so Mr. Cramer could get a good look at her reflected frontal image. The CEO simply sat there smiling—taking it all in.

With her hands on both sides of her barely covered bosoms, the woman pushed inward as hard as she could, bowing out her cleavage from her body toward the mirror. The other women cooed some more, and a few even applauded the act. Mr. Cramer raised his right hand and extended his thumb upward in a gesture of approval, which generated more applause.

It was then that Andy realized that the "see-see-see" referenced by Randy Neymeier was in fact the legendary and mythical C.C.C.: a "Cramer Cleavage Check." It was known in some circles as a tall tale; until now, that is, with Andy witnessing the entire bizarre event himself.

One of the women in the semicircle suddenly noticed Andy standing in the soft light near the shower stall. This caused all of the other women to look his way. It was an awkward moment for Andy, feeling as though he had just been caught by his mother while looking at pornographic magazines. He could only clear his throat. Mr. Cramer then turned to him, his facial expression growing stern.

"Andy, did you get the beer?" Mr. Cramer asked, using a tone that had a standard clipped professionalism normally reserved for board meetings and contract negotiations.

Andy kept his cool. "Yes sir. It's right out there." He nodded toward the door.

Mr. Cramer turned away from him, looking back at the mirror. "Thanks, Andy." An uncomfortable beat followed.

"Good night, sir."

"Good night."

Then, as though someone had just changed the universe's channel, the group looked away from Andy in unison just as another participant in a low-cut dress and wearing white pearls broke from the crowd and sauntered over to the mirror. The woman smiled into the reflection, her hands cupped her breasts, she squeezed, and Andy quickly left.

SEVENTEEN

The rain was falling so hard that Wil could barely see the illuminated short-term parking sign at the entrance of the Minneapolis-St. Paul International Airport complex. The sound of the rain that pounded his windshield drowned out the sounds from the radio as he drove up the concrete ramp. He paused just long enough to grab the ticket stub from the entry kiosk, causing his sleeve-covered left arm to get completely soaked.

    The car rumbled up the parking ramp and he immediately found an empty spot near the terminal entry doors. He sprinted inside and examined a bank of arrival monitors that flickered with information on dozens of inbound flights. To his relief, he discovered the flight from L.A. was only 10 minutes late despite the lousy weather. He got through security with ease and was waiting at the gate moments later.

He felt good about the snap decision to fly Lanny to Minneapolis and was glad to pay the $1,400 fare. He wasn't completely sure what Lanny was going through, but Wil would have paid any amount to save his friend from what sounded like the depths of despair.

Lanny was one of the last passengers to disembark the aircraft. When Lanny emerged in the jet way door, Wil thought he looked especially pale and noticed that he had lost weight. Wil gave him an awkward, brief hug, and little was said between the two men for quite some time.

They were headed north on I-35W toward downtown Minneapolis when Lanny finally loosened up. "Shoe's on the other foot, huh? Now you're picking me up."

"The very least I can do for you," Wil said softly.

Wil pulled the car into a parking stall at North Country Bar, his favorite evening hangout on Second Avenue in Minneapolis. He led Lanny through the rain and up a rickety flight of stairs to the rear entrance of the joint. They headed to an unoccupied corner of the long bar and ordered two beers from a beautiful Hispanic bartender. Within moments, two frosty mugs appeared in front of them.

"I want you to know something," Wil said, nervously rubbing the condensation off the side of his mug. "I may have an opportunity for you."

Lanny just finished chugging his beer and stared down at his empty mug. "C'mon, man. Last I heard, you weren't working for a charity organization."

"I'm serious," Wil said, looking Lanny straight in the eyes. "This outfit I'm going to work for, they need help. They employ a lot of people, but they're kind of old-fashioned. They need solid project leaders and innovators. Your programming background will probably get you hired right off the bat."

"Oh, come on."

Wil signaled the bartender to refill Lanny's mug. "Midwest Federated is a big company with great earnings and a lot of growth potential," Wil said confidently. "And the gloves are off for them. I think they really want to make a difference."

"So, what'd this Midwest Fed guy give you, anyway?" he asked. "Sounds like you got a good deal."

Wil looked away from Lanny.

"Come on. You can tell me."

Wil smiled. "Oh...great salary, bonus...and a car."

Lanny stopped his beer mug short of his mouth. "A car?"

Wil nodded, a bigger smile swelling on his face.

"They gave you a car? You son of a bitch."

"We can probably get you the same deal. Do you think your wife would move to Minnesota with you?"

Lanny shrugged. "I don't know. But let's find out. Give me your cell. I'm way too far over on my minutes." Lanny hopped off his bar stool and took Wil's cell down a dark hallway that led to the restrooms.

With Wil alone at the bar, the bartender walked up. "One more?" she asked.

"Why not," Wil answered, pushing his empty beer mug closer to her.

The bartender pulled a draft. "I couldn't help but overhear. You work at Midwest Fed?"

"I will soon. Monday."

"New hire?" she asked. "Where you coming from?"

"Union First."

"Oh, lots of changes over there."

She put the refilled beer mug down in front of him and he took a big swallow. Wil looked up at her to notice how black and shiny her hair appeared in the low light of the bar, which provided an attractive complement to an equally attractive Hispanic face.

"Felicia Cortez," she said.

"Wil Fischer." They shook hands.

"I hear they're changing their name to Continental-American in a few weeks."

Wil studied her for a moment. "For a bartender, you seem to know a lot about banking."

She smiled. "I work at Midwest Federated too. I'm a branch manager by day, bartender by night."

"Interesting concept. How long have you worked at Midwest Federated?"

"Couple of years. But I've got to warn you, things aren't all that great there either."

He furrowed his brow. "Don't tell me..."

She nodded. "They don't treat people very well. I mean, I'm just a lowly branch manager, so I can't expect much. But many people complain about working there. Lots of old guard running that place."

Must be a phenomenon in banking, he thought.

"What are you going to be doing for the bank?" she asked.

"I'm your new marketing director."

"Marketing?" Her voice went up an octave, and she raised a hand to her mouth to cover a chuckle.

Wil sat his beer mug down with a thud. "Why is that funny?"

She waited until the grin disappeared from her face. "You're not responsible for that ad in the paper, are you?"

Wil frowned. "Oh...that ad? Absolutely not. I haven't started there yet, remember?"

She laughed again, toying with him. "Those ads," she said, shaking her head. "We all had a good laugh about them at the branch."

Wil nodded and slurped the foam off the top of his fresh mug. As Felicia stepped a few feet away to serve a newly seated customer, Lanny finally returned. He grabbed his beer mug with both hands and sported a renewed, contented look on his face.

"Well?" Wil asked.

"Jill said she'd follow me anywhere if it meant a new start."

Wil turned to him and grabbed his shoulder. "That's great, Lanny. Give me a few days to get my feet wet over there, and we'll be talking."

EIGHTEEN

June 2000

The traffic report indicated that there were several accidents clogging up the main arteries feeding the Twin Cities, and Wil didn't want to be late for his first day of work. The Midwest Federated regional building on Third Avenue in downtown Minneapolis was just a few short blocks from the Union First Bancorp Tower—soon to be known as Continental-American Place—so he knew the back streets well. He had often avoided being part of the assault of vehicles that charged the downtown area every morning, and today was no different.

Wil arrived a few minutes before 8 a.m. and was to report to Human Resources on the tenth floor. There he was to spend part of the morning learning about the Midwest Federated benefits package, the 401k, and filling out the necessary paperwork that comes with starting a new job. After that, he was certain that he was going to spend time with Regional President Barney Jennings, who would undoubtedly introduce him to the marketing staff and other key players in the bank.

He stepped off the elevator and turned right, dutifully following a gray and white sign with an arrow that indicated the direction of the HR department. He got just a few steps down the hall when he was greeted by Jane Duprey, the Midwest Federated Human Resources director. Short, athletic, with the deepest, bluest eyes Wil had ever seen, Jane was 49 years old and wore a tailor-cut dark blue suit trimmed with a white blouse. Her naturally brown hair revealed a slight suggestion of gray and was cut at shoulders' length. Expensive silver jewelry adorned her neck and ears.

"Is that Wil Fischer?" she asked, pausing in mid-tracks.

"Wow, am I that obvious?" he asked jokingly.

"It's that power suit. A dead giveaway," she said, chuckling. "I'm Jane Duprey, Midwest Federated Human Resources." They shook hands. "We're going to have a change of plan this morning." Her bright, welcoming facial expression suddenly turned serious. "Something last-minute has come up and, well, we might be able to use your expertise."

Wil had just met the woman, but he thought that she suddenly looked very uneasy. Jane grabbed his elbow and gently prodded him back toward the elevator.

"All right," he answered with a shrug. "I'm up for that."

They boarded the elevator and she pushed the button to the first floor, their descent starting immediately. They soon arrived nine floors down, and Jane guided Wil into a small conference room at the end of a stubby hallway. The room contained a huge round table, too large for the space it was occupying, with a speakerphone sitting in the middle.

She shut the door behind them and motioned for him to sit down. She positioned a pair of designer reading glasses on her nose and removed a small notebook from her jacket pocket. She opened the book to a page in the middle and located a phone number. With her index finger, she slowly punched the number into the speakerphone's keypad.

Wil sat silent, watching her. She seemed so focused and in her own little world that he hesitated to say anything for fear of breaking her concentration. As she continued her methodical dialing, Wil could wait no longer for more information. "Can I ask who you're calling?" he asked sheepishly.

Jane paused in mid-dial and looked up, as though realizing just then that someone else was in the room. "I'm so sorry," she said. "Of course." She turned toward him. "We have a bit of a situation...a media situation that we think you might be able to help with. I'm getting Duke Slaytor on the phone. He's in Miami with the rest of the management team and board members, and there's...this...a reporter...who is making things interesting for us." In a nearly robotic motion, she looked back at the keypad and punched in the remaining numbers.

Uh oh, Wil thought. "What kind of reporter?" he asked her, folding his hands nervously in front of him.

"Do you read the 'My Sources Say' column in the Minneapolis Daily Post?" she asked.

He nodded. "Sometimes." He answered with a lie. Wil didn't care too much for gossip columnists, but Candy Luther from the *Minneapolis Daily Post* was the most popular muckraker in town, so he wanted to acknowledge that he at least knew of her. Wil figured that if Candy Luther was writing something about Midwest Federated, it probably wasn't good.

Jane kept dialing. "Seems that Candy is convinced she's got a bit of juicy gossip on an executive of ours, and she called John Gale, one of our board members, on his cell to confirm it. What she didn't know is that John is also in Miami, so he was able to alert the guys down there."

Wil blinked. "What is the gossip that she's trying to confirm?"

The ringing finally began, blaring over the speakerphone. "That's what you're about to find out." After the third ring, the call was answered.

"Duke Slaytor."

Duke R. Slaytor, age 57, was the head of Midwest Federated's Information Technology Division. Divorced as many times as Dick Cramer, he was an unwavering Cramer loyalist and held the auspicious honor of being the first person to be hired when the CEO assembled his executive team in the 1980s.

"Duke!" Jane said loudly in a tone that Wil took as reverence.

"Hi Jane," Mr. Slaytor said.

"I have Wil Fischer here with me."

"Good," he said. "Say, Fischer, sorry I couldn't meet you in person. Our meetings down here ran long."

Wil cleared his throat. "No problem."

"Listen, Fischer, do you know Candy Luther?"

Wil glanced at Jane, who kept her eyes fixed on the speakerphone. "I don't know her personally," Wil answered. "But I know of her."

"Yeah, well, Candy Luther somehow got a tip that makes her think she has some information on the goings-on during the meetings down here. Seems she thinks that there was some improper behavior among executives."

Wil's eyes grew wide. *What the hell?* Craving some kind of non-verbal communications, he looked again at Jane, but her eyes stayed locked on the phone in front of her. "What kind of behavior?" Wil asked tepidly.

"It's not important what it was," Mr. Slaytor said loudly. "It's all baloney, anyway. She makes this stuff up. Listen, we're all down here, and you're more available there. I know you're new, and I don't know what you're capable of. But Fischer, do you think you could get her off our back?"

Wil felt the hairs on his neck rise. He fancied himself as a marketer and manager, but despite having worked in the TV industry, damage control was not his forte. He looked again at Jane, her eyes steadfastly avoiding him. Wil cleared his throat again. "I suppose I could try," Wil stammered. "What exactly should I say?"

"You're the marketing guy, so you tell me," Mr. Slaytor said. "All you need to know is that we're having great meetings down here about the company's future. She's just trying to sell papers. That's all."

Wil struggled to swallow as his throat went completely dry. "But it would be most helpful if I knew what she thought she was writing about," he squeaked.

"Look," Mr. Slaytor said with an angry shortness evident in his voice, "you just need to work some magic with her and tell her to get off of it. Can you do that, Fischer?"

Wil looked at Jane. She still didn't look at him. "Uh, sure," he said meekly. "I will, but I have to meet with Barney Jennings later this—"

"Barney's down here with me," Mr. Slaytor snapped. "I'll tell him you're working on it."

Wil was suddenly very annoyed at finding out that his boss was not in town on his first day. He was led to believe that Mr. Jennings was planning to spend the afternoon with him, getting him acclimated to his new job. "I understand," he said softly. "I'll see what I can do."

"Good," Mr. Slaytor said. "Call me back with an update as soon as you have one."

Jane finally looked at Wil with an apologetic expression on her face. Wil's heart sank.

They all said their goodbyes and Jane reached over to shut off the phone.

Wil sighed. "I suppose we don't have a public relations person?"

Jane Duprey shook her head.

Wil couldn't hide his concern. "Wouldn't it make more sense if Mr. Cramer or someone else handled this instead?"

Jane forced a smile and shrugged. "Feel complimented," she said, gathering up her notebook and standing. "They want you."

NINETEEN

The newsroom of the *Minneapolis Daily Post* was a sea of cubicles. The clacking of computer keyboards filled the air, and the barely audible sound of various news channels that barked from numerous wall-mounted TV monitors created a methodical background hum.

The *Post* was the highest daily circulation newspaper in the Twin Cities, boasting some 450,000 households as measured from Monday to Saturday, with the Sunday edition growing to 1.3 million households. It was widely regarded as a politically liberal paper. Mr. Cramer himself often used his local clout to write letters to the editor and guest editorials on topics that ranged from politics to government programs, and they all received prominence in the *Post*.

Candy Luther stood among the piles of paper stacked indiscriminately on her desk in the oversized cubicle she had occupied for years. Candy had worked in newspapers all of her adult career, and spent the last 18 years with the paper. At the age of 49, she had attained the honorary title of the longest running gossip columnist in the paper's 98-year history. Just five years before, Candy had generated gossip of her own when she was often seen leaving the downtown condo of Abbott Van Kirk, the prominent Minneapolis attorney who was a likely future candidate to be Minnesota's Attorney General. The gossip subsided when she finally married him in a wedding day spectacle that was befitting a queen.

A well-dressed woman with blonde hair and darkened roots, Candy bounced from paper pile to paper pile, the phone being held to an ear in one hand while she rifled through paper stacks with the other. Angry that no one answered her call, she pitched the phone through the air and into its cradle with scientific accuracy, something she had plenty of practice doing. The handset hit the cradle, bounced, and nestled itself into its predetermined slot. A moment later, one of the phone's lines lit up with a blinking red light.

She bent down to get a closer look at the caller I.D. screen. She didn't recognize the number, but she did recognize the three letters that were positioned above it: M.F.B.

She removed a pen from her mouth. "This is Candy."

"Yes, Miss Luther, I'm Wil Fischer, vice president in charge of marketing at Midwest Federated Bank." Sitting alone in the conference room on the first floor of the building—Jane Duprey had long since left—Wil was doing his best to sound robotic and unaffected.

"Fischer? Fischer? I don't know a Wil Fischer." She scribbled his name down on a piece of paper.

"Yes, you see, I am new to this position," Wil said hesitantly. "I understand that you were attempting to contact one of our board members today regarding official Midwest Federated business."

Candy's guard was up. She knew immediately when she was being handled. "Mister Fischer, I have it on good authority that your executive management has been in Miami. Can you confirm that they were there?"

"Yes, I can confirm that. They are often attending meetings around the country." Wil wasn't sure of that fact, but he was reasonably sure that such a statement was within the realm of probability.

"And, Mister Fischer, can you confirm that Chief Executive Officer Richard Cramer was there as well?"

"Sure. I can confirm that."

"Mister Fischer, I'm working on a story about the fact that there was a get-together with your executive group on Saturday night in the presidential suite of the Beachside

Resort and Hotel in Miami, where the meetings were being held."

Wil swallowed hard. Sweat was breaking out on his forehead. "Okay. How is that relevant to anything worthy of your column, Miss Luther?"

"Mister Fischer, my sources tell me that there were some hired hands in attendance at that meeting."

Wil paused. *Hired hands?* "Can you be more specific?"

"On which part?"

"The hired hands part."

"Yes," she answered. "I have it on good authority that they were hired females."

"Excuse me?"

"Mister Fischer, your executive management group had a so-called official bank meeting on Saturday night, and I happen to know that there were paid women on site."

Wil's heart was racing. *What the hell kind of a situation have I walked into, anyway?* He paused again, thinking. "Miss Luther, can you please tell me the source of your information?"

"Of course not. I never reveal my sources."

Wil did his best to sound lawyerly. "Miss Luther, you are obviously reporting erroneous information. There was no such meeting on Saturday night, nor were there any hired hands or other impropriety that you are asserting. Until you reveal a source, your facts are incorrect, irresponsible and if you print them, I regard them as libelous." Wil's blood was coursing through his system at warp speed. It was only 9 a.m., and he was already wishing he had brought along a fresh change of shirts.

"Sir, you are a publicly-traded company, and I don't have to reveal my sources. I am going to run with this in my column tomorrow, and I'm giving you the chance to comment on this situation."

Wil sat back in his chair. The early June sun was still low enough on the eastern horizon that it peeked between two tall buildings and blinded him as it radiated through the conference room window. He felt it warming his face as he paused.

"Let me get back to you."

Sensing that he was cornered, he ended the connection and quickly hit another line, redialing the last number he called, which was the switchboard of the *Minneapolis Daily Post*.

"Good morning," he said loudly. "I'd like to talk to Gene Danielson." Wil hadn't seen Gene for over a year, ever since Wil was plucked from his previous employer's marketing group to join its product group. Gene served as the executive director of the *Post's* display advertising for many years. At the time Wil was working with him while still at Union First, he always felt Gene had some influence over many levels of the newspaper. Wil knew now that he was about to find out how much.

"Gene, it's Wil Fischer calling, formerly of Union First Bank, now with Midwest Fed."

Gene was glad to hear from Wil. After some chitchat, the man explained to Wil that he wasn't very happy about the fact that Union First didn't buy as much display advertising after Wil left the company's marketing group, and there was very little advertising dollars now coming out of the L.A.-based Continental-American marketing unit. Wil listened patiently, letting Gene say his piece, despite the fact that he could do nothing about it.

"I want you to know that I've been hired here for a reason," Wil said. "These guys at Midwest Federated want to take this bank to the next level. The only way I'm going to be able to accomplish that is by changing the brand. And you know what that means."

"More advertising," Gene shouted. "You're talking my language, Wil."

"I'll need to buy plenty of newspaper space." Wil knew he was out on a limb. He didn't even know where this bank's marketing department was located, much less how big the ad budget was, but he needed to butter up Gene as much as possible. "You have it on my personal authority that I'm going to be tossing a lot of new business your way in my role."

"That's great!" Gene said. "Midwest Federated Bank has been buying some remnant space in the paper here and there lately, but nothing consistent. I always take care of Mister Cramer, you know. I give him good rates, but nothing like I could give you if you'd lock into a contract. When can we get together to discuss it?"

"Soon, Gene. Real soon. But first, can you do me a favor?"

"Name it."

"Can you check on something with Candy Luther?"

"Uh oh. Does she have the crosshairs on you?"

"Not on me. But she doesn't have her facts right."

Wil could hear a few papers rustle on Gene's end.

"What a surprise," Gene said.

Wil smiled. "Any chance you can get in the middle of it?"

There was a pause. "Let me see what I can do."

TWENTY

Wil awoke especially early the next morning and groggily descended the staircase toward the front door. Still squinty-eyed, he slowly navigated the carpeted steps, recalling that his first day as Midwest Federated's marketing director was more lively and eventful than he thought possible. He had spent part of the morning with the Miami crisis, and then was holed up in HR to sign forms and get answers to his benefits-related questions. After that, he spent the remainder of the day meeting individually with the current staff of six marketing officers, assessing their strengths and getting to know them. Somewhere in between all of that, he had called Miami to leave Duke Slaytor a message, updating him about the Candy Luther story. Because of being so busy on his first day, he remembered with frustration that he didn't even have time to review the consumer research findings that he had convinced Mr. Jennings to commission some weeks before.

"Where are you going?" Jessica called from the bedroom.

"Newspaper," he said. The paper was wrapped in a blue plastic bag, a sign that told Wil the paperboy had probably expected rain that morning. As he leaned over to grab the package off the front step, he spun around long enough to notice that the sky looked free of all clouds.

Once back inside the foyer, he isolated the Metro Section from the thick packet of newsprint and turned to the page that contained Candy Luther's gossip column. Her article was unusually verbose that morning, running three full columns in the upper right-hand corner of page five. The amount of copy in the column made him cringe. He feared that his efforts to squash the story by leveraging his friend Gene had failed miserably. *Shortest amount of time on the job—ever.*

He scanned the column, using a speed-reading technique that he learned from a local anchorman while working in television. But he didn't see anything about Miami, or Dick Cramer, or Midwest Federated at all. He had to be sure, so he quickly rescanned the column, this time at a much slower speed. Still nothing. He let out a long breath and closed his eyes.

Thank you, Gene.

Wil opted to take the I-35W route, watching the gleaming skyline of downtown Minneapolis slowly growing larger in his windshield. He felt exuberant, giddy almost, for he had just achieved an incredible first-strike victory, dodging the proverbial bullet—perhaps two. He had kept his company out the paper, avoiding the embarrassment of potentially libelous news, while also demonstrating to his management that he could be an effective part of the team, even on his first day! He had won the equivalent of the World Series, he felt, and he was enjoying the personal victory as he drove toward downtown.

With Mr. Jennings expected back in Minneapolis by now, Wil was convinced that he would be treated as a hero as soon as he walked in the building. But as he thought more about the situation, something was nagging him, spoiling his triumph for more than a moment.

What if the story is true? he wondered. *Is this the kind of thing that happens all the time at the bank? And if so, what does that make me now—an accomplice?*

Wil drove his car into the Midwest Federated parking ramp and took the first stall he could find. He was looking forward to arriving someday in his new company car, something that Jane Duprey promised to make a reality in the next few days. He headed into the building and took the elevators to his office on the sixth floor.

It was early, 7:30 a.m., so human presence was still rare on his floor. Wil knew that most marketing people were usually late sleepers, and while he didn't know his staff that well yet, he figured that he would always be the first one in the office from now on.

His office was spacious with a decent view. The furniture overwhelmed the room but seemed fairly new and unscathed from its previous occupier. The bank's Marketing Department shared space with the Legal Division, and because the bank had operated without a marketing director for many years, Wil presumed that his office was likely a recent home to an attorney.

Wil flipped on the lights and booted up the computer on his desk. He was pleasantly surprised to find a sheet of instructions nearby that told him exactly how to log-in to the bank's computer system. After keying in the proper passwords and codes, he was finally into his new email box.

No messages...yet.

He turned his attention to the drab wallpaper and gritty windows of his sixth-floor space. His office had potential, but it wasn't as bright and cheery as the one he left at Union First. He then noticed a large bouquet of flowers that was centered on the small meeting table in the corner, and he was dumbfounded about why hadn't seen it when he first walked in. He got out of his chair and ambled over to the table to open the small card dangling from the clear glass vase.

Congratulations on your new gig! Love, Jessica. The card made him smile.

He returned to his desk and picked up a fat blue folder that contained a label with the words *COX RESEARCH GROUP* printed on the front. The folder was several inches thick, and he fanned the pages to get a sense of what was inside. He noticed charts, graphs, tables of numbers, and lots of text. He loved research, so he hoped that he could find the time during the day to dig into it thoroughly.

He opened the first page and read the description of the survey criteria:

> *A total of 1,002 adult consumers in the Minneapolis and St. Paul metropolitan area were randomly surveyed via paper and phone interviews for this confidential research project to gain knowledge of their attitudes, beliefs and biases as they relate to their personal banking experience.*

He got that far, and his phone rang. The phone's I.D. screen indicated that the call was coming from the executive floor, so he picked it up immediately.

"Good morning, Wil," the familiar female voice said. "This is Victoria Kline, Mister Jennings' assistant on the fifteenth floor. Mister Jennings wants to speak to you. I'll put him on."

Wil realized that the only time Mr. Jennings had ever personally called him without the help of an assistant was when he offered Wil the job some weeks ago. All subsequent conversations were fronted quite formally by Victoria, an approach that struck him as being presumptuous and old-fashioned. He never ran into such formality at Union First, even from the bank's highest levels.

"Hello, Wil," Mr. Jennings said. "How did the first day go?"

"Other than our little crisis with Miss Luther, it went great."

There was a pause over the phone line. Wil had expected some accolades instead.

"What about it?" Mr. Jennings asked, apparently confused.

"I think the pressure that was put on the paper worked," Wil beamed, hoping that Mr. Jennings connected the dots and gave him credit for squashing the story.

"Oh, yes, we have Dick to thank for this one. He called his buddy, Gene Danielson, at the paper. He-he-he threatened a little retaliation, telling him he'd pull all of our advertising if they ran such fiction."

Wil was stunned. "He did what?"

"He-he-he told the paper that we'd never advertise with them again." Mr. Jennings voice was flat and matter-of-fact.

Wil had a nauseating feeling wash over him. He was asked to follow-up with the paper to shut down the story himself, and he felt that he personally applied the appropriate pressure on Gene Danielson. But now he realized that Mr. Cramer beat up on his contact after Wil had already talked to him. *I have an apology to make,* he thought.

"So, Mister Slaytor didn't tell you that I was the one who...?" Wil stopped, realizing that his new boss had no idea that Mr. Slaytor had involved him in the fiasco. Wil finally went on to explain the whole story.

"Sounds like you both had a hand in it," Mr. Jennings said in his usual, non-emotional tone.

It was the emptiest compliment that Wil had ever heard. *What did they think—that I just ignored the whole thing so that Cramer had to step in and save the day?*

After hanging up, Wil decided to shake it off, chalking it up to poor timing and miscommunication on the first day of a new job. He wanted to get back to reading the research findings, but he had to quickly turn his attention to other things. He met again with several staff members, who updated him on the various marketing projects that were in the queue. He was happy to learn that the anti-merger campaign had just ended; he didn't want any of his friends or former colleagues to think that he had had anything to do with it.

As lunchtime approached, Wil decided he would grab a sandwich and head back to his desk to read his research report. He walked out the door of his office suite and was approached by a white-haired man in a plaid sport coat. "Have any lunch plans?" Duke Slaytor asked.

TWENTY-ONE

Mr. Slaytor led Wil down a steep, darkened staircase in a building that Wil was certain he had never visited. The outside sun had constricted his pupils, so he held the railing to avoid falling down the steps and into his 57-year-old luncheon host. Wil focused his eyes onto the top of the man's head, reasoning that the extreme whitish locks he sported must be artificial. The men finally reached a heavy oak door at the bottom of the steps, and Mr. Slaytor swung it open with ease.

"Table for two," Mr. Slaytor said to a young hostess, who recognized him immediately.

"Right this way, Mister Slaytor." The hostess sat the two men in a red leather booth near the back of Ollies, a steakhouse restaurant Wil had never even considered to be on his own list of eateries. This place, he thought, smacked of old guard—and old money.

"Have you been settling in okay?" Mr. Slaytor asked as he adjusted his glasses to read the menu.

"Very much so," Wil said. "Of course, it's only day two, but I'm glad I made the move."

"Lots of changes over there at Union First, I'm told. Were you affected by the merger?"

Wil didn't want to tip off anyone that he had been severed from the bank. "I had a chance to move to California, and I much preferred to stay local. My mom lives in Sioux Falls, and I need to keep a close eye on her. California was out of the question."

Mr. Slaytor nodded. "Understandable."

The two men chatted easily through lunch with Mr. Slaytor doing most of the talking. Wil was waiting for the Candy Luther conversation to come up, but it was being avoided for the time being. As the conversation wore on, Wil learned that Mr. Slaytor was first among the original five men brought in by Mr. Cramer in the early days, and he was struck by Slaytor's broad knowledge of banking, information technology and bank regulations. He was obviously highly regarded by senior management, a fact that Mr. Slaytor made Wil well aware of.

"I have a big stake in this company," Mr. Slaytor said. "As long as Dick Cramer's at the helm, I'll be running Information Technology. We watch out for the shareholders around here, Fischer. We don't spend money frivolously. It's not our style to develop systems and products by ourselves. You're probably not used to that from your Union First days. But here, we wait until such things are developed by other banks, and then we buy the technology off the shelf. We may be late to the market, but it saves us in the long run."

How ironic, Wil thought, *that the head of I.T. would brag about buying tech off the shelf and being late to market.*

"You won't see us advertising a lot either," Mr. Slaytor added. "But I think that's about to change. I know Barney wants to step it up in this market. I suppose that's the right thing to do."

It was then that Wil realized Mr. Slaytor was no fan of marketing. *A tightwad in I.T., and a penny-pinching watchdog for the rest of the organization,* Wil thought.

"So...how did things go in Miami?" Wil blurted out during a lull in the conversation. The question seemed to backfire. Wil was anxious to hear some kind of acknowledgement of his efforts to kill the Candy Luther story, or hear more about Mr. Cramer's decision to beat up his contact, but now he felt he had accidentally dropped a pin-pulled grenade onto the table.

Mr. Slaytor slowly removed his glasses and set them down on the table. "Why...they went very well," he said in a measured fashion, folding his arms in front of him. "I thought we discussed that fact when we first spoke over the phone."

Wil sensed Mr. Slaytor's irritation. "I was just curious, because—"

"Because of the Candy Luther rumor mill?" Mr. Slaytor waived his hand dismissively, and his eyes darted. "Don't worry so much about her. She's been after us since the early days. She loves to make up dish and write about it. It sells papers. In any case, it's something we need to keep under wraps. You know how damaging these things can be."

Wil interpreted Mr. Slaytor's tone as a threat, and that made him feel especially queasy. He was having an even harder time reconciling what Candy Luther had told him about the goings-on in Miami with the trivializing attitude of Slaytor and Jennings. *Would even a gossip columnist risk libel by making up such personal attacks to help sell papers?* he wondered.

It was an odd moment. Wil was looking intently at Mr. Slaytor for any outward signs of deceitfulness, while Mr. Slaytor was staring Wil down to determine how much of the truth he knew. Wil was certain that his own expression revealed his true feelings: there had to be more to the story.

The conversation just hung there, a black cloud of tension hovering over the table. Smelling an opportunity, Wil decided to blink first, looking away from his white-haired lunch host and down at his water glass. "Despite the fact that you don't develop your own systems and products, I'm sure you still look for good people in I.T.," he said, awkwardly changing the subject. "You need solid managers, right? You know the type."

"Yes," Mr. Slaytor answered in a suspicious tone. "That's right, Fischer. We do." Just then the waiter showed up with the check and seemingly out of character, Mr. Slaytor handed off his credit card without even looking at the bill's amount. "We always need good people."

"Duke," Wil said, deciding to assume the risk of sounding too personal, "I have someone in mind who you'll want to hire. In fact, I'd owe you a big favor if you'd hire him in the next few weeks."

TWENTY-TWO

July 2000

Jill Taylor couldn't believe how beautiful and expansive the Twin Cities looked at night. Her night view from the jet's window could have been seen above Los Angeles, San Francisco or any other major California metro area. She had never visited Minnesota before, and she readily admitted that she didn't know what to expect.

With the kids being watched by her parents back in Anaheim, she was looking forward to the time away. Despite the anxiety that her husband was exhibiting, she was viewing the opportunity as a mini-vacation, paid in full, and all courtesy of Midwest Federated Bank.

Lanny held her hand as the jet grew closer to the ground on its final approach. "I'm glad you decided to come," he said. "I need you here with me."

"It's great to get away," she said, squeezing his hand. "I know you'll do just fine."

After checking into a downtown hotel and grabbing a late dinner, they immediately went to bed. But Lanny had a fitful night's sleep. His interview with Mr. Slaytor was scheduled at the regional headquarters building in Minneapolis early the next morning, and he was worried that his travel alarm clock might not rouse him in time. As a backup measure, he called the front desk to schedule a wake-up call, just in case.

As the sun finally rose, the travel alarm clock beeped, followed by the ringing phone of the wakeup call. Jill groaned as she rolled over. Exhausted, Lanny struggled to get his feet over the side of the bed.

"How'd you sleep?"

"Great."

She noticed Lanny's face looked drawn and pale. "You're lying. You didn't sleep at all."

Lanny stretched his arms and walked to the bathroom. Jill got up to peer out the twenty-second-floor hotel window and down to the streets below. It was a beautiful July morning, and she could see that Minneapolis was already bustling, even at this hour.

Lanny eventually appeared in the bathroom door, showered and shaved, nicely dressed in a new suit.

"You look much better."

"You like?"

"I like very much." She kissed him.

"Wish me luck," he said. "I'll come back to get you as soon as I'm done. I can't wait for you to meet Wil Fischer. After my interview, he's taking us to lunch."

Barney Jennings had informed Wil that Mr. Cramer was not a fan of formalized research. In fact, Mr. Jennings had told Wil how Dick Cramer had often conducted his own research by simply asking friends, acquaintances, relatives, even waitresses, what they thought about a particular banking issue. Mr. Cramer was known to make big decisions with heavy financial impacts that were based solely on input from a few random interviewees.

Wil felt confident that he was a step ahead by keeping his research presentation materials short and to the point. The last thing he wanted to do in his meeting with the top man was to overwhelm him with a lot of distracting and unnecessary gibberish.

Wil was also confident that he was an expert on the consumer research findings. He studied the thick packet of results for several weeks, and Mr. Jennings insisted that the material be presented to Mr. Cramer as soon as Wil was ready. It was finally show time.

Wil was looking forward to meeting Mr. Cramer. He was on the job for just a month, and he couldn't wait to start having ongoing, meaningful interaction with him. He had the feeling that the man at the helm of Midwest Federated Bank was bigger than life.

It was to be a good day. Once he was done with his presentation at the Saint Paul HQ office, Wil planned to drive back to Minneapolis to meet Lanny Taylor and his wife for lunch.

Wil arrived at the Saint Paul headquarters on time and immediately headed to the second floor. He decided to visit the executive bathroom near one end of the opulent hallway to ensure his dark blue suit and red tie looked crisp. Once inside, he was immediately greeted by an elderly man dressed in a white jacket. The man could have been well into his 70s, and he simply nodded at Wil, standing statuesque. Wil felt uncomfortable. *An attendant in the bank's executive bathroom?*

Wil leaned in toward the huge mirror above the double sink and self-consciously straighten his collar. He washed his hands, and the man in the white jacket promptly handed him a soft white hand towel. "Thank you," Wil said, not knowing if it was proper to show gratitude for such a mundane service. The man nodded again and swiftly returned to his stoic position. *What does someone like him get paid?* Wil wondered.

Wil bounded back into the hallway and approached the large waiting area that was halfway down the corridor, which was surrounded by beautiful, light-colored ornate woodwork. He introduced himself to Marci, Mr. Cramer's assistant.

"Mister Cramer will be with you in a moment." Her smile was friendly, her face welcoming.

"Has Barney arrived yet?" Wil knew Mr. Jennings was going to meet him here for the presentation, but Wil didn't see his car in the parking lot when he drove in.

"No. I'm afraid Mister Jennings won't be here. He called a little bit ago and said you should go on without him."

Wil suddenly felt weak. While he was looking forward to meeting with Mr. Cramer, he had heard many stories about the man's uneven temperament. He would feel more comfortable if Mr. Jennings was in the room during his first presentation to the man in charge.

After a few minutes nervously waiting outside of the CEO's office, Wil was finally led inside by Marci, who instructed him to sit in an elegant guest chair that faced the front of Mr. Cramer's huge desk. He noticed immediately that the chair was lower than normal, making him feel diminutive despite his six-foot frame.

"It's a pleasure to finally meet with you, Mister Cramer," Wil said with a smile on his face.

"Yes," Mr. Cramer grunted. The man was seated comfortably behind his desk in a black leather chair. But he was distracted, making no eye contact with Wil, choosing instead to dig something out of the wastebasket that was located under his desk.

As Mr. Cramer dug, Wil opened his leather satchel and extracted two of the three presentations copies he had prepared. He gingerly laid a copy on Mr. Cramer's desk, expecting him to grab it immediately. Instead, Mr. Cramer ignored it, opting to look at a single spreadsheet he had rescued from the trash and was now perched in a landscape position at the end of his fingers.

For what seemed like a lifetime, Wil's printed presentation sat untouched near the edge of the huge desk. Wil nervously eased the packet ahead an inch at a time with his fingers, pushing it toward Mr. Cramer. As Wil inched it forward, Mr. Cramer suddenly seemed satisfied with whatever it was he was looking at on the spreadsheet, and he quickly deposited it back in the wastebasket. He then snagged the presentation with one hand, drew it toward him, and spun it around on the desk. He rebalanced his pair of reading glasses on his nose and opened the presentation to the first page. A frown immediately developed on his face.

Wil nervously cleared his throat. "I guess Barney won't be here this morning, so I guess we can just get started." The tenseness in the room was killing Wil. He wondered if Mr. Cramer even knew that Barney Jennings was supposed to be present in the first place. He also wondered if Cramer even knew the subject of the meeting.

"I've tried to keep this fairly short and in summary form," Wil said with forced confidence, watching the brow on his CEO's forehead wrinkle up. "So, if you turn in your presentation packet to page—"

"Marci!" Mr. Cramer interrupted. "Get in here!" He closed the presentation cover with force and held the packet at one corner, letting it dangle off of his stubby fingertips.

Marci was a middle-aged brunette, attractive and smartly dressed, and Wil's growing discomfort diminished slightly when she appeared in the doorway with a smile. She seemed so relaxed, and her expression was somehow reassuring to him.

"This thing has staples," Mr. Cramer snapped. "Get rid of them."

"Yes, Mister Cramer." She looked at Wil. "Do you want anything to drink while you wait?"

Wil was starting to sweat. The only drink he wanted now contained a hundred proof, so he simply managed to shake his head.

Cramer looked at Wil and glared over his glasses with steely eyes. "Hate staples," he harrumphed. "Next time, no staples."

Wil was embarrassed. Barney didn't mention anything about a staple fetish. He knew the man had some eccentricities, but staples? He was mortified that he had gotten half a sentence out of his mouth, only to be interrupted by the thought of a quarter-cent fastener.

Marci returned mercifully fast with the packet, sans staples. She handed it to Mr. Cramer and he immediately reopened it to the first page. "Continue," he commanded to Wil.

Wil cleared his throat a second time and tried to boost himself up in the squatty chair. "More than a thousand customers and non-customers were surveyed in the Twin Cities on their attitudes toward banking," he said, keeping his voice steady. "The results clearly show three key trends from their attitudes. First, they don't want to pay a lot of fees. They're willing to pay something when there is concrete value for the service, but they are quickly turned off when they get dinged just for checking their account balance over the phone or for seeing a teller.

"Second, they want accuracy. Nothing pushes them over the edge more than a wrong statement or an inaccurate address on a pack of new checks.

"And third, they want better access to their money. The research clearly shows they want to be able to bank when they want, and where they want. Consumers want better hours, better Internet access and ATMs that have more functionality, like check-cashing or postage stamps."

Mr. Cramer paged through the presentation fitfully as Wil talked. Wil could tell the man wasn't following along; Mr. Cramer was obviously one of those people who skipped ahead rather than stay engaged with the pacing.

Despite the rudeness, Wil kept going. "The research also allowed us to find out what our own customers are thinking. Unfortunately, they don't see our branch people as being very competent. While they like our multiple locations in the metro area, we're losing some relationships because some customers feel our staff isn't very well trained on products and services."

Cramer abruptly stopped flipping the pages and closed up the packet. He held it with both hands and glared at Wil as he talked. Wil couldn't tell if Mr. Cramer was interested or irritated. He decided to continue.

"They also think we're not open long enough, that our operating hours are inconvenient," Wil said. "Work patterns have obviously changed over the past few years, and being open from nine to five doesn't cut it anymore. People want to bank when they're running errands after work or on the weekends. Midwest Federated, and all other banks for that matter, need to have extended hours of operation. We shouldn't close at noon on Saturdays. Branches should stay open much later."

Mr. Cramer plopped the packet onto his desk. He removed his reading glasses and laid them on top of the packet, then folded his arms in front of him and leaned back in his leather chair. Wil paused.

The CEO's eyes blinked slowly. "What does the research show about our latest anti-merger campaign?" Mr. Cramer asked pointedly, his eyes gazing up toward the ceiling in an obvious attempt to intimidate his guest.

Wil quickly tried to make sense of the question. The anti-merger campaign was over, but it was so poorly done that up until now, he had put it completely out of his mind. "We didn't ask specific questions about advertising," Wil said, "but the trends clearly point to an opportunity for us to take advantage of the Union First Bank name change. People don't like their banks changing ownership. It makes their heads spin."

Cramer unfolded his arms and placed his palms down flatly on the desk. "So," the CEO asked impatiently, "what did you think of our campaign?"

At last, he wants my opinion, Wil thought, misreading the situation. Wil had decided he was always going to be honest, so he was. "While it struck on an interesting angle, I think it was poorly executed."

Cramer didn't bat an eye. "How so?"

"It didn't speak to consumers at their level. It was just banking gibberish."

"Oh?" The CEO remained stoic except for a thick black eyebrow rising over one eye.

Wil plowed ahead. "The ads didn't look professional, in my opinion. Some of the people I talked to agree. In this market, we need to look better than that and raise the bar in quality." Wil felt good that he was being brutally honest. He hoped to gain points for his transparency, even if he had wandered into a hostile situation.

"What does your little survey say about friendly bankers?" Cramer asked acidly. "What does it say about that?"

Wil played nervously with the packet of paper in his hands. "Friendliness doesn't come out as a primary attribute. Being friendly is really a bi-product of being competent. Our customers want bankers who perform their jobs well, who know the products, and who don't make mistakes.

Friendliness won't cover that up. Competence has to be a priority when it comes to handling people's money. That's what they're asking for first."

Mr. Cramer pushed himself back from his desk and stood. He took several purposeful steps until he arrived at the mounted steel I-beam near his office door. Wil thought it was inappropriate to stand, so he twisted his body around in the chair to ensure he kept the man in view.

"I come from an extremely humble background," Mr. Cramer said, admiring the beam's sheen. "I came up through the ranks by knowing my business, and knowing my customer." Mr. Cramer glided his right hand over the top of the steel, a movement that Wil took as a caress. "I never had to pay for research to find out who my customer was," he continued, his tone becoming more patronizing. "You simply look them in the eye and shake their hand. That's how you find out what they want."

Wil realized that he was in trouble. Mr. Cramer didn't believe anything Wil had said, and true to form, the man was discounting research that was conducted by one of the best consumer research firms in the Midwest.

"I also believe that asking people what they think is the right thing to do," Wil said, fighting to keep his voice from wavering, twisting his waist in the squatty chair even more. "But this research has a statistical significance of plus or minus two percent. You can't get that kind of accuracy with just a couple of individual interviews."

Mr. Cramer looked over at Wil and stared at him for moment. Wil's tall body was uncomfortably contorted as he struggled to keep his face pointed at the powerful man wearing the canary-yellow shirt. Somehow, Wil held the man's gaze.

"Okay." Mr. Cramer took his hand away from the steel beam and dropped it to his side. "That will be all. Thanks." With that, he stepped over the threshold of his office door—and left.

Wil felt his legs go numb from being in such an awkward, unnatural position. He sat there stunned, his brain flooding with thousands of thoughts, his warped body all alone in the empty office of the Midwest Federated Bank CEO.

Oh my God, Wil thought, *I'm dead.*

TWENTY-THREE

Ron Mayville had the hangar all to himself. He liked these moments alone when he could spend quality time inspecting his aircraft. It was a trait taught to him by his father, who was a commercial pilot decades ago for Pan American prior to its bankruptcy, and a corporate pilot for many years before he passed away. His father was often on Ron's mind. It was he who had given Ron his first flying lesson at the age of 14, and from then on, he was hooked. Before leaving college he knew that desk jobs were not for him; flying was his ultimate fate. His father was also a stickler for safety. *Check it, check it again, and then again,* he remembered his father often telling him.

He walked slowly around the Gulfstream business jet, its white fuselage gleaming under the hangar lights. He looked under the wings, carefully inspecting the flaps. He dragged his fingertips along the wing, feeling the smoothness of the aircraft's lightweight skin.

As the new company copilot, Ron couldn't believe he was in charge of such a beautiful craft. His career skyrocketed from the moment he got his first corporate job at the age of 28, flying insurance company executives back and forth between Minneapolis and the east coast. Now here he was, a corporate copilot working for one of the largest banks in the Twin Cities.

He wanted to make one final inspection of the interior of the craft before he left for the day. Some routine engine maintenance and instrumentation upgrades were completed during the summer downtime, so Ron knew that Andy would appreciate the duplicate review.

After completing a thorough pass around the outside of the jet, Ron ascended the aircraft's steps and ducked as he entered the cabin. He flipped on the interior lights and looked to the right, toward the tail section. He loved the leather smell of the inside of the craft, and he stood there taking in the luxurious cabin. It reminded him of his grandfather's motor home, a beast of a vehicle in which he often traveled when he was a kid. But he was certain that even that "overgrown bus," as his grandfather used to call it, was no match for the deluxe accommodations of this multi-million dollar aircraft.

Ron walked to the jet's tail, looking for anything out of place. He knew Andy had probably made sure the interior was clean after the last flight, but it was a tradition for pilots and copilots to ensure that no stone was left unturned, either inside or outside the craft.

As he walked back toward the cockpit, a glimpse of something white caught his eye: A corner of a magazine was sticking out of a leather pocket on the side of one of the passenger chairs. He stopped and shoved it down, but it got caught on something as he repeatedly pushed on it. He decided to pull it out so he could reorient it and try again, and that's when he discovered it wasn't a magazine after all. It was a long white envelope, blank and unsealed, with several large color photos sticking out above the flap.

Ron removed the photos and flipped through them. They were dark and grainy with a green hue that indicated they were taken in low light, without a flash. Despite the poor quality, the details were easy enough to make out.

Ron blinked repeatedly and rapidly, letting his eyes adjust in the cabin's lighting. He could see that the images were shocking and disgusting, and they became even more disturbing when he recognized the man who was in all of the shots. As Ron absorbed the voyeuristic images, his eyes grew wider, and his breathing became more nervously shallow.

He sat silent in the passenger chair, stunned. In the solace of the empty cabin, Ron realized that returning the photos was not going to be an option. With the stack between his two hands, he instinctively shoved the wad back into the envelope and returned it to the chair's leather pocket where he had found it.

At all costs, he wanted to ensure that no one ever knew that he had seen such appalling and private photos of Richard Edmund Cramer.

TWENTY-FOUR

It was the longest day of Wil's life. First he had a near disastrous encounter with the CEO of Midwest Federated Bank. Then his planned luncheon with Lanny and Jill Taylor was put off because Lanny's interviews ran long. The rest of the day was filled with dread from the morning encounter, made worse by the fact that Barney Jennings hadn't even bothered to call to see how things had gone.

That evening, Wil was looking forward to a stiff drink. He picked up Jessica after work and told her all about his bad day, and then headed back to downtown Minneapolis to the North Country Bar. Lanny and Jill met them there and after introductions and shaking hands, the four of them sat at a table near a window that overlooked the street.

"I'm anxious to hear about your interview, Lanny," Wil said after swallowing a mouthful of chilled beer. "It had to be better than my day. How'd it go?"

"You, my friend, are my hero," Lanny said. "That was probably the best set of interviews I've ever had. There's no doubt in my mind that I'll get the manager job."

"Let's not start picking out houses yet," Jill said. "We need that offer first."

"It'll come. And we have Wil Fischer to thank."

"Shut up and buy more beer," Wil said in jest, raising his beer mug to prompt a toast.

After a swig of their drinks, Jessica leaned in, fidgeting to keep her long brown hair off of her shoulders. "Kind of a contrasting day for both of you, though," she said. "You had a great day, but Wil's day wasn't so much."

"Never mind about it," Wil said frowning.

"What happened?" Lanny asked. "I thought you met with the head honcho, what's his name…?"

"Dick Cramer. Yes, I met with him. And it didn't go all that well."

"Wasn't that on your research project?"

"Yes."

"Let me guess. He doesn't like research."

"Precisely."

Lanny took a shallow sip of his beer. "Doesn't surprise me," he said. "Guys like that are all ego. They don't want to be told what to do, so they listen to nothing other than their own instincts. I think it's a requirement for being a mucky-muck."

"I don't understand it," Wil said, shaking his head. "This research is thorough, right on the mark. Customers want better access to their money, longer hours, and more competent people in the branches. It's not rocket science. These executive types need to realize that retail is changing. Banks can't just operate from nine to five anymore. They need to be open and available just like the big-box retailers. People want to be able to bank when and where they want. That's what this research proves."

"Sounds like a good idea for an ad campaign," Jill said.

"It was, until I talked to Dick Cramer. He seemed offended by the whole thing."

"Don't worry about it," Jessica said. "Maybe he'll think more about what you said. I bet he'll come around."

Wil doubted it.

After draining his glass one more time, Wil raised his hand to alert the waitress to bring him another drink, desperately trying to create an alcoholic buzz that would severely dull his senses.

TWENTY-FIVE

Late September 2000

The Minnesota summer was fleeting, but its warmth held on longer than usual. With the days growing shorter and the weather quickly changing, the blue skies and warm sun were finally being replaced by the grayish, cool clouds of late September.

Corporate pilot Andy Gerhardt had just drifted off to sleep in his own bed when the phone jarred him awake. It was 12:41 a.m. His wife, Margaret, who was a light sleeper for most of their marriage, didn't flinch. They were both getting on in age, and sleep was something that the two of them enjoyed.

"Hello," Andy said groggily.

"It's Dick," the curt voice said. "We're going to head down to Vegas by morning. Can you get the jet ready by then?"

There was a lot of background noise and what sounded like giggling as Mr. Cramer talked, but Andy couldn't distinguish the voices. Andy squinted at his watch again. He looked over at his wife, who was snoring soundly.

"This morning? Shouldn't be an issue, Mister Cramer," he said, pushing out his voice to sound as alert as possible, a habit after all these years. "What time would you like to leave?"

There was more noise and giggling. "Let's get going by six," Mr. Cramer said quickly. "I'll see you then."

The call ended abruptly and Andy was tempted to put his head back on his pillow. But that was a dangerous thought, as he knew he'd fall right back asleep. He removed the covers instead and swung his aching legs over the bedside. Rubbing the sleep from his eyes, he retrieved his cell phone from the night stand, powered it up, and hit the memory button to call Ron Mayville.

Wil's alarm buzzed him awake at 5:45 a.m. He leaned over to kiss Jessica, who joined him in bed after a late night at the restaurant. He'd let her sleep by trying to get ready for work as quietly as possible.

After showering and dressing, Wil grabbed a days-old bagel from the fridge and headed out the door, arriving in his downtown Minneapolis office by 7:15. It was to be a big day for him: He was close to signing a deal with a local home builder to give away a lakefront cabin in northern Minnesota. The cabin and property were worth more than $250,000, and all that Cabin Lake Construction, Inc., required to make the deal happen was that their name be plastered on all of the bank's advertising during the promotional giveaway.

Wil was convinced that this promotion was going to put Midwest Federated Bank on the map. Consumers who opened an account were to be automatically entered to win, and due to sweepstakes rules, those who didn't want to make a purchase could simply fill out an entry form in the bank. Wil was well aware that a lake cabin was considered gold in Minnesota. Residents were considered true Minnesotans only when they joined the weekend ritual of heading "up to cabin" on some northern body of water. A promotion where a free cabin was the ultimate prize was sure to create a lot of buzz—and a lot of new accounts.

Barney Jennings was thrilled with the idea, and Wil felt he was finally making progress in his quest to make more noise in the market. He had been on the job a few months now, and despite a weird but forgotten meeting with Mr. Cramer during the summer, Wil was certain that things were starting to look up. He had weeded out some of the dead wood in his department, and his marketing staff was getting stronger and more credible.

He had also hired Kari Bender, early 30s, newly married, and extremely talented in all things marketing. Wil had known her from his corporate marketing days at Union First, and he realized how lucky he was to get her. She was fast becoming Wil's right hand. Her creativity and ability to put logistics together were a godsend, especially when it came to operating in the Midwest Federated culture. Wil understood that to be successful, he would have to create a department that was the equivalent of an internal ad agency, with resources that could field a variety of marketing requests from all over the bank.

Just after lunch, Wil had finished reading his emails that piled up during his morning meetings when Kari appeared at his door. "I got the call from Cabin Lake Construction," she said, a smile on her face.

"Tell me they said yes."

"You got it. It's all locked down. They've agreed to give away their model cabin on Lake Mille Lacs in exchange for the equivalent of three-hundred-thousand dollars in cooperative advertising."

Wil had negotiated that point himself, knowing that to properly kick off this campaign he needed to spend upwards of $300,000 in newspaper, radio, billboards and direct mail just to get the word out.

"When can we get started?"

"As soon as the contract is signed. All the advertising is ready to go."

Wil could not have been happier. He wanted to share his good news, so he picked up the phone to call Barney Jennings.

Andy had landed the Gulfstream jet in Las Vegas by 10 a.m. local time. It was now early afternoon, and all he could do was to sit and listen to his stomach rumble from a lack of food. He hadn't had time to grab a bite to eat before takeoff at Holman Field in Saint Paul, and he was regretting it.

The car he had reserved from the Vegas airport barely registered 100 miles on the odometer, and the new car smell was practically overwhelming. To tamp down the factory odors, he ran the air conditioning on full blast, which eventually become a requirement as the day's heat rose; the Nevada sun baked on the idling black car as it sat outside in the Vanguard Hotel's parking lot.

Andy was switching channels on the radio, trying to keep the volume low, when Ron awoke and leaned his passenger seat forward, his eyes slow to open.

"I really needed that," Ron said, yawning.

Andy shook his head. "How can you sleep in this thing?"

"I can sleep anywhere." Ron rubbed his eyes and squinted at his watch. "Time for some grub, don't you think?"

"Thought he'd be back by now," Andy said. "Normally he doesn't take this long."

Ron shot Andy an inquisitive look. "What the heck are we doing here, anyway?"

Andy smirked. "You're kidding, right?"

"I have an idea, but..."

"But you don't want to admit that you're working for a guy who can't keep it in his pants?"

Ron rolled his eyes. "I've seen his wife. She must be getting too old for him."

"Harriet?" Andy asked. "She's a terrific person. You'll get to meet her some day. He'll take her to their New Mexico ranch occasionally, probably only when he has to. I've had the chance to spend time with her on those trips. Although sometimes I do admit that I feel like an executive's spouse-sitter."

Ron looked over at the entrance of the hotel, which was well within visual range even from their remote spot in the vast parking lot. He then thought of the pictures he had seen on the plane. "Do you think she knows? I mean, does she even suspect his...indiscretions?"

"I'm sure she does," Andy said. "Don't know how she couldn't know. Maybe she's hooked on his money. Or maybe she doesn't care. Hard to know what goes through the minds of the rich like that. They're all so disconnected from the real world, and they're certainly out of my league."

Ron could see the figure of someone who looked like Mr. Cramer emerging from the Vanguard's main entrance. "Think that's him."

Andy leaned forward to get a better look out of the car's window. Even from extreme distance, he immediately recognized Cramer with the thinning black hair and canary-yellow shirt. Several gorgeous women surrounded him, but the young and beautiful one in her 20s, who was right on his heels, stood out. A desert breeze was blowing, and her long hair was flaring out from her body, waving gently with the wind. She turned to Mr. Cramer and planted a short kiss on his cheek. The other women kissed him more passionately, right on the lips. The whole scene could have been a TV commercial, Andy thought, for a professional service—or for erectile dysfunction.

"I recognize the one with the long hair," Ron declared. "She was at that party."

Andy instantly smirked and nodded in agreement. "The one in Miami with the tattooed rose."

"That's right. Man, she's gorgeous."

Andy was annoyed. Every time Mr. Cramer made him go on one of these junkets, Andy felt dirty somehow. He just wanted to fly jets and finish his career in a few years as the corporate pilot he had become. He didn't want to be some taxi service for an oversexed executive. Ron's hanging tongue didn't help that feeling.

Andy put the car in drive and moved it into the roundabout that was filled with cabs. By the time he had gotten close enough for Mr. Cramer to see the car, the tall brunette and the other women had left. The car came to a halt, the rear door opened, and Mr. Cramer got in.

TWENTY-SIX

The Lanny Taylor family had enjoyed several weeks of occupancy in their new 3,900 square foot home in Bloomington, Minnesota, when Jill Taylor had finally unpacked her way to the last moving box. Following Lanny's acceptance of the job, their relocation went well, with the contents of their California homestead packed and shipped by a national moving company hired by Midwest Federated Bank.

Jill was getting used to her new surroundings. While she considered herself first and foremost a Californian, she marveled at her newfound convenience of living in Minnesota. Compared to the congested area she called home, the Twin Cities boasted a relative lack of traffic whenever she headed out during the day to run errands. There was no smog and no visible crime that she could detect. The cost of living was also significantly cheaper than in Alameda. The four-year-old house in which they now lived—on a quiet cul-de-sac in Bloomington—would have cost four times what they had paid, had it been comparably located in California. And of course, the Mall of America was just minutes away from their front door, which meant plenty of distractions were awaiting her.

Jill was glad that she had had the luxury of the last several weeks to unpack the boxes from their move. With the kids in the local elementary school and Lanny off to full-time work as an I.T. manager at Midwest Federated in downtown Minneapolis, Jill could concentrate on putting things away in an organized and thoughtful fashion. Having repaired the strained marriage she had with Lanny, Jill was finally energized to get her new household put together as a new start.

The box cutter slid easily through the packing tape that held together the lid of the last moving box. The box was tall—nearly four feet high—and she didn't have to bend at all to open up the top cardboard flaps. One by one, she removed the eclectic contents stored inside, including folded blankets, comforters, an old VHS player, and several wall pictures.

There was something heavy at the bottom of the container that she couldn't reach, and she didn't want to tip the box to get to it. Instead, she took the box cutter and slit one corner of the cardboard vertically from top to bottom. She separated the halves and discovered the object to be a square wooden storage container, about the size of a small briefcase.

The wooden container was heavier than she anticipated, so she had to wrestle it out of its cardboard cage. She positioned it on the beige carpet in her living room, and then sat on the floor next to it. As she examined her find, she could not remember what the wooden container was used for, or even where it was previously stored in their former house in California. She had recognized nearly every item that she unpacked during the past few weeks, even the ones that were in storage for the majority of their marriage. This one, though, definitely had her stumped.

She noticed that the wood box's lid contained a small gold keyhole, and her tug at the lid confirmed that it was locked. She lifted the box again, and this time she slowly shook it. There was a heavy clunking noise inside, so whatever it was, it had mass. *Probably a drill or some power tool,* she thought.

Giving up, she stood from her squatted position and carried the box downstairs. She was placing items that she didn't need on two metal shelves that stood in one corner of the long basement. As she approached the shelves, she realized that they contained mostly junk.

Fodder for a garage sale some day, she thought.

There was a narrow opening on the bottom shelf and she wedged the wooden box into it, right next to a cardboard box of old garden tools. She turned, switched off the lights, and ascended the narrow stairs to the home's main level.

"That's-that's-that's great news, Wil," Mr. Jennings stammered over the phone. "When can we get started?"

"Most of the advertising time is secured," Wil said. "I still have some work to do with the Minneapolis Daily Post. I'm working to get their display rates down a little lower. Should be ready to go by Monday."

"You're working with Gene at the paper?"

"Yes. I've known him in my previous role at Union First. He'll come around on the rates."

"Great, great," Mr. Jennings said. "Keep me informed. Good work, Wil."

Finally some affirmation for my hard work.

Wil was quick to realize that recognition was not something that was easily dispensed from Midwest Federated's management. When it did come, it meant a lot.

The lobby area of the *Minneapolis Daily Post* looked just like Wil had remembered it. Its smooth round walls and white woodwork reminded him of a private Washington tour he'd taken of the Oval Office in the White House. As Wil followed the curved wall to the reception desk that afternoon, he passed several front-page mats of the *Post* that studded the walls. *Kennedy Assassinated, Man on the Moon,* and *Berlin Wall Down!* were headlines that caught his eye.

The reception desk was more like a fortress, protected with bullet-proof glass from counter to ceiling, with only a small opening through which the receptionist could communicate. *Must be lots of threats in the newspaper business,* Wil thought.

Wil noticed that the young receptionist who sported a fluffy gray sweatshirt was talking to a tall, well-dressed blonde woman who looked to be 50ish. The woman was barking something at her, but Wil couldn't make out the dialogue due to the clear protective barrier that separated him. For several seconds he was completely ignored, and he was becoming annoyed until the receptionist spotted him out of the corner of her eye and turned toward him.

"I'm sorry...may I help you?"

"Yes. I'm Wil Fischer to see Gene Danielson." The older blonde woman next to the receptionist heard him say his name, and Wil noticed that she immediately left the space.

The young receptionist moved her long, frizzed hair away from her face by pinning one side of it behind an ear, and looked down at a clipboard that was on her desk. "I see on here that he's expecting you. You can have a seat."

Wil thanked her, turned and walked to a group of empty waiting-room chairs on the far wall. He grabbed a complimentary copy of the day's paper and sat down. As he turned to the Sports Section, a female voice from the other end of the lobby got his attention.

"Mister Fischer? From Midwest Federated?" It was the woman who he saw chatting—or arguing—with the receptionist when he walked in.

"Yes, that's me." He stood as she approached. As the woman got closer, Wil thought it was odd that this person, who was obviously a newspaper employee, didn't extend her hand in greeting.

"I'm Candy Luther."

Wil stood there staring a moment, ashamed of himself for not recognizing her sooner. Even though he was not a fan of her gossip column, he had seen her headshot in the paper for years. But now that he was up close and personal with her, he reasoned that her photo must have been taken in her much younger days.

"Pleased to meet you," he said forcefully, extending his hand. But she merely nodded, opting instead to hold onto an oversized red coffee cup with both hands.

"I must tell you, Mister Fischer, I didn't appreciate the business practice that your bank uses for squashing editorial content." Her eyes narrowed as she finished her sentence.

Wil remembered that he himself had attempted to kill the Miami fiasco with the stick and carrot approach: *Treat us well and we'll buy more advertising.* It was a tactic used by many a company as long as newspapers had been around, albeit to various degrees of success. But he also remembered that Mr. Cramer had gone around him—or had barreled right over him—on Wil's first day of work. He was never sure what actually did transpire back then to kill the story.

"Miss Luther," Wil said, "I'm afraid I have no idea what you're talking about."

"I find that hard to believe. Such threats are unethical, and if Richard Cramer wasn't such a good friend of this paper..." Her voice trailed off as she looked over her shoulder to see a visitor enter the lobby and move toward the reception desk.

"I want to make this clear, Miss Luther," Wil said, keeping his voice low to avoid a scene. "I have absolutely no idea what you're—"

"Wil Fischer!"

The voice that interrupted was deep and loud, and Wil knew it could only belong to Gene Danielson. Wil turned to see the portly man in a rumpled tan shirt and creased silver tie bounding through a door marked *EMPLOYEES ONLY*.

Candy Luther's posture suddenly went limp, and she lowered her head in retreat. She shot him an awkward look. "It was nice to meet you," she said, glaring at Wil, turning to leave as Gene walked up.

Gene's hand was fully extended. "It's great to see you face-to-face again, Wil." They shook hands and both men watched as Candy Luther walked away. He shrugged. "Sorry," he said. "I hope I wasn't interrupting."

Wil could only manage a smirk. "No. Don't worry. You weren't."

TWENTY-SEVEN

The Midwest Federated corporate jet was back from Vegas and on the ground at Holman Field in Saint Paul by 5:30 p.m. As the rushing noise of air and engines subsided and the jet turned onto the taxiway, Andy knew his wife would be pleased to have him back for dinner. Daylong junkets with Mr. Cramer often turned into later-than-planned events, and he found himself apologizing to her a lot. *Not tonight,* he thought.

The jet worked its way toward the cluster of corporate hangars and pulled up in front of the one marked *MFB*. The engines slowly wound down to a dead quiet, and Ron leapt out of his copilot seat. "I'll get the door," he said, straining to keep his head low in the cramped cockpit.

Andy stayed in his seat to finish shutdown procedures. He loved this state-of-the-art cockpit, but as he methodically reset the switches and dials that surrounded him, he found himself thinking that it would be okay if someday he never saw the inside of an aircraft again. His wife constantly worried about his safety, and her repeated nagging about wanting him to stay home permanently was finally sinking in.

Finally finished, Andy exited the cockpit and headed back into the cabin. But he was surprised to see Mr. Cramer, the jet's only passenger, still sitting in his leather chair, talking on his cell phone. It was unusual for Mr. Cramer to remain on board so long after the plane had shut down. He was normally itching to open the door before the aircraft even stopped rolling.

Andy looked to his right and out of the opened cabin door, and saw Ron standing on the tarmac, waiting. Ron just shrugged. As Mr. Cramer jabbered away on the phone, Andy headed back to the lavatory to straighten up the cabin before putting the aircraft away for the evening.

Mr. Cramer was loud while talking on the phone, apparently in the middle of an argument. "Don't care," he shouted. "You have thirty seconds to explain it!"

Andy had seen Mr. Cramer angry plenty of times before, but the man's tone was now particularly acerbic.

"We can't miss those numbers in the fourth quarter," he continued in an angry rage. "We'll take a beating if we miss the Street's expectations. You better find something we can cut right now that'll reduce our cash outlay."

With the CEO's voice getting louder, Andy was feeling like he shouldn't be lingering inside the cabin any longer. He headed to the aircraft door and stooped to get his 5-foot-nine-inch frame through its opening. Andy could still hear Mr. Cramer's booming voice even as his head cleared the fuselage and emerged into the chilly outside air.

"Then institute that salary freeze, and pull the pension plan, like we talked about," he heard Cramer say. "Stop screwing around. We need to make those numbers."

Salaries? Pension plan? Andy wondered if he had heard him right. He wasn't sure what Mr. Cramer meant by pulling the pension plan, but Andy knew full well that even if the company stopped funding the pension accounts and left the balances in tact, his planned retirement would have to wait. While a salary freeze wouldn't be a huge setback for him, he needed a few more years of pension contributions to make his retirement numbers work out.

Andy joined Ron on the tarmac at the bottom of the stairs. Ron immediately noticed his look of concern.

"What happened? Something wrong?"

Andy bit his lower lip. "If I just heard correctly," he said, looking up toward the jet's doorway, "everything is wrong."

The sun was low on the horizon with a bank of gray clouds opening just enough to allow a filtered stream of light through Gene Danielson's small office window at the *Minneapolis Daily Post*. Gene spun in his chair to grab the freshly printed contract off his printer, and then handed it to Wil.

"That should be everything you asked for," Gene said. "Dick's a good friend. I'm sure he'll appreciate this."

Wil took a moment to review the advertising rate information on the page and allowed a smile. "I appreciate the competitive rate. I've got to make my ad budget stretch as far as I can, and this really helps." Wil pulled a pen from his black suit jacket and scrawled his signature on the paper. He handed it back to Gene. "I have one more question."

"Anything," Gene said.

"Can you tell me what really happened?"

Gene raised an eyebrow. "Happened? When?"

"Back in June. The whole 'Candy Luther' thing."

"Oh, that," Gene said flatly, straightening out some of the piles of paper that littered his well-worn desk. "What is it that you want to know?"

Wil leaned forward, not wanting to lead the conversation too much. "As I remember it, I had called you about that story she was planning to run."

Gene sat back in his chair, which squeaked in protest against his weight. "I appreciated that. I really did.

Otherwise, I wouldn't have known about the story when I got the other call."

"Which other call?" Wil already knew the answer.

"The call that killed the story," Gene said, evasive.

"C'mon. It's me!" Wil hoped that Gene might respond better if pressured under the pretext of their friendship.

"Listen up," Gene said with an admonishing tone. "Candy Luther attends a lot of functions, all over town. She's a gossip columnist, after all."

Wil waited for more, but the pause stretched on. "And?" Wil prompted.

Gene grinned. "Sometimes, she finds herself even mingling with those she reports on."

Wil was expressionless. "What are you trying to tell me?"

Gene scooted his chair forward until his wide belly squished against his desk, and then carefully folded his hands in front of him. "Sometimes she's even attended functions at CEO's houses, where pictures can be taken." Gene didn't blink, didn't flinch. He just stared at Wil.

Wil examined Gene's face carefully. With Gene's look and serious tone, Wil figured that despite an urge to know more, there was to be no more conversation about it. Wil held his gaze for a moment, and then abruptly stood from his chair.

"Thanks for the contract rate," Wil said. "We'll get the ads over to you tomorrow."

TWENTY-EIGHT

October 2000

"Daddy's leaving."

Jill always called for her three boys to say goodbye to their dad each morning before he left for his job at Midwest Federated. The boys were home today, a vacation from school due to district conferences. But they were up at the normal time anyway, and on command they all came running, their bare feet padding atop the tile flooring of the home's foyer. Leading the way was Kevin, their eight-year-old and oldest son, followed by Zack, who was seven, and Jonathan, who just turned six.

"Goodbye kids," Lanny said, squatting down to hug each boy one at a time. "Have fun with mom today." He stood and planted a kiss on Jill's lips.

"I'll have dinner ready late, around six-thirty," she said, smiling.

"I'll try my best to be here by then," he said, bending down to grab the handle of his black leather briefcase that sat upright on the tiled floor.

She was glad to see Lanny so happy, and as he made his way to his car, she realized that it had been a long time since their lives seemed so...normal. As soon as Lanny left, Jill shooed the kids downstairs to play while she started her cleaning and laundry regimens.

"Too cold to be playing outside," she told them as the three boys rumbled down the steps to the basement.

The Great Cabin Giveaway was in full swing. The advertising was now all over the Minneapolis-Saint Paul metro area, appearing in the newspapers, billboards, on radio, and in direct mail. The first 40,000 full-color direct mail pieces were in consumers' homes, and Wil had high expectations that the bank's business would start ramping up, all due to his first major marketing initiative at Midwest Federated.

Wil was engrossed in his email when Kari Bender appeared at his door. "They're standing in line in Apple Valley," she said, dumbfounded.

Wil looked up quickly from his computer screen and stared at her with a hopeful look. "What?"

"New customers...they're responding. We're getting calls from all over the metro. I just got a call from Cindy, the branch manager at Apple Valley. That branch has a line of people out the door!"

Wil stood up. "You're not kidding?"

Kari shook her head and sifted through a stack of messages in her hand. She paraphrased the messages aloud. "They're completely out of entry forms in Lakeville. The Minnetonka branch had to call in more staff to handle the waiting customers. Maple Grove already hit their checking goal for the month!"

"That is just great news," Wil said, a huge smile lighting up his face.

"Just as you predicted," Kari said. "This thing's going to be a huge hit."

That ought to get some people's attention, he thought.

Little Jonathan was the first one to find the cowboy hat sitting atop a box in the corner of the basement. He quickly donned it and grabbed a garden hose sprayer from another box on the shelf. Instinctively he aimed the sprayer at his two brothers and shouted, "Stick 'em up!"

Zack ran over to him and rummaged through the box, finding a cracked squirt gun near the bottom. He, too, was into the mock fight and made popping noises with his mouth as he dodged and weaved around a make-believe shower of bullets.

"I got you!" Zack yelled. "I got you fair and square."

"Nuh-uh," Jonathan replied as he stomped his feet defiantly, the cowboy hat concealing his eyes. "You missed me, Zack!"

While the two brothers continued to spar over who shot who, Kevin rummaged through the boxes of newfound treasure stacked on the two shelves. He quickly uncovered an old video game console. As he lifted up the toaster-sized instrument to examine it, he remembered that it was the first gaming system he had ever played. He had mastered nearly every game his parents had bought for this system, and the pleasant thoughts of conquering those old challenges motivated him to look even harder for the game cartridges in the boxes of stuff.

Meanwhile, Zack and Jonathan ran around the empty basement, guns blazing, each hiding behind a wardrobe box, the water heater, then the furnace, all in an attempt to avoid the whizzing bullets of each other's imagination.

"BLAM-BLAM-BLAM," Zack shouted, his green plastic water pistol with a cracked handle aimed skillfully at his brother.

Everything came to a screeching halt when a heavy wooden box with a gold lock crashed to the concrete floor. As it hit, there was a loud, sharp crack.

"What was that?" Jill shouted from upstairs.

As if on cue, the three boys were instantly quiet. "They're just goin' bananas," Kevin said, after a beat.

"We didn't do it," the other two boys cried in unison.

As she put another load of laundry into the washing machine, Jill could only hear the overlapping yells from downstairs of three boys who always played rambunctiously. "Play nice down there," she bellowed, knowing that even if they did hear her, she would most certainly be ignored.

"What'd you do?" Zack asked of Kevin, seeing the broken wooden box on the floor.

"Never mind!" Kevin shot back. He leaned over to pick up the box, but the lid was broken, its lock and hinges clearly separated from the wood. Suddenly, out spilled a red velvet bag onto the floor. The bag thudded as it met the concrete, making a dull, but clearly metallic, sound as it hit. Kevin bent over and picked up the velvety bag.

"What's in there?" Zack asked.

"Let me see! Let me see!" Jonathan yelled excitedly.

The bag was cinched up tightly with a white strap. Kevin picked at the strap with his fingernails, but he couldn't figure out how to make it looser. He then tried to force it open by jamming his fingers into the small hole at the top of the bag. It was such a narrow hole that he could only get one of his fingers inside. He wriggled it back and forth, and the hole eventually got larger, but not by much.

"What's in there? C'mon! Let me see!"

Kevin held the bag up to his right eye and tried to look inside the opening. The hole was still too small and the basement light too dim to see anything significant. Holding the top of the bag with his left hand and resting the bottom of the bag in his right palm, he realized that he could push the contents of the bag partially up through the hole.

"Let me see! Let me see!" Jonathan stood on his toes, crowding Kevin as he tried in vain to get his small body tall enough to see the bag's contents.

"Get away," Kevin said, shoving his little brother back with his right elbow.

"Owww! Hey!"

With some trial and error, Kevin figured out that he had to loosen his grip around the top of the bag to allow more of the object to poke through. He pushed as far as he could with his right hand, forcing the stubby black shaft of metal out into the light.

"Wow! What is that?"

"C'mon! Let me see!"

Kevin pushed his two brothers back again by widening out both of his elbows, resembling a hawk stretching its wings to take flight. But the effect of his defense was fleeting as the smaller boys quickly crowded in even closer; the prospect of finding hidden treasure in the boys' new basement was simply too tantalizing to ignore.

There it was, peering out at them, a black metal treasure that was surely worth millions, maybe billions of dollars!

"Oh cool, look at that! What is that? Is it real silver?" Zack asked.

The three boys hovered around the object, just like all kids did whenever a firecracker was lit or a turtle was found in the backyard. Kevin pushed the object as hard as he could in an attempt to pop it free of the velvet bag, but the hole was still too tight. He pushed and pushed with his hand, all the while waiving the metallic object at the faces and chests of his two brothers.

Real danger lurked in that bag, and none of them even knew it.

Unwittingly, the three boys were looking straight down the long barrel of a British-made Enfield Mark 1 revolver.

TWENTY-NINE

CEO Dick Cramer started his weekly conference call with the usual demand from his regional bank presidents to give him an update on checking account production in their individual markets. "You have two minutes apiece," Mr. Cramer said, using his familiar countdown command.

One by one the presidents gave their updates, interrupted on occasion by a question or two from the CEO. The Minnesota region was last again to give an update. Barney Jennings sat behind his desk, a broad smile on his face as he stared at the speakerphone, primed with good news. He was in fine stuttering form today.

"We-we-we have experienced substantial checking account growth with this new promotion," he said. "Our-our numbers for the Minnesota bank are up nearly twenty percent compared to the same period last year. Account balances are also higher. There-there appears to be great demand for this promo. A lot of people in this state want a lake cabin, and when we can give one away for free, they're-they're lining up in droves to open an account to get in the drawing."

A few questions on logistics came from the other bank presidents, which Mr. Jennings delightfully answered. Strangely, Mr. Cramer remained quiet. At the end of the questioning, Mr. Jennings simply said, "That's my report."

"Listen up," Mr. Cramer said. "We need accounts that produce revenue. Checking accounts with higher balances mean fewer bounced checks. We need customers who bounce checks, because that means we collect more fees. Am I clear?"

Mr. Jennings cleared his throat, which echoed across the phone lines to five states. "It's-it's-it's up to us to cross-sell those accounts to make them highly profitable, Dick. The-the-the branch staff needs to do their jobs and make sure those accounts are active. The-the-the important thing is that we sell more services, because that can translate into higher revenue for the bank, too."

Mr. Jennings stopped talking, and there was an instant crackle of sharp static that shot through his speakerphone. For a moment he thought that either he had lost the call—or that Dick Cramer was pounding his fists on his desk in Saint Paul.

"I want accounts that produce revenue," Mr. Cramer demanded. "We need a more compelling draw, something that softens the blow when we charge them for fees. We need to appear to be the friendliest bank around. Midwest Federated Bank should stand for something. It should be the Midwest's friendliest bank!"

Mr. Jennings piped in again, keeping his voice steady. "Re-re-remember that survey data from last summer? Friendliness wasn't-wasn't-wasn't a priority on the—"

"That's it! The Midwest's Friendliest Bank!" Mr. Cramer repeated, loving the idea even more as it came out of his mouth again. "Let's make that work. Barney, can your marketing guy do something with that?"

Mr. Jennings swallowed hard. "Well, I-I-I think that we should first try to—"

"Good," Mr. Cramer interrupted. "We need to be the friendly bank, the Midwest's friendliest." Overlapping voices of agreement chimed in from the yes-men presidents on the line.

"And we should do things to prove that we're friendly!" Mr. Cramer said, each word accompanied by a thumping sound from his fist hitting the table as he talked. "For example, we should get closer to dog lovers." *Thump, thump.* "Dog lovers are loyal." *Thump.* "We should give away dog treats with every single transaction." *Thump, thump, thump.*

"Not everybody likes dogs, Dick," Randy Neymeier, the bank president from Kansas City, said in his grating, cartoon-like voice.

Mr. Cramer was unfazed. "We should go for kids, too. With lollipops. Give every kid a damn lollipop! That's it. I want us to be the Midwest's Friendliest Bank!"

Accolades normally reserved for brilliance poured in through the phone lines from across the Midwest Federated states. But behind a single oak desk in downtown Minneapolis, Barney Jennings could only cover his face with his hands, all the while dreaming of the ocean blasting the rocks along the coast of his vacation property in southern Georgia.

Wil was perusing a spreadsheet that was delivered to his office that morning. It showed new checking accounts, listed by branch, for the entire Minnesota operation.

"Look at that," Wil said. "The numbers are up all over the board. Balances, too."

Kari Bender sat in a guest chair in Wil's office, looking at her own copy of the report. "They haven't seen this much growth in years," Kari said.

"How much advertising is left?"

"A few more weeks. We're still heavy in newspaper and on radio."

"We might want to consider sending more direct mail. This thing is smokin' hot."

The door frame of Wil's office was suddenly filled with the short and wide body of Mindy Munroe, Wil's temporary administrative assistant. He was too busy to find a permanent assistant, so he was relying on temp agencies to fill the void. Ironically, Mindy's vast, squatty body also filled every physical void she happened upon.

"I have a delivery for you," Mindy said.

"Oh, what is it? Flowers?" Wil looked at Kari and grinned jokingly, knowing that he shouldn't be expecting any trophies or rewards—at least not yet.

"No," Mindy answered. "Just this memo. It came from the executive floor."

Wil waived her over to his desk. She handed him a white envelope, its flap sealed with clear tape. The front had two words written in blue ink: **WIL FISCHER**.

Kari continued looking at the spreadsheet in her hands while Wil tore open the envelope. It was an interoffice memo from Duke Slaytor, written to the state's divisional leaders, of which Wil was one. It read:

TO: MFB Divisional Management Team
FM: Duke Slaytor, Executive Vice President
RE: Senior Level Directives

In a meeting today with CEO Richard Cramer and MFB executive management, it was decided that two major initiatives will be undertaken to ensure that Midwest Federated Bank becomes known as the "friendliest bank" in the Midwest. In order to support this initiative, two projects need to be started immediately:

1. Adopt a tagline in all of our advertising, brochures, and on signage where possible and appropriate. This new tagline will be "The Midwest's Friendliest Bank" and will accompany the MFB logo in all cases.

2. All branches should get a supply of dog treats and lollipops to be distributed to customers who either have dogs with them in the drive-through lanes (dog treats), or children with them in either the drive-through or the lobby (lollipops).

Mr. Cramer wants to ensure that these projects are completed immediately. I share Mr. Cramer's enthusiasm for the timely completion of these initiatives.

Wil was beginning to realize that Duke Slaytor, the head of the bank's information technology functions, was also Dick

Cramer's heavy. Wil's heart beat rapidly as he absorbed the information in the memo. *The Midwest's Friendliest Bank? Lollipops? Dog treats?* To Wil, these things were just a simple confirmation that Mr. Cramer ignored all the findings of Wil's consumer research, and that the bank was quickly heading into obscurity. He couldn't help but worry that people he knew in town might think that he alone was responsible for such lame ideas. Disgusted, he handed the memo to Kari, who was still reviewing her spreadsheet.

"Oh my God," Kari said after speed-reading the memo. "Is this for real?"

Wil threw his hands up. "Welcome to Midwest Federated, the Midwest's friendliest bank."

"But…this goes completely against your findings from last summer," she said, her pitch getting higher. "We can't just say that we're friendly. We have to prove we're friendly first by being competent and mistake-free. I mean…dog treats? Lollipops? Those things just cover up the symptoms."

Wil stood up and walked over to his sixth-floor window. "This is crazy," he said, shaking his head and crossing his arms. He was silent for a time as he looked down at the traffic coursing the street below.

"What are we going to do?" Kari asked. "We'll have to cancel our promotion that's running. This just doesn't make any sense."

He turned toward her. "We don't need to cancel it. We just need to make it work, somehow."

"So what's your plan?"

Wil turned toward the window again to notice the buildings across the street being silhouetted against a cloudless October sky. He turned back to Kari. "My plan? I guess you and I are going to make a trip to the grocery store."

Kari raised an eyebrow. "Huh?"

"For dog treats...and lollipops."

THIRTY

Night came fast at the end of chilly October days in Minnesota, with the sun losing its strength shortly after 5:30 p.m. The soft orange glow of the sun's final moments over Holman Field bathed the white hangar in an eerie luminescence, and Andy thought that it was somehow appropriate that it looked almost radioactive. He and Ron had stowed the aircraft after a short hop to Chicago, and they were starved.

"Since my wife's out of town, what do you say we have a good dinner tonight?" Andy asked as he eased into the driver's seat of his car. "My treat."

"How can I say no?" Ron answered. Twenty minutes later, the car was pulling into Currell's Restaurant in Richfield.

"Been here before?" Andy asked.

"No, but I don't want that to stop us. I'm famished."

Andy bounded through the front door first and approached the hostess stand, which was guarded by a skinny blonde-haired woman dressed in a white shirt and dark pants. "Two tonight?" she asked, grabbing two menus from a shelf behind her. Andy nodded, and she led the men to a window table on the street side of the restaurant. "Jessica will be your waitress tonight," the hostess said with a smile before returning to her position at the front door.

Ron put his napkin in his lap and immediately opened the laminated menu. After a quick glance at it, he looked up at Andy, who seemed distant, staring blankly at the wall near the table.

"I need to ask you something," Ron said.

Andy blinked. "Shoot."

"You've seemed a little...distracted lately. Like something's bothering you."

Andy nervously started playing with the salt shaker on the table, spinning it back and forth as though it was a knob on a panel in his aircraft. "My wife will tell you that I'm not a very good liar."

"I don't know you that well, Andy, but I'm getting better at it. That's important among pilots. I can tell from your moods. Ever since that day last month when you overheard Mister Cramer talking on the plane...something went wrong, didn't it?"

Just then an attractive waitress interrupted. "Good evening," she said with a broad smile on her face. "My name is Jessica and I'll be your server this evening. May I get you something to drink to start off?" Jessica Tolkin had worked at Currell's for several years now, and she knew a lot of the regulars, even remembering the faces of people who had only infrequently visited the restaurant. She quickly concluded that these two gentlemen didn't fit either description.

The two men ordered diet colas, and Jessica spun around toward the bar. With her back turned and lingering a moment as she wrote on her order pad, she overheard one of the men say the words "Dick Cramer." *Must work at Midwest Fed,* she decided as she stepped away to fill their order.

"To answer your question," Andy said to Ron, "it is because of Dick Cramer that I've been in this funk."

"Why?" Ron asked. "What happened?"

Andy sat up straight in his chair. "I've been flying this guy around the country for years. I've put up with the late nights, the last-minute flight schedules, the elongated visits, and all the shenanigans. Hell, I've even put up with the poor salary of this job knowing that I'd get a chance to fly, and that at least my pension was safe. But now, everything's messed up."

"How so?"

Andy leaned in. "He's screwing us. Guys like me, I mean."

Jessica appeared again with two large glasses of diet cola in her hands. She put each one down in front of Andy and Ron, and then took their food orders. After scribbling their requests onto her order pad, she lingered a bit by clearing away the two empty place settings at the four-person table.

Ron talked over the clatter. "Screwing you? How?"

"Cramer's got numbers to make," Andy said. "He and his cronies over there have a big fat stock bonus awaiting them if they hit certain financial targets. And apparently, the only way to get there is to cut expenses, no matter who's affected by it."

"Cramer's cutting the pension?"

"Sounds that way. I still have a couple years to go, and to maintain my lifestyle in retirement, I'll be cutting it close, even under current conditions. But take away the pension grants, and I'm working even longer to make up the difference."

Jessica fumbled with the placemats and extra silverware, and in slow motion, she left the table. *Another member of the Dick Cramer fan club,* she thought as she walked away.

Lanny was beat. He came through the front door of his home around 7 p.m., and after a long day of meetings, he was looking forward to one of Jill's meals.

"Daddy's home!"

As was the ritual, his three boys came running to the foyer as soon as the door opened. Jill was close behind, a welcoming look on her face.

"A long day for you?" she asked.

"The longest." He leaned over and kissed her on the cheek.

"Dinner's ready for us. The kids already ate PBJs."

Lanny followed Jill into the spacious white kitchen and smelled the distinct odor of lasagna and garlic bread baking in the oven. The kids' peanut butter jar was still sitting on the table, lidless.

"How'd your day go?"

"Got lots of cleaning done," she answered. "Kids stayed out of my way all day."

"Yeah, we played cops and robbers downstairs!" Jonathan said excitedly.

"No! Cowboys and Indians," Zack said.

"Wow!" Lanny said, patting Zack on the head. "You guys certainly covered all the genres."

"Dad?" Kevin piped in. "Can we buy some more guns?"

Lanny sat down in his usual chair at the kitchen table as Jill placed the steaming pan of lasagna near him. He looked at Jill while simultaneously reaching for the serving spatula. "Didn't we bring those plastic guns from Alameda?" he asked.

"Oh yes," Jill said, sitting down next to him. "They're downstairs somewhere."

"Those broke, mom," Zack said.

"Can we get some more real ones, like on the cop shows?" Jonathan asked.

"Yeah!" Kevin yelled. "The real ones are so cool!"

"Absolutely not," Lanny said. "No one's going to be playing with anything that looks like a real gun in this house."

"I have an admission," Ron said, gulping the last bit of cola from his glass.

"Too much artificial sweetener will do that to you," Andy said wryly. He turned his head to see if he could spot the waitress. The food still hadn't come.

"There's something I saw on the plane."

"I've seen a few things, too, but none worth mentioning." Andy's grin melted away as fast as it had appeared.

"What I saw was a little more disturbing than the usual shenanigans," Ron said. "I don't know what to do about it, if anything."

Andy put down his glass and looked quizzically at Ron. "What is it?"

"A few weeks ago I was cleaning up the jet's cabin, doing the final sweep inside before heading home, and I saw something in the leather pocket of one of the chairs." Ron kept talking even as he saw the waitress appear out of the corner of his eye. She carried two plates of food and put one in front of each guest.

"Sorry for the wait, gentlemen," Jessica interrupted. "Is there anything else I can get for you right now?"

"Bring the check any time," Andy said, digging into his pasta. "This won't take us too long."

Jessica nodded, then took her pad out of her apron pocket and spun around to step away from the table. The two men resumed their conversation, with Ron telling Andy everything he had seen in the stack of pictures aboard the aircraft.

Jessica loitered purposefully a few feet from the table, and continued her lingering long enough to overhear the juiciest part. Her eyes grew wide.

Did he just say something about pictures of Dick Cramer?

THIRTY-ONE

By noon the next day, Wil and Kari had filled the Midwest Federated delivery van with $50,000 worth of lollipops and dog treats from a wholesale distributor they had found in Maple Grove, northwest of Minneapolis. Wil was grinding the van's gears as he pulled the vehicle out of the distributor's parking lot.

"Good thing you're in marketing and not in the courier business," Kari laughed from the passenger seat, her head getting jerked back and forth by the lurching vehicle.

"If nothing else, it keeps us extremely humble," Wil said, finally engaging the van's correct gear more smoothly.

"We haven't really talked about what we're going to do next with this stuff," she said. "You don't have it in your head that we're going to deliver these to every branch, do you?"

"Hell no," Wil shot back. "Barney's admin said there's a group of retirees who get together to help with things like this. We'll have them mail them out."

"Want me to get Mindy to start calling?"

"Good idea. Here, use my cell." Wil dug the phone out of his pocket and handed it to Kari. She had punched in most of the numbers when the van lurched sharply to the left, throwing her against the passenger door.

"What are you doing?" she yelped.

"Change of plan. We're taking a detour. Let's get some real perspective on this project before we do anything."

The Maple Grove branch of Midwest Federated Bank had all the classic styling of Roman architecture, the bank's adopted brand look. As Wil and Kari entered the dark lobby through the glass door, Wil noticed the ornate inlaid designs and high arches of the space, which he thought contrasted sharply with a collection of eclectic and haphazardly placed marketing brochures, posters, and directional signs. He made a mental note that this was something his own department needed to correct.

Wil approached the teller line. "Is Dale here?" Wil asked.

The young male teller who wore the name *TODD* on a badge that was pinned to his black shirt got off his chair and knocked on the window of the manager's office. Within moments, Dale appeared in the lobby, nicely dressed in tan pants and a black shirt—the Midwest Federated Bank logo smartly stitched on the breast pocket. Dale was of medium build, light brown hair and in his early 30s.

"Hi Wil," he said. "What brings you out here to Maple Grove?"

"Dale, meet Kari Bender, Midwest Federated Marketing." The two shook hands. "We have a couple of questions for you."

"Sure. Come into my office where there's more privacy."

They followed him into his office, which was small and claustrophobic. Dale's desk nearly filled the room, and the guest chairs were crammed between it and the scuffed-up wall. There was barely enough room for Wil and Kari to squeeze in.

"What can I do for you?" Dale asked, dropping into the chair behind his desk.

"I have a question," Wil said.

Dale nodded. "Okay."

"Do you have many kids coming through here?"

Dale paused a moment. "Kids? You mean...with parents?"

"Yeah. Little ones."

"The sticky lollipop kind," Kari interrupted with sarcasm in her tone.

"Yeah, of course," Dale answered. "We get kids in here all the time. Why?"

Wil looked at Kari, then back at Dale. "We received a bit of an edict from the higher-ups," Wil chuckled nervously as he spoke. "Turns out that all branches need to start handing out lollipops to kids."

Dale looked down at his desk for a moment, and then frowned. "Let me tell you something about that idea. We've had trouble on similar giveaways. We gave away candy one weekend last year, and it was disastrous. Kids were crying when they wanted one, but the parent wouldn't let them. Parents got ticked when a teller gave one to a kid without permission. That's not even counting all the litter in the parking lot, wrappers flying all over, and so on. And then there's the occasional family of eight that comes back for more on the same day."

"Then I suppose dog treats aren't any better of an idea."

Dale's eyebrows arched up. "Dog treats, too?"

"Bet you don't get many dogs through the lobby," Kari said with a smile.

"I suppose dog treats wouldn't be a bad thing through the drive-through," Dale offered. "You'd be surprised at how many dogs ride along with their owners. I'd go for that over lollipops any day of the week," Dale said.

Dale stopped talking suddenly when he realized there was a disruption inside his branch lobby. Even through the closed door of his office and the thick pane of glass of the interior office window, he could hear quick screams and gasps erupting from the employees and customers.

"Everybody DOWN!"

The request from the male voice was loud and commanding. The intruder was dressed in jeans, a flannel shirt, tan jacket and leather boots. He wore a brown cowboy hat and had one hand in his jacket pocket, implying the presence of a gun.

"You!" the man yelled with a slight slur to his voice, looking toward Dale's office. "Come outta there. Now!"

Dale looked at Wil and Kari and gestured with a nod of his head for them to walk to the lobby.

"Now GET DOWN!" the man commanded as they entered the area.

Dale motioned for Wil and Kari to lie facedown on the lobby carpet. Wil noticed that two customers had already complied, and the three bankers who were once behind desks were also prostrated on the floor.

"Now you," the robber shouted, pointing at Todd behind the teller line. "Give me everything in the drawer. EVERYTHING."

Wil's face was pressed so tightly to the floor that he could smell the commercial cleaner that was used to scrub the carpet. He closed his eyes out of fear. He found enough confidence to slowly open them again, and craned his neck enough to see young Todd calmly obliging the intruder by taking the money out of the cash drawer and piling it on the counter.

The robber grabbed the stacks of money and dumped them into what looked to be a pillowcase. Dale and Wil could hear Kari whimpering softly.

"He'll be gone in a second," Dale whispered from his floor-bound position.

Wil closed his eyes again. He didn't want to be noticed by the robber, and closing his eyes somehow made him feel invisible. Most of all, he just wanted the incident to end like Dale was predicting.

But the dull footsteps of sneakers on carpet were getting closer, not farther, away. "You. Mister suit-and-tie!" the man slurred.

Wil knew instantly that the robber was addressing him, as he was the only one in the entire branch wearing formal business attire. Wil unclasped his hands from behind his head and looked up. "Me?" he asked, tentatively. Wil looked right into the man's eyes, noticing that the robber's face was red, sweaty, and heavily pitted from acnes scars.

"Gimme the keys."

"The keys?" Wil looked to his side at Dale, who was glaring up at the man. He then looked over at Kari, who continued her whimpering and was shaking uncontrollably. With the man's eyes fixed solely on Wil, it became apparent to Wil that the suit he was wearing created the impression that he was the branch manager. "I don't have the keys to the vault," Wil said weakly. "There are no keys. It's locked." Wil didn't even know if the branch had a vault, much less if it opened with keys—or a combination code.

"No, idiot," the man said, slurring his words. "Gimme the keys to your van outside."

Wil realized that the man must have stalked the branch before the robbery, watching every move, including Wil's and Kari's approach through the parking lot. Wil thought he had no choice but to give in. "I have to reach in my pocket and get them."

"Then do it. Now."

Wil nervously reached into his pocket, a tough maneuver while sprawled on the floor. *They're not there*, he thought, sliding his hand to the bottom of his right-hand pocket. He switched hands and tried the other side of his trousers. *Oh no*, he thought, panic racing through his brain. *They must still be in the van.* He swallowed hard. "I don't have them. They're outside."

There was stony silence, followed by louder whimpering from Kari. The robber pushed his right hand deeper into his jacket pocket and forced it out toward the floor, implying the use of force with his still unseen gun.

"They better be," the man slurred, "or I'll be back." The man turned to address the lobby one more time. "No one triggers any alarms, or I come back and kill all of ya." His gaze was steely, and with one hand in his jacket pocket and the other hand tightly holding his bulging bag of cash, he turned and left the branch.

As soon as he exited, Dale leaped up from the floor. "Hit the alarm!"

Todd obeyed and punched a button hidden under the teller line. The silent alarm immediately notified police that a robbery was in progress—or in this case, just ending.

Wil stood quickly, and then bent down to help Kari stand. "You okay?"

She was breathing nervously and brushed off her pants with her trembling hands. "I think so."

Wil took two tentative steps toward the front windows of the bank to get a better look at the robber's current location.

Dale stepped up next to him. "So...are the keys in there?"

Wil instinctively felt his empty pockets again, and then realized he was hyperventilating. "I think so," he said, holding his chest to calm his breathing. "They must be. I don't have them."

"Oh no!" Kari shouted, a hand over her mouth, looking in the direction of Dale's interior office window. Dale and Wil followed her panicked gaze with their own eyes. Both immediately recognized what she saw: The van keys that were being sought outside by the robber were perched on the edge of Dale's desk.

"Holy—"

"Get down!" Wil yelled to the customers and employees. "Get down, everybody. He's going to come back!"

Everyone got lower to the floor, this time mostly squatting to avoid getting into a vulnerable position. Dale, however, remained standing, his arms crossed.

"Don't worry. He won't be back."

Wil lowered his tall body to the floor, ducking as though bullets were flying over his head. He slowly looked up at Dale. "What do you mean? Are you crazy? Get down!"

Dale looked over at Todd behind the teller line. "Did you give him the pack?"

"Yep."

Dale looked at Wil with a smile and shook his head. "He won't be back."

Wil slowly came to an upright position. "What's a...pack?"

"Dye pack. It's a brick of money that contains a small explosive charge. There's one in every teller drawer. Now it's in his bag. As soon as he left the building, the pack armed itself from a small chip that's embedded in the door's frame. It'll trigger in a few more seconds and spoil the money with nasty red dye."

Wil was amazed. For as long as he had been in banking, he never heard of such a thing. "But where is he?"

"He must have gotten distracted. I think he's in the back of your van. You guys don't have any money in there or anything, do you?"

Just then, the van lit up from the inside with a quick, sharp, white flash. Within moments, the back double-doors of the vehicle flew open, followed by the robber, who was coated from head to toe in wet red dye.

"There he goes."

The man fled on foot, dropping the blood-colored pillowcase onto the pavement. Inside the branch, everyone burst into laughter, the kind of nervous giggles that accompany relief at the conclusion of a stressful situation.

"Where's the cops?" Kari asked, keeping her distance from the front window.

"They won't be here in time," Dale said. "Never are."

Wil looked at him. "You mean this happens often?"

"Oh yeah," Dale said with a nod. "You could say we're in the banking and robbery businesses." Dale walked over to the customers to ensure that each was all right, and then spent several minutes talking to staff. Dale then asked Wil and Kari to stay until the police arrived.

Once the first police cruiser pulled into the branch's parking lot with its lights flashing, Wil's cell phone rang.

"Hey, it's me," Jessica said as soon as he answered the call.

"Jessica," Wil said unevenly, "this isn't really a good time."

"I'm sorry I didn't call you last night," she said, ignoring his dissuasive tone. "I worked very late. But do I ever have something to tell you."

Wil watched as two police officers entered the lobby. He turned his body away and lowered his voice. "Believe me, Jessica...whatever it is...I have something that is sure to top it."

THIRTY-TWO

Andy decided to get to the hangar just 15 minutes earlier than normal. He figured that was plenty of time to look for the incriminating photos that Ron had discovered and still get the aircraft ready for takeoff. The trip to New Mexico was a simple run from Saint Paul to Albuquerque, and there was just one passenger on this trip today: Mrs. Harriet Updike Cramer.

Andy unlocked the heavy steel door of the hangar and flipped on the lights. It still seemed too dark in the hangar on such a cold October day, so he promptly punched the hangar door button to raise the giant aluminum shield off the ground. The light from the filtered overcast sky slowly spilled into the cavernous room as the huge door rumbled to its fully-opened position. Satisfied that he now had enough illumination, Andy bounded up the steps and opened the aircraft's fuselage hatchway.

Once inside, he clicked on the cabin lights and began checking the side pockets of each of the six leather chairs. He worked his way to the back of the aircraft, coming up empty each time. After some digging to the bottom of the pocket of the chair that was closest to the aircraft's bathroom, it seemed he had found the item that Ron had described.

Andy lifted out the white envelope and removed the pictures. He briskly flipped through them. Despite the natural light from outside of the hangar and the cabin lights overhead, the illumination was too low and the pictures were too dark, making it initially difficult for Andy to comprehend what he was seeing. He sat down in the chair and clicked on the reading light above him for a better look. Nervous, he looked out the window to make sure the coast was still clear.

He brought the first picture in the stack closer to his face and paused, letting his pupils adjust. He immediately recognized that the photo was taken in very low light. It had a greenish tint to it, and it was of a quality that looked as though it was snapped in a hurry from a cloaked location.

He saw that there was a man seated in a chair in the center of the picture, with only his upper back and head visible, and a bombshell of a woman with bare breasts standing in front of him, facing the camera. Other women were also visible in the picture. He squinted as narrowly as he could in an effort to get the sharpest possible resolution out of his 61-year-old eyeballs.

That is Dick Cramer, he thought, *in the Miami resort bathroom!*

There were seven more pictures, and each one was more revealing than the first. While Andy had witnessed the event himself, he did not stay long enough that night to see how events transpired, and it was obvious that Mr. Cramer had enjoyed himself. *The man apparently loves his lap dances,* Andy thought.

What puzzled him most was the fact that these photos had to have been taken immediately following his departure from the bathroom, and snapped from a variety of angles. With that in mind, he concluded the pictures weren't taken from a hidden camera in a fixed position; someone must have taken them while roaming undercover. *But who in that room could have taken these photos, and not be seen?* He felt a wave of paranoia suddenly wash over him. *The only person in that room who could have gotten away with this...was me!*

Andy looked up at the ceiling of the aircraft, shaking his head in disbelief, regretting that he even set foot in that suite in Miami. But Andy knew he had nothing to do with the pictures that he held in his hands. *Who else could it have been? And who put them on the plane?*

Andy wracked his memory banks about that night. He shuffled through the eight photos again. Then he figured something out: *That woman in the blue cocktail dress—she's not in any of these shots,* he thought.

"Hello?"

The faint female voice startled Andy, and he nearly dropped the photos to the floor. He recognized the voice immediately.

Harriet Updike Cramer was bent forward as she appeared in the open doorway of the cabin, stooping to avoid messing up the cream-colored hat that was affixed to the crown of her head.

"Andy, are you in here?"

"I'm here, Missus Cramer." Andy panicked. He tried to shove the pictures back in the envelope, but he couldn't find the dexterity to get it done. Instead, he fearfully shoved the whole wad, with the pictures on top of the envelope, back into the leather chair's pouch.

"Sorry, I was just...catching up on some paperwork," he said, nervously standing.

"That's all right," Mrs. Cramer said. "Is it okay that I'm early? I want to get going."

"Certainly, certainly. Ron should be here any moment now. We'll get the plane out of the hangar and we'll be underway. Did you bring your luggage?"

Mrs. Cramer pointed down the stairs where her luggage was sitting, and Andy shakily moved aside as she worked her way toward the back of the aircraft. "I'm just going to sit and catch up on a little sleep, if you don't mind."

"Sure," he said. *Just don't sit in the number five seat,* he thought.

Mrs. Cramer was 55 years old, the oldest daughter of the well-to-do Updike family. Her 91-year-old father had always been her idol. Now wheelchair-bound, her father became too ill to attend meetings of the Midwest Federated Board, of which he was still an honorary member. Randall Updike also harbored a majority number of shares of Midwest Federated's stock, and that kept the family fortune fresh.

Harriet Cramer's hair was nicely arranged, but Andy always thought it was done up in such a way that it made her look 10 years older. She was always neatly dressed, but she usually wore the type of clothes that one might wear to a PTA meeting.

Andy watched as the CEO's wife headed to the seat in which he had just been sitting. He was relieved when she abruptly veered to the left and sat down in the number six leather chair on the starboard side of the aircraft. "You can just relax," he said as she sat down and buckled herself in. "We'll take care of everything."

Andy watched as Harriet leaned back on the headrest and closed her eyes. He looked nervously over at the pocket of seat number five, wondering if he should recapture the photos right then and there. He looked back at her and paused momentarily. Deciding against it, he quickly spun around and exited the aircraft, hustling down the steps to retrieve her luggage.

"You were what?" Jessica asked.

"Robbed," Wil said. "The bank, I mean."

"How? Are you okay?"

"Yes, yes, we're fine. A little shaken, though." Wil went on to explain what had just occurred in the Maple Grove branch that day. He was keeping his voice calm and steady, and he realized that Jessica may not comprehend the intensity of the situation because of his artificial composure.

"I'm glad you're okay. But I called to tell you something juicy."

"Hang on." Wil was standing near a group of people in the lobby who were talking to the police. He stepped a few feet away from them to gain some privacy. "Okay. I'm ready."

Jessica's tone turned to one of glee. "Last night, at the restaurant, these two guys came in. I think they're pilots or something for Midwest Fed."

"They didn't hit on you, did they?" he asked, trying to force some levity. He knew Midwest Federated had a company jet, but so far he hadn't been fortunate enough to ride on it or even meet the pilots.

"No, no. I accidentally overheard their conversation."

Wil smiled whenever Jessica said she "overheard" something. In the consecutive months that they had spent together, he had heard more mundane restaurant gossip from her than he thought was humanly possible. He knew that overhearing conversations was less accidental and more of a hobby for Jessica, so he decided to go along with it. "What did they say?"

"First of all, the older guy is not a fan of your Dick Cramer."

"Now that's hard to believe." Wil glanced over toward the group of people in the lobby as the police continued their questioning.

"They also said something about pictures. Naked pictures."

Wil turned to make sure no one around him could hear. "Say again? Naked pictures? Of who?"

"I thought he said something about Cramer."

"Dick Cramer? Can't be."

"I admit I didn't hear all of it, so I can't be sure. But I do know that the older guy is pissed because they're cutting expenses at the bank."

"Doesn't surprise me. Not in the least." Wil was no stranger to such talk. Cutting expenses in big corporations was a way of life. Jessica was a smart woman, but he couldn't expect that she'd take news like that as casually as him.

"That's not all. It's the way Cramer is cutting expenses. He's cutting the pension."

This caused Wil to pause. He had read that pension-cutting was becoming more and more common, but it was usually a maneuver of last resort, a way to manipulate the bottom line at the expense of the masses.

"It also sounds like Cramer's freezing salaries," Jessica said casually, as though she was reading from her grocery list.

Wil raised an eyebrow. "You heard all of this?"

"Yes. It wasn't easy."

Wil grinned at her mild confession. Overhearing conversations was an art form that his girlfriend constantly hoped to perfect.

His mind raced. This news did sound serious after all. While pension-cutting was one thing, he knew that salary-freezing was certainly another. In all his years of professional life, Wil never experienced a freeze in pay, even when he worked in television. "You say these two guys are the corporate pilots?"

"Yes. I'm sure of it. They were talking about flying Cramer around the country. I don't think they like carting him around too well."

Wil noticed that one of the two police officers was waving him over, so he raised his index finger as a way of asking for another minute. "I've got to go, Jessica. But first, can you do me a favor?"

"Sure."

"Kari and I need a cab to get back downtown. Can you call one for me?"

"A cab?" Jessica asked. "Why? What happened to your car?"

"My car is fine. It's the van we rode here in. It's now part of the official robbery investigation."

At 29,000 feet and heading due south, Andy leveled off the Gulfstream IV and gave control to Ron, who happily took over. Andy unbuckled from his captain's seat. "I'm going to check on our passenger."

He entered the cabin to find Harriet Cramer awake and still in seat six at the rear of the aircraft, looking into a small hand mirror, reapplying her lipstick.

He sat in the nearby seat and leaned toward her, raising his voice enough to be heard above the roar of the

Gulfstream's engines. "We're running ahead of schedule," he explained casually. "We're at our cruising altitude now and the weather looks good all the way down."

"That's so nice," she said, snapping her pocket mirror shut and replacing it into her purse. "I'm looking forward to some warmer weather at the ranch."

Andy adopted a comfortable smile on his face. "I haven't seen the flight schedule for later this week. I presume we'll be flying your husband down in a few days." Andy didn't feel the least bit guilty about his trolling for information. He was curious about their relationship.

"Oh yes, yes, yes. Dickie will come down this weekend."

Dickie, he thought, *is such an appropriate pet name.*

"I want to get a good start on my projects," she continued. "I'm remodeling the entire great room at the ranch. I suspect it'll take me a few weeks, so I'll be down here a while."

Andy forced a grin. "That sounds ambitious." He briefly glanced down at the leather pocket of his chair. He knew he had to figure out a way to retrieve the photos soon, as he didn't want to be implicated in some devious plot for which he had no good alibi. "If you need to use the lavatory, now would be a good time. It's smooth sailing." He grinned again.

"No. I'm just fine, Andy, thank you." She leaned over and dug into the leather pocket of her own chair.

Andy's heart skipped a beat. He didn't want her searching each chair's pockets to stumble onto incriminating photos of her own husband. "Need something to read?" Andy asked hastily.

"Yes, that would be nice. I guess I forgot to bring my book."

Andy got up and took one step into the restroom where magazines were housed in a wall-mounted rack. He grabbed an entire stack of magazines and clumsily thrust them at her.

"My heavens," she said, mildly alarmed. "This will keep me busy. Thanks, Andy." She crossed her legs and shuffled through the pile of periodicals.

Andy nervously glanced down once more at the pocket of his chair, but he concluded that it would seem clunky to retrieve the pictures just then; he wouldn't know what to say if she asked him what they were. Defeated, he remained stationary for a moment, turned, and then slowly strode back to the cockpit.

Wil's day wasn't getting any better. After spending more than two unplanned hours at the Maple Grove branch, he and Kari called a cab and returned to downtown Minneapolis, their delivery van full of dog treats and lollipops temporarily impounded.

As soon as Wil entered the sixth-floor Marketing Department, Mindy handed several letters to him. "These came in your afternoon mail," she said.

He sifted through them, noticing that two of the three envelopes were addressed by hand, and one was typed.

"Wait a minute," he said, confused. "These are addressed to Mr. Cramer, the CEO."

"Yes, I know," Mindy answered quickly. "However, I'm told it's the Mailroom's policy to ferret out complaint letters from his personal and business mail."

"And exactly how do they know this is a complaint letter?" Wil asked.

"It's been opened."

"I can see that. Why do I get the complaint letters?"

Mindy shrugged. "They tell me that's just how it's done."

"You're joking."

"No. You're not just the marketing guy. You're also the Complaint Department."

Wil rubbed his eyes with his free hand and exhaled after taking a long, deep breath. He strode to his office and placed the letters on his desk. Plopping his body down into the chair, he removed the letter from the first envelope in the stack and read it:

Dear Mr. Cramer,

    I recently opened a new checking account at MFB. I did so in response to your advertising campaign that promotes the fact that you're giving away a lake cabin. I thought this was as good a time as any to open an account at your bank. After all, who wouldn't want a chance to win a free lake cabin?

    Unfortunately for you, I have decided to close my account as fast as I opened it. The banker who opened my account was rude. When I asked her questions about your promo, she just shrugged her shoulders. She couldn't remember the details! Then she kept pushing free checking on me, but I didn't want free checking—I wanted checking that earns interest. I eventually gave in and opened the account anyway. A week ago I received my checks. However, my address was printed wrong. Later I got my ATM card. I tried to take $40 cash from one your ATMs, but the keypad was so damaged and gritty that I could barely press the buttons. Then the screen said "access denied."

    The service at your bank is terrible. Please let someone know that I want my account closed and my $1,500 balance returned to me."

    Sincerely,

    Samuel H. Rose

Wil shook his head in disbelief and opened the next letter. After reading it, he took out a yellow highlighter and went back to outline several of its key handwritten sentences:

> *I recently received an incorrect bank statement. I went to your branch in Bloomington to straighten it out, but I discovered that your branch is closed on Saturday afternoons. Don't you people know that customers want to bank on the weekends?*

He put the letter down and opened the last letter, the one that was addressed to Mr. Cramer with a typewriter. Inside was a yellow sheet that was torn from a pad of line paper. He unfolded it and knew immediately it wasn't a letter at all: It was instead a pen outline of someone's right hand, the middle finger extended.

So much for being the Midwest's friendliest bank, he thought.

The Gulfstream jet screeched to a halt ahead of schedule on the runway at Albuquerque, New Mexico. Andy taxied the jet to the usual spot in front of the hangar and shut down the engines. He leapt out of his seat. "I'll get the door," he told

Ron, who remained to shut off instruments on the cockpit panels.

Andy entered the cabin and opened the hatch to the outside world. The warm, dry air of New Mexico rushed into the aircraft, but it was soon replaced with the familiar smell of jet fuel—and hot tire rubber.

He grabbed the two red luggage bags from the front closet and carried them down the stairs, setting them on the pavement below. He rushed back up the stairs and extended a hand to the waiting Mrs. Cramer. She gingerly descended the steps, all the while holding the tips of Andy's right-hand fingers.

A black limo was waiting for her, and after picking up her two bags, Andy led the woman to it. He greeted the driver, who assisted Mrs. Cramer into the car's back seat.

"Have a nice stay, Missus Cramer," Andy said. "Good luck on your remodeling projects." Andy backed away from the car and executed a quick salute with his fingers on his forehead. Through the tinted glass of the rear door, he could see the woman waving. He watched as the limo sped away.

With the car quickly receding into the distance, Andy turned back toward the aircraft and bounded up the stairway. Reaching the top step, he could see that Ron was still in the cockpit.

"Get her on her way?" Ron asked, unbuckling his seatbelt.

"Yes. Package delivered." Andy turned to his right and took several long steps, quickly reaching seat number five near the tail of the aircraft. He bent down to reach the leather pocket and fished out the empty white envelope. He remembered shoving it into the pouch separate from the pictures, so he lowered his right hand back into the pocket to feel for the photo stack.

"Did you find them?" Ron asked, now standing in the cockpit doorway. The two didn't talk at all about the photos on the trip down, and Andy hadn't even yet admitted seeing them. But Ron knew exactly what he was searching for. Andy ignored his copilot for the moment and kept digging.

They're not here!

Andy immediately sat down in the chair to get better leverage. He grabbed the top of the leather pouch and stretched out the elastic band to its limits. There was nothing inside. He forced his hand back down to check it again. And again.

"What's the matter?" Ron asked, stepping closer. "Can't you find them?"

Andy glanced up at Ron, who looked genuinely concerned. "I put them right back in here," Andy said. "The envelope's still here. But the pictures—they're gone."

"So you did see them after all?"

Andy nodded weakly. "Yes, before we took off."

Ron walked over to the seat where Mrs. Cramer was sitting and opened the pocket, but only magazines were in it. He then started checking the pockets of every chair.

As Ron came up empty one seat at a time, Andy sat silently in seat number five, wondering what he should do next. It was obvious to him that Mrs. Cramer was now in possession of eight damning photos of her powerful husband. And if Dick Cramer ever found out about the existence of such photos, no one other than Andy was more keenly aware that both men would certainly be in a heap of big, big trouble.

THIRTY-THREE

Wil stood by Mindy's desk looking at more customer letters that had come in the mail. The basic pattern was the same: The more business the cabin sweepstakes campaign brought in, the more customer service complaints were received by the bank. Wil just finished reading the last letter in the batch when Kari walked up.

"The FBI called," Kari said, grinning. "They've released the van and it's being driven down here as we speak."

"Finally," Wil said, glancing at the date on his watch. "It only took them three days."

"We should probably get the retirees in soon. We don't want those dog treats to get stale."

Wil smiled. He liked Kari's sarcastic sense of humor. "Except we don't know what shape they're in. Fifty-thousand dollars worth of dog treats and lollipops covered in red dye might not be too appealing."

"They were in boxes, so they should be okay. Besides, it'll give the old geezers something to talk about."

Wil looked at Mindy. "Hop on the phone and call the retirees in," Wil said. "And I want to know the minute that van arrives."

Prior to heading to Holman Field to board the company jet that was bound for his New Mexico ranch, Dick Cramer needed some weekend money. The high-end, cherry-red sports car pulled into the outside drive-through lane of the Midwest Federated branch along Snelling Avenue in Saint Paul. He lowered his driver's side window and punched the call button on the black kiosk. He grabbed the cylindrical money carrier and put a check made out for five-thousand dollars inside of it, sealing up the carrier with a snap of its cover.

"May I help you?" the young male voice asked, crackling over the tinny speaker.

Mr. Cramer couldn't see the person behind the drive-through window to whom he was talking; the glare from the midday sun was too bright against the glass, so he merely stared at the speaker. "Cash this for me, would you?" Mr. Cramer asked, putting the carrier into the tube and hitting the send button. The carrier shot up the tube quickly, accompanied by a loud whooshing sound.

A few seconds went by and the speaker crackled to life again. "I'm sorry, sir," the young, disembodied voice said confidently. "We cannot cash this much money and send it through the tube. You'll need to come inside."

Mr. Cramer leaned over the top of his driver's side door to get closer to the speaker. "Did you *look* at the check?" he asked, his condescending tone cutting the air like a knife. "Did you see the name that's on it?"

The voice from the speaker became almost robotic. "I'm sorry, sir. It's against our policy to send this much cash through the drive-through tubes. If you come into the branch and show us your identification, we can accommodate you in here."

Mr. Cramer grunted with extreme irritation and grabbed the steering wheel to gain more leverage to adjust his blocky body. He tried hard to position his bloated torso at a correct angle in a fruitless attempt to eliminate the glare that was hitting the bank's drive-through window. He wanted to see for himself what young punk his company had hired who didn't recognize the commander-in-chief.

"Listen here," Mr. Cramer said, his voice getting louder and his head bobbing violently as he adjusted his sightline. "Don't you know who the hell I am?"

A pause ensued, followed by more static from the speaker. "Your check says Richard Edmund Cramer," the voice answered flatly. The kid had no idea.

Mr. Cramer thrashed wildly in his vehicle's seat. "And I suppose you still want me to come in? Is that right?"

"Yes sir," the voice said. "This is our policy. Please come into the bank, and we'll accommodate you."

The drive-through-lane's crackly speaker went silent. After another obnoxious grunt of displeasure, Mr. Cramer threw the car into drive and squealed the tires as he rounded the front of the bank at lightening speed. The car rocketed into a parking space, and within seconds the man was bounding into the lobby on a mission, heading directly for the teller line.

"Who is the manager here?" Mr. Cramer barked gruffly, addressing Felicia Cortez, the first person he saw.

"That is me," she said. Felicia was good at calming irate customers, given her years of experience at being both a teller and a bartender. But she knew instantly that the man in front of her was no ordinary customer. Even though she had never met Dick Cramer personally, she had seen him speak at various company meetings, and she was fully aware that the CEO now stood in her branch, livid and red-faced.

Mr. Cramer leaned toward her. "I want to know why the CEO of this company can't get a five-thousand dollar check cashed and sent through the drive-through. Why is that? You have thirty seconds to explain this to me!"

Felicia stared back at him, undaunted. "It's Midwest Federated Bank policy, Mister Cramer. We simply don't want customers to risk getting that much cash potentially stuck in the equipment. After all, five-thousand dollars has some weight, and—"

"Stop the doubletalk," he yelled. "Five-thousand dollars should be no problem to handle!"

Felicia looked to her right side and noticed several customers at the other teller stations who moments ago were minding their own business, but were now focused solely on the man who was having a conniption fit in the middle of her lobby.

Felicia glared back at him. "Mister Cramer," she said loud enough for all to hear, "I'll gladly accommodate your request for five-thousand dollars in cash. Please provide me with the check and your account number."

"I don't have the damn check," Mr. Cramer shot back, angrily tugging at the lapels of his suit coat. "That ignorant drive-through teller has it."

Felicia kept her voice steady and loud. "Do you know the name of that ignorant drive-through teller?" she asked, sarcasm leaking into her tone. "I can retrieve it from him." Customers chuckled. They didn't know who this irate man was, but they did know that he had met his match in Felicia Cortez.

Cramer leaned in closer. "Get my check and cash it," he said, taking his voice down an octave and inflecting an evil, sinister tone. "Now."

Felicia fought hard to show no emotion, and then turned away. She exited through the door that led to the drive-through teller stations located at the back of the bank. Moments later, she reappeared with his check in hand. Without saying another word, she masterfully keyed in Mr. Cramer's account information on the terminal in front of her, and then opened her cash drawer.

As Felicia calmly counted out the money, Mr. Cramer snooped around like an old lady, craning his neck over the teller line to look behind it, then stepping back to get a frontal view of each station that studded the long wooden counter. "Where the hell are they?" he asked.

Felicia was in the middle of counting out $5,000 in $100 bills, and she paused. "Where is what, sir?"

Mr. Cramer banged his fist on the counter. "The lollipops," he snorted. "Aren't you handing out the lollipops?"

Felicia slowly moved her eyes up to meet the man's steely glare. "The lollipops?" she asked tepidly.

"Yes, yes. The lollipops. The lollipops! You people are supposed to be handing out lollipops. And there are kids in here!" Mr. Cramer's face was morphing from one shade of red to another, eventually ending in a purplish hue.

"I'm sorry, Mister Cramer," she said calmly and professionally, shaking her head, resuming her count of the money he had demanded. "I don't know what you're talking about. Is there supposed to be a supply of lollipops around here somewhere?" Felicia kept counting, but felt completely out of the loop.

Mr. Cramer slammed his fist down again and strode over to the closed teller gate, a short wooden door that was the only way through the teller line. He put his hand on the gate's silver knob and attempted to turn it, but found it to be unmovable, secured by a pushbutton lock system. His head jerked back with anger. "Open this."

Felicia put down the stack of money and walked over to the gate. She punched in the four-digit code and swung it open. Mr. Cramer stepped through and immediately bent down sharply at his waist, maniacally looking behind the teller counter for his would-be supply of lollipops.

One of the female tellers observed Mr. Cramer's doubled-over posture and approached Felicia. "What in the world is he looking for?" she asked, keeping her voice to a whisper.

Felicia shrugged. "Something sweet, I guess."

Mr. Cramer stopped behind each teller station, methodically bending over each time to get a look at the knee-high shelves behind the counter in what looked like a dance routine gone awry. Sometimes he even resorted to looking straight through a teller's legs in order to view what was on the shelves beyond. To his sheer disappointment, there were no lollipops to be found.

He made a beeline back to Felicia. "Take me to the drive-through area," he commanded, forcefully punching his forefinger at her.

She motioned for him to follow, and they walked through the door at the back wall. Mr. Cramer then inspected the two stations that faced the drive-through lanes.

"No dog treats either?"

Felicia looked at him with a raised eyebrow. "Did you say...dog treats?"

"Yes, yes, dog treats. This branch does not have its supply of lollipops and dog treats! Damn it! Who is responsible for this?"

The two tellers manning the drive-through stations stopped what they were doing, frozen there like statuettes, staring with incredulity at the hotheaded CEO of Midwest Federated Bank.

"Mister Cramer," Felicia said softly, breaking the painful silence, "I'm sorry, but we just don't know anything about dog treats or lollipops. Should we?"

"Yes, yes!" he said, stomping his right foot onto the brown industrial carpet in unison with each word. "You all should know about this. I wanted this done immediately. Someone's head needs to roll!"

Felicia followed Mr. Cramer out of the drive-through area and back to the lobby's teller line. In complete silence, she efficiently counted out the remaining $5,000 in cash. Then, after stuffing the bundle into three cash envelopes, she handed the whole wad to him.

He grabbed it with both hands, nodded to her with a nasty snarl on his face, and then turned on his heals to leave the building.

The gleaming jet was gently towed out of the hangar and onto the pavement. Andy and Ron inspected the underside of the aircraft in the midday light, busily readying the Gulfstream for the run back to New Mexico.

"Think he'll say anything?" Ron asked. "Think he knows?"

"We'll know soon, although it will be tough to tell, unless he comes right out with it."

"What do you mean?" Ron asked.

"Cramer's always in a bad mood when he goes to see his wife at the ranch. Either way, he's sure to show up ornery."

Ron grinned and opened the aircraft's door. Andy continued his external inspection of the aircraft's underbelly, carefully examining the flaps, the wheel wells, the tires. Andy knew he was completely innocent of the picture-taking, and he still couldn't comprehend why the woman in the blue cocktail snapped them in the first place. But he felt overwhelming guilt nonetheless.

He knelt down to get a closer look at some dirt that he spotted on the nose gear strut. *Maybe I should play my cards,* Andy thought, picking at the debris with his fingernails. *Perhaps he'd pay me off if he thinks I did it.*

"I'm sorry, Mister Cramer, but Mister Jennings is out meeting this afternoon with a business client," Victoria said. "I don't think I'll be able to reach him until after four." As Mr. Jennings' assistant, Victoria knew the moods of each bank executive by heart, and she could easily sense when Mr. Cramer was upset about something. But she learned through experience that the best course of action was to stay as calm and professional as possible.

"Damn it," he said, a spike of static punctuating his words over his weak cell phone connection. "Then get me that marketing guy...what's his name...?"

"Wil Fischer?"

"Yes, yes. Get him. You have thirty seconds."

"Yes, Mister Cramer. One moment while I connect you."

Wil could see on his phone's I.D. screen that Victoria was calling. *Unusual,* he thought, *for a Friday afternoon.* He had come to know that most of the executive floor was AWOL on Fridays, and that meant few interruptions, even from executive administrative assistants. He plucked the phone from its cradle. "Wil Fischer."

Victoria's voice was steady and calm. "Wil, I have Mr. Cramer for you."

Mister Cramer?

Wil felt his stomach flutter. His disastrous summertime meeting with the CEO was a distant memory. He had never heard directly from the man since then, and he certainly didn't expect a direct call from him under any circumstances; Wil reasoned long ago that he was just too lowly for executive interactions.

"Put him on," Wil managed, swallowing saliva that seemed to dry up as soon as it hit the back of his throat. After a few clicks, Wil could tell he was now connected to a cell. "Hello?"

"Fischer? Dick Cramer." His voice was clipped.

"Yes, Mister Cramer. How can I help you?"

"Are you the one working on the lollipops and dog treats project?"

Wil quickly exhaled in a failed attempt to relax. "Oh, yes, that's me, mister dog treats and lollipops," Wil chuckled with aplomb, trying to sound lighthearted.

"Then where in the hell are they?" The man's voice was instantly patronizing.

Wil's stomach fluttered again. *He must not know what happened.* "Oh, there's an explanation for the delay."

"There damn well better be," Cramer yelled. "You have twenty seconds!"

Wil felt his posture wilting against his leather chair. He tried to straighten himself up to sound more confident, but he couldn't fight the urge to slump. "We just finally got the van back from the authorities."

"The authorities? What van?"

He doesn't know any of this. "The Midwest Federated delivery van. We filled it with the lollipops and dog treats, but the investigation of the robbery took—"

"What investigation?"

Doesn't this guy know we were robbed? Wil tried to swallow again, but his mouth and throat felt as though they were stuffed with cotton balls. "The robbery. At Maple Grove. You see, the guy left the bank and got into the van—"

"What guy?" Mr. Cramer's impatience was approaching critical mass.

"The robber."

"A robber got into our delivery van?"

"Well, yes, in a sense. I left the keys on the manager's desk and, well, after he took the loot from inside, he went to the van and tried to—"

"Let me get this straight," Cramer interrupted. "You drove our delivery van to a branch, left it unlocked, and a robber was given an opportunity to steal it?"

Wil felt his lower muscles cramping. "Yes."

"Why were you driving *my* delivery van?" Mr. Cramer asked, his voice rising over the intermittent bursts of cell static.

"We were trying to get the dog treats...we wanted to...it was going to take too long to..." Wil's voice trailed off. He knew how ridiculous the whole thing sounded. He decided it was no use. He opted to simply stop talking and hoped that Mr. Cramer would be merciful.

A long pause followed with nothing but a cacophony of static and road noise filling the void. Wil felt beads of perspiration popping out all over his body.

"Hear me and hear me good," Mr. Cramer said through obviously gritted teeth. "This kind of crap shouldn't happen. Do you understand? Fischer? Never! Good *BYE*!"

There was a loud click, and with that, the man was gone.

Wil sat silently with the phone still pushed against his ear, his eyes staring blankly out the window of his sixth-floor office. A thousand bees had just stung him in the face. He got chewed out by the CEO of Midwest Federated Bank, and he couldn't help but wonder if it was the last time he'd ever talk to the man.

Foul weather in New Mexico had kept the Gulfstream IV jet grounded at Holman Field in Saint Paul for several hours longer than planned that afternoon, which ultimately created a nighttime approach into Albuquerque. After waiting as long as they dared for takeoff from Minnesota, Andy and Ron finally executed a leisurely flight south, the winds calming enough to bring the jet safely onto the New Mexico runway.

They taxied to the hangar and shut down the engines. Ron got out of his copilot's seat and found Mr. Cramer already standing at the fuselage's door, waiting impatiently to be exited.

"Sunday night for departure?" Ron asked, deftly opening the door for his passenger.

"Make it Sunday afternoon," Mr. Cramer grunted. "Three."

Ron grabbed Mr. Cramer's single suitcase and led him down the stairs.

Andy stood in the doorframe of the aircraft, watching as the men descended. It didn't take long for Mr. Cramer to get into his car, start the engine and leave. *The shorter amount of time with the missus, the better,* Andy thought while shaking his head, the car quickly disappearing into the distance.

THIRTY-FOUR

Hallie Jordan was a godsend for the Taylors, the kind of reliable babysitter that is equivalent to solid gold—all due to Jill's networking in the neighborhood. At the tender age of 15, Hallie was cute, smart, articulate, and responsible. Better still, she only lived two doors away and was available on a late October weekend.

Hallie stood near the Taylor's kitchen island, pushing her strawberry-colored hair from her face with one hand. Jill's freshly applied perfume wafted through the house as she handed a list of emergency contact numbers to Hallie. The handwritten list included the cell number of Wil Fischer, with whom the Taylors, along with Jessica Tolkin, would be rendezvousing to spend most of the evening together.

"We'll be at dinner until around eight, and then we'll probably stop somewhere for a few drinks after that," Jill said. "Should be back before midnight."

"Not a problem, Missus Taylor," Hallie said. "The boys and I will have a great time."

Jill thought about correcting Hallie to have her address her as just "Jill," but she liked the formality. Jill had once commented on how kids were often disrespectful to their elders these days, so she found it enjoyable when the few teenagers she had encountered addressed her with a formal title—especially when such teenagers babysat her three boys.

"Let's go, love," Lanny said urgently from the door. "We're going to be late, and I hate being late."

"Coming," she said. Jill turned to her boys in the family room who were each eating their TV-dinner macaroni meals while crouched around the coffee table, watching a cartoon.

"Good night, boys," Jill said. "Bed by eight for all of you." The boys barely registered the command, too engrossed in the animation that flashed across the TV screen. Jill turned to Hallie and grinned. "They shouldn't give you any trouble. If they do, I want to hear about it."

Hallie returned the smile and wished the Taylors a good time. Within moments, the couple was out the door.

It didn't take long for the three kids to stop eating and turn their attention to the babysitter.

Hallie cleared away their half-eaten food. "You boys want to play a game?" she asked as she came back from the kitchen.

"Yeah!" they shouted in unison. The middle boy, Zack, instantly produced a deck of cards on the family room coffee table.

"Go Fish! Go Fish!" Jonathan yelled.

"Good idea." Hallie took the deck and distributed five cards to each of the players, and then spread the remaining cards randomly across the center of the table.

Several hands ensued, all won by Kevin, the oldest. At the age of eight, he was an accomplished Go Fish player. The start of the fourth hand was interrupted by the phone ringing.

"Hang on guys," Hallie said, standing from her legs-crossed position to reach the phone on a nearby table.

"Oh, hi Trevor."

Her boyfriend was the overly-jealous type, often calling her wherever she happened to be, especially on a Saturday night when the two weren't together. "Just babysitting," she explained, watching as the three boys tried to continue the game without her.

Only a minute into her conversation, the boys lost all interest in cards and fled to the basement for more nighttime adventure.

"It wasn't a stellar week," Wil said, talking more to the glass of red wine in front of him than to the three people seated at his table. The Color Red was a trendy new restaurant in downtown Minneapolis, but Wil was too preoccupied to realize that his red wine was just one small piece of a giant themed ensemble that swirled around him. The staff sported red shirts, walls were accented with red paint, and dinner plates were trimmed with red rims and flanked by red napkins, all creating an odd effect that bathed the whole place in a kind of pinkish, bloody light.

"Trouble in paradise?" Lanny asked, flinching as Jill playfully swatted him on the shoulder with her hand.

"I think Mister Marketing is finding out that the grass isn't always greener on the other side," Jessica said as she took a sip of wine.

"Really?" Jill asked, looking at Wil. "Things aren't getting any better at work?"

Wil kept staring at his wineglass. "I just feel like I'm off by half a beat. I can't seem to find a groove over there."

"Know what you mean, buddy," Lanny said, trying to make misery love company. "We've got some real technology issues. I've discovered some programming on Midwest Federated systems written so long ago that no one knows how to read it anymore, much less know what to do with it. The email firewall for the company is so thin that I have no doubt that a virus could bring the whole place to its knees. Then there's Duke Slaytor. That guy doesn't seem to give a hoot, even if he is the head of Information Technology. It's his way, or no way, and his way is stuck somewhere back in nineteen-eighty-seven."

Jessica grabbed her wineglass with both hands and propped it up with her elbows resting on the table. "Both of your problems are just beginning, if what I overheard at work is true."

Wil winced and shook his head. "Jessica!" he blurted with admonishment. "It's just rumor...hearsay. We can't prove what you heard is true."

"What'd you hear?" Lanny asked.

Jessica was fidgeting in her chair, impatient to let everyone know what she learned at the restaurant. "These two guys—your company jet pilots I think—were at Currell's the other day. I overheard them say the pension was being cut. And salaries, too."

"Frozen," Wil corrected.

"Ouch," Lanny said. "They'd probably be the ones to know. I hear they fly Cramer and his entourage all over the place. They probably learn a lot of stuff on those trips." Lanny shot Wil a look. "What's the matter? You don't think it's true?"

Wil shrugged. "Who knows. I have to admit that management is acting kind of desperate to hit their numbers.

I keep getting beat up about checking accounts, checking accounts and more checking accounts. Trouble is, the more accounts we bring on, the more customer service problems we get. I've got a stack of complaint mail now about this tall." Wil held his right hand up to the top of his wine glass.

"They've never been known for their great customer service," Jessica said. "You've known that for a long time."

"Yes," Wil nodded, "but now I feel like I'm in a position to do something about it. No one at the bank management level seems to want to acknowledge there's a problem." Wil took a long gulp of wine, draining the glass. "I'd be willing to divert my entire marketing budget for a year if it would get the branches better trained, but you can't throw money at a problem that apparently doesn't exist."

Lanny raised his hand to recall the waiter to the table. "This man needs more wine. Keep it coming." The waiter moved in to swiftly refill Wil's glass. "Our troubles deserve a toast," Lanny said. "Here's to the Midwest's friendliest bank." Lanny raised his wineglass, followed by Jill, Jessica and then Wil.

Wil looked intently at his refilled glass and noticed the wine's deep red color, the liquid swirling within, his mind filling with ridiculous thoughts of red-dyed dog treats and cherry-flavored lollipops.

"Bang, bang, bang!" Jonathan was at the top of the steps, carrying the green plastic squirt gun with a broken handle. He scurried out of the doorway and ran into the middle of the family room, followed closely by Zack, who returned fire with an old garden hose sprayer.

"Keep it down, boys!" Hallie said, trapping her left ear shut with an index finger to hear her boyfriend's phone voice more clearly.

"Bang! I got you! I got you!"

"Boys! Boys!"

The two kids ran wildly around the house exchanging the rapid gunfire of young imaginations. Zack and Jonathan screamed in delight as Kevin suddenly appeared at the top of the basement steps wearing a blue baseball cap and holster. "All right, you varmints! You're all under arrest!"

Click. Click. Click.

The Enfield revolver made a loud metallic sound each time the trigger was pulled. The boys took off running, and Kevin gave chase.

"Kevin, I'm on the phone here," Hallie yelled, covering the mouthpiece with her hand as she verbally scolded the boys.

At the end of the long hallway that led to the bedrooms, Kevin had his two brothers effectively cornered. *Click, click.* The revolver was pointed at little Jonathan's face, then at Zack's head. Kevin pushed the long barrel closer to the targets in front of him, waving the gun slowly back and forth. "Die, you varmints...DIE."

Dinner was followed by dessert, a fine crème brulee topped with plump red strawberries. As Wil and Lanny divvied up the bill, Jill dug inside of her purse for the cell phone.

"While you're figuring out the check, I'm going to step out and call home." She looked at the phone's display screen and noticed a poor signal. Nudging her chair back, Jill stood and headed for the front door in search of a stronger connection.

"Stop it, you guys." Hallie's appearance at the other end of the hallway created groans from all three boys. "It's after eight. You heard what your mother said. Bedtime at eight for all of you."

Jonathan and Zack did an end-run around their armed brother, avoiding the gun that was pointed their way. The two boys went to their individual rooms to change into pajamas, but not before they dropped the squirt gun and hose sprayer to the floor.

Kevin turned toward Hallie, the real gun now being held at his side. "Me, too?" Kevin asked.

"You too," Hallie said. "Come on. First pajamas. Then to the bathroom to brush your teeth." Hallie pointed toward Kevin's bedroom, and Kevin obediently walked in and closed the door to change. Just then, the phone rang again.

"Yes, everything's fine, Missus Taylor," Hallie said assuredly from the kitchen phone. "They're just now heading to bed."

The two couples walked several blocks in the chilly air to the North Country Bar, but found they had to wait a short while for enough seats to become available at the busy counter. Lanny was eventually able to stake his claim on four stools before any competition nuzzled in.

Wil was heading to grab a seat when someone recognized him.

"Mister Wil Fischer!" Felicia Cortez's beautiful facial features were accentuated under the low lighting of the bar. Her high cheek bones, black hair, dark skin and deep brown eyes looked stunning to Wil as he approached.

"Why, if it isn't my favorite bartender."

The boys had all used the bathroom and brushed their teeth, with Kevin being the last one out. After he retreated to his bedroom again for the night, Hallie went down the hallway, making sure each kid was properly tucked in.

Farthest down the hall was young Jonathan's room. Hallie immediately noticed that he had opened the closet door slightly, leaving the closet light on.

"Everything okay in here?" Hallie asked as she entered the room.

"Yeah," young Jon said. "Mom lets me sleep with a light on."

"Okay," she said, pulling the covers up to his neck.

"But I need something," he said.

"What's that?"

"Can you find my toys?" he asked in his little voice. "I don't want Zack taking my squirt gun tomorrow."

"Sure thing." Hallie walked out the bedroom door and saw both the green squirt gun and the hose sprayer on the carpet. She bent down and collected them, and reentered the boy's bedroom. "Here you go." She dropped them next to his bed and stood in the doorframe. "Good night."

"G'night," Jonathan said.

Walking down the hallway toward the living room, she noticed the bathroom light was also still on. Instinctively she reached in through the door without fully entering the room, but she couldn't locate the light switch with her hand. She pushed the door open a little more and stepped inside. On the edge of the vanity was the gun that Kevin had been using. Hallie picked it up. "Jeez, they make these things so real," the 15 year old mumbled under her breath.

With the weapon in one hand, she flipped off the light and walked back down the hallway. She strolled into Jonathan's room and stuffed the Enfield revolver under his bed. "There you go," she said, patting his covers with her right hand. "You now have control of all the toys."

With all three guns in Jonathan's possession, Hallie knew she had scored an abundance of points. She was certain she had just become the kid's most favorite babysitter.

"So, did your head roll?" Felicia asked over the loud music of the bar.

"Excuse me?"

"Your head. Did it roll?" Felicia was smiling as she sat a beer in front of Wil.

"Sorry. Not following."

"I had a visit at the branch from Mister Cramer himself yesterday. He was looking for his lollipops." Felicia snickered as she said it.

Wil's expression sunk. He hadn't mentioned this fiasco to anyone, including his own girlfriend. But now here he sat, the bartender of North Country about to spill the beans about the biggest confrontation he ever had with a higher-up.

"Oh, that." He then managed a faint smile. "You were at the branch where this all started?"

"Was I ever! Boy, he was not a happy man," Felicia said, delivering drinks to Wil's friends. "Apparently, he likes his lollipops."

"And his dog treats," Wil said flatly, noisily sipping the foam from his beer glass.

Questions about the incident started coming from Lanny, and Wil began explaining what happened, opting to skip many of the pertinent details. Halfway through the story, Jessica started tapping Wil on the elbow.

"That's them!" she said, pointing to the end of the bar.

"Who?" Wil asked.

"The two pilots. The ones who were in the restaurant."

"Hi gentlemen. Remember me?"

After a full day of routine maintenance at the hangar, Andy and Ron had decided to stop on their way home for a quick beverage. Jessica stood behind them, sexily flipping her hair so that it flared and landed on her shoulders. Ron was the first to turn toward her, but he furrowed his brow, not recognizing the woman. Andy just kept looking down at the bar; he always tried to prevent being recognized in drinking establishments, even if he was just drinking a cola. It was something that was drilled into the man during his days as a commercial pilot.

"I'm sorry," Ron said, extending his hand. He never missed a chance to interact with the ladies, especially those as beautiful as the one who stood next to him. "You are...?"

"Jessica Tolkin," she said, returning the handshake. "I was your waitress a while back. At Currell's."

"Oh yes. Of course, of course." Ron was in a stage of near-drool, so Andy finally succumbed to his own curiosity and turned to have a look at the woman. He remembered her instantly. He also remembered that he hadn't been terribly impressed with her service that night. "You miss us already?" Andy asked, a smile finally cracking his tired face.

"You're pilots, right?" she asked, pouring it on, swaying her hips back in forth in a full bodily gesture of approval.

"Yeah, we are," Ron said, feeling he was scoring well with just the mention of his occupation.

Andy leaned over to Ron. "Down boy," he said softly, knowing all too well that bars had eyes—and ears.

"There's someone here I want you to meet." Jessica turned and motioned to Wil.

Wil was sometimes annoyed at the openness and extreme approachability of his girlfriend. He thought she often liked to create situations that were uncomfortable, just to see how they might play out. The situation that was unfolding had all the ingredients for just such a scenario. He reluctantly slid off his bar stool, and with beer glass in hand, he walked up.

"Gentlemen, I'd like you to meet Wil Fischer," Jessica said as he approached. "He's the marketing director at Midwest Federated Bank. I think you'll find that the three of you have something in common."

As Wil became engaged in conversation, Lanny and Jill joined them, and the entire group was introduced. After some brief small talk, the Taylors decided to use the distraction as a reason to call it a night. After Lanny and Jill said their goodbyes, Wil, Jessica and the two pilots moved to a more intimate table, away from the bar.

"Andy, you've been flying for a lot of years?" Wil asked, simultaneously signaling the waitress for another beer refill.

"Thirty-three."

"You're looking at one of the last great Pan Am pilots," Ron said. "Just like my dad."

"And you admit that?"

The group laughed, and Ron grabbed the pitcher of beer that he had placed in the middle of the table, refilling his glass. He raised the pitcher toward Andy, tempting him with the chilled golden liquid.

"Why not," Andy sighed, giving in. "I've had too much pop sugar anyway." Ron filled Andy's glass with beer.

"How long have you worked for Mister Cramer?" Jessica asked.

"I've been his company pilot for fifteen years."

"And the way things are going, he may be the company pilot for only fifteen minutes more," Ron said smiling, toasting his glass of beer in the air.

Wil sat up straight. "Oh? Not a fan?"

"Let's say the man has some nuances about him," Andy said, swirling the beer in his glass before gulping it.

"Deep convictions about his money," Ron said out of one side of his mouth, the alcohol doing more of the talking.

Wil grabbed the pitcher and refilled Andy's glass. "I've been hearing some rumors," Wil said. "I wonder if either of you can confirm them." Wil looked over at Jessica, who raised her eyebrows in a mischievous manner when she realized exactly where Wil was going with this line of questioning.

"Rumors? What rumors?"

"The pension, for one," Wil said to Andy. "A guy like you probably has a lot of cash built up in the pension fund. I hear they might be discontinuing it. That can't make someone like you very happy."

Andy adopted a stony look on his face and took a long swallow of beer. He set his glass down loudly on the wooden table. "I am sixty-one years old. I wanted to retire in four years. But by discontinuing the credits into the fund, that's no longer possible. I'll need to work probably ten more years to make up for it. That's too old for a pilot."

"Salaries are being frozen, too, I'm afraid," Ron said, leaning back with his arms crossed. "No more raises for a while."

"And if salaries are being frozen, like they did two years ago, that means bonuses go away again," Andy said.

"You mean they've done this before?" Jessica asked.

"It goes in cycles like this," Andy explained. "I've seen it go on and off like a faucet over the years. The bank gets near the end of the fiscal year and management starts to panic. They slash here, burn there. Now that Cramer and his buddies in the other states have a huge stock award awaiting them, they want to do whatever is necessary to hit their numbers by December. If that means cutting the pension and punishing us, then so be it. It's obvious they don't care about you...or you...or you," Andy said, pointing at Wil, then Jessica, then Ron, his voice starting to slow from the effects of rapid consumption of alcohol. "They only care about their big, fat paychecks to feed their big, fat wives." Andy picked up the pitcher and drained what little beer was left into his glass, and promptly downed it. Due to his profession, he was a lousy drinker.

"Too bad we don't have those pictures," Ron said, tipping his chair back on its two hind legs.

Fascinated, Wil looked at Jessica, who nearly sent a mouthful of beer through her nose.

"Pictures?" Wil and Jessica asked simultaneously.

Ron wiped his lips with his hand. "We had a nice collection of color photos before Captain Pan Am here lost them," he snickered.

"Let's get one thing straight," Andy said with an alcohol-induced grin on his face, "I didn't lose them. They were confiscated."

Wil leaned in. "What, may I ask, were the pictures of?"

"Oh," Ron said, biting his lower lip, "this and that." After a moment of struggle to keep a straight face, both Ron and Andy disintegrated into a hysterical fit of laughter.

"So there really are pictures of Mister Cramer?" Jessica asked.

"A pale Mister Cramer and a few of his feline friends," Ron snorted. More laughter from the pilots ensued. Ron got under control long enough to blurt out a full sentence. "However, that man is not quite as pale from the waist down."

While the two men laughed uncontrollably, Wil felt sober. "These pictures," he asked softly, "they weren't taken in Miami by any chance, were they?"

Andy and Ron melted with more laughter. "Yep."

"Taken back in June?"

Laughter. "Yep."

"Taken during a Board of Directors' trip?"

Belly laughs. "Yep!"

Wil felt sick. "With...prostitutes?"

The two pilots were now doubled-over in their chairs in laughter, nearly collapsing from being out of breath. Wil watched as the men held their stomachs to try to get their guffaws to subside.

Wil looked sadly into Jessica's eyes, his thoughts filled with memories of his first day of work at the bank, of the PR nightmare he found himself in that day, and of Candy Luther. Over the past few months since the incident occurred, he sought every reason to doubt her story, which was the only fuel he had in order to deny the whole thing to the *Minneapolis Daily Post* columnist.

That doubt was now shattered with a sudden, harsh dose of reality.

What have I gotten myself into?

THIRTY-FIVE

November 2000

An early snowfall had coated the Twin Cities with a fresh layer of frozen precipitation. As a result, the glare from the sun bouncing off the whitened landscape was too much for Wil's blue eyes as he headed northbound in his company-leased car. A morning dental appointment had him running late, but fortunately the traffic was light during the post-rush hour period. Wil was driving with one hand and grasping for his sunglasses in the glove compartment with the other when his cell phone rang.

"This is Security," the deep male voice on the other end of the phone said as soon as Wil was able to open the receiver. "I'm calling to report that one of the branches has been robbed."

Ever since the October robbery that he had witnessed, Wil was placed on MFB's Security notification list so that he didn't get surprised if the media ever called for comment on an incident. This latest call was the fourth one he had received since October, and each robbery was perpetrated by the same cowboy-hat-wearing suspect.

"Was it our man?" Wil asked, pushing up his sunglasses over the bridge of his nose.

"Yes."

"Which branch?"

"Chaska."

"Anyone hurt?"

"No."

"Money taken?"

"Yes. Twenty-three hundred."

"Any video?"

"Grainy. Nothing usable."

Wil was frustrated that the security technology being used by Midwest Federated Bank was so antiquated. He remembered back in his Union First days that on the rare occasion a branch was robbed, the pictures were always crystal clear and the perpetrator caught almost immediately.

Wil was further frustrated that the media had given a name to this serial bank robber, and he thought it only helped glamorize a very unglamorous, and potentially dangerous, activity. References to "the Cowboy Bandit" were in every newspaper headline that reported on the rash of robberies, and Midwest Federated was becoming synonymous with the robber's name and the crimes he committed. Despite the efforts of local police and the FBI, the Cowboy Bandit remained at large, with Midwest Federated branches being his most favorite target.

"Any media inquiries yet?" Wil asked.

"None. What would you like us to say if we do?"

"Same as always," Wil answered. "No comment."

Barney Jennings waited nearly an hour in Saint Paul for Mr. Cramer to be freed up. He had plenty to do himself that day, and he always despised being called out to the headquarters at the last minute, only to be forced to cool his heels and wait.

The double doors of Dick Cramer's office eventually opened, and the CEO waived him in. Mr. Jennings walked in and sat in one of the guest chairs while Mr. Cramer walked to the large windows that faced the freshly snow-covered sidewalks of downtown Saint Paul. Mr. Cramer folded his arms, gazing out at the footprints being left in the snow by passers-by who scurried near Sixth and Wabasha. "Barney, you need to communicate to your troops today that salaries for all exempt employees will be frozen, effective immediately."

Mr. Jennings hated communicating issues he couldn't control. But when Duke Slaytor wasn't assigned to deflect bad news or otherwise protect the CEO, it was normal for Mr. Cramer to push the bank regional presidents straight into the line of fire to do the dirty work.

Mr. Cramer kept looking out the window and down at the street. "I'm also discontinuing the funding of pensions," Cramer continued. "Companies aren't going to be supporting pensions anymore. We'll be ahead of the curve. Figure a way to soften that, will you Barney?" Mr. Cramer's voice remained flat as he unfolded his arms and picked up a pair of binoculars from a small nearby table.

Mr. Jennings frowned. "It's-it's a big impact on people, Dick. Is-is-is there another way?"

"We're going to hit those numbers," Mr. Cramer said. "I just know it. I can feel it." Cramer put the binoculars up to his eyes and tracked a flock of geese that flew in perfect formation high above the MFB building.

Mr. Jennings sat silent, opting to stare at the wall of personal photos that hung in neat rows behind Cramer's desk.

Mr. Cramer noticed the stillness and turned to him, donning a broad smile. "Don't panic, Barney. My guys are all exempt from these changes."

Mr. Jennings broke from his stare and returned a forced smile. Mr. Cramer strode confidently back to his huge oak desk.

"There's one more thing I want you to do," Mr. Cramer said, plopping down in his high-backed chair.

"What-what's that?" Mr. Jennings asked.

Mr. Cramer threw on his reading glasses. "We need to put the heat on, Barney. We need checking accounts, the kind that bounce checks and produce revenue for us." He opened a drawer in his desk and pulled out a white business card. "There's a lady I want you to contact. I've known her for years. She's in Little Rock, Arkansas, and I want you to call her." He handed the business card to Mr. Jennings.

Mr. Jennings read the card. "What-what-what exactly is she going to do for us, this woman?"

Mr. Cramer didn't blink. "Maybe you didn't hear me," he said pointedly. "She's going to get us checking accounts."

Mr. Jennings clenched his jaw. He looked down again at the name on the business card. "Once I call her, what do you want me to do?"

Mr. Cramer leaned back in his chair and rested his hands behind his head. "Then, Barney, it's simple," the CEO said, putting his shiny black shoes up on his desk, "I want you to hire her."

Jill Taylor picked up her three boys from school and immediately dropped off Kevin at hockey practice. With Zack and Jonathan in the back seat, she headed to the Midwest Federated branch in Bloomington on Old Shakopee Road. She pulled up her SUV as close as she dared next to the drive-up ATM, but she was quickly disappointed when she saw the words *TEMPORARILY UNAVAILABLE* on the machine's screen. She needed cash, and the only way to get it now was by going inside the branch, so she drove her vehicle into the first parking spot she could find.

"Come on, boys. We're going on a little adventure." The vehicle's doors opened and little Jonathan led the way, still wearing his blue school backpack. They darted across the wet blacktop through the chilly November air and entered the dark bank lobby of Midwest Federated Bank.

Jill saw that two teller lines were staffed, and although she picked the row with the shortest number of customers, she was still fourth in line. Knowing that she had to write a check to get cash from a teller, she frantically dug in her purse, looking for the checkbook. Zack and Jonathan soon lost interest in standing in line, so they ran across the lobby to a small plastic picnic table that was designed for such emergencies. It was stacked with a vast selection of kids' puzzles and games.

After a few more minutes, Jill finally found herself in front of a teller. She had just finished writing on the payable-to line when everything went into slow motion.

"EVERYBODY DOWN!"

The voice was loud and sharp, and the lobby's patrons reacted with screams. Jill turned toward the door to see a man in a flannel shirt, jacket, boots, and cowboy hat, his legs slightly apart, his right hand buried deep inside his jacket pocket.

All seven customers instantly hit the floor, followed closely by Jill. As her face hugged the floor, she kept her eyes locked exclusively on her boys, who were still sitting at the small plastic table on the other end of the lobby. They sat motionless, their eyes wide with fear, confusion gripping both of their faces.

From her horizontal position, Jill could hear the robber's footsteps on the carpet as he neared the teller line. She trembled uncontrollably as her sightline was disrupted by the man, his boots blocking a clean view of her two sons.

"Empty the entire drawer into this," the Cowboy Bandit said to the teller as he held open an empty pillowcase. "If ya give me the dye pack, I promise ya, I'll come back and shoot ya."

Hearing this, Jill let out a yelp and burst into tears, her eyes darting desperately to see past the man's footwear in an effort to get a glimpse of her boys.

The man looked down at her. "Quiet. Shut up!"

Jill knew that the Cowboy Bandit was speaking directly to her; it only made her yelp again and cry harder. She tried to calm herself, but her efforts made her hyperventilate.

"I don't like no crying," he yelled with a slur. "No crying! I said shut UP!"

Jill couldn't catch her breath while pressed flat against the floor. She struggled to control her airflow, but she was most concerned about the safety of her young sons. She hoped they were sitting as still as possible.

Per the Cowboy Bandit's instructions, the young female teller calmly and efficiently filled the pillowcase with the entire contents of her money drawer.

The process seemed to take forever. Jill could only wait and watch as the man's boots finally moved, turning a full 180 degrees, but still blocking the view of her kids. As she tried to quiet her whimpering, the boots took several steps closer, and she realized that the man was standing directly over her.

"Get up."

Slowly and deliberately, she craned her neck to get a look at the man's pitted face. Tears were streaming down her cheeks.

"I...said...GET...UP!"

One of the man's boots pressed slowly against Jill's ribs, deeply penetrating her side. Pain shot into her body. She was shaking so hard and so violently, she thought she had lost complete control of her functions. Her brain commanded her right leg and knee to move so that she could get leverage to make her body upright, but she found herself frozen to the floor in fear.

"Listen, lady," the man said, "when I say get up, I mean get UP."

KA-BANG!

Time stopped. The blast was sharp and unexpected, like a firecracker detonating at close range. Everyone inside the branch screamed simultaneously. Jill snapped her eyes shut.

The sound was accompanied by something hitting the ceiling, and shards of white plaster fell like Minnesota snow onto the lobby floor, Jill's back, and the brim of the hat worn by the Cowboy Bandit.

A gunshot!

Feeling the plaster striking her head, Jill thought she was hit by a bullet. She felt no new pain, so she slowly opened one eye, expecting another shot to ring out. But the man's boots had disappeared.

The Cowboy Bandit had fled.

Jill couldn't process what had happened, and she concluded that she definitely had not been hit.

But who was? she wondered, panic gripping her. *My God. My boys!*

Jill mustered enough courage to lift her head from the plaster-strewn floor. Across the lobby were Zack and Jonathan, seemingly unharmed, a tight cloud of smoke from a gunshot hanging near them.

While Zack was still seated at the colorful plastic table, six-year-old Jonathan was standing rigid, frozen in place, his arms outstretched, his tiny hands still gripping the vintage British Enfield revolver.

Little Jon's face was white; his eyes were wide as saucers. For his weapon had just discharged a single bullet into the ceiling of the Midwest Federated Bank.

Wil and Kari Bender sat at the small conference table in Wil's office reviewing the final numbers on the Great Cabin Giveaway.

"Looks like the news is good, and bad," Kari observed, pointing to a small line of numbers at the bottom of a long spreadsheet. "Twenty-two percent increase in accounts, year over year." Kari took a pen and circled a number on the page under the heading labeled *CLOSED ACCOUNTS*. "Look at this," she said, pointing to the pen mark. "A nine percent increase in attrition."

Wil shook his head. "The faster we put those accounts on the books, the faster we seem to lose them," he concurred. "We have a real service problem."

"I'm sure those lollipops and dog treats will help to make all those accounts stick," Kari said, rolling her eyes.

Wil smirked. "Those things have been at branches a while now. Do we know if they're even being used?"

"Judging by the size of some of our tellers, I think they're mostly being eaten by staff," Kari laughed.

Wil allowed a chuckle. "Check the usage reports for me. I want to make sure those branches have a constant supply before you-know-who visits another branch."

"Sure thing. You'll also be glad to hear that we finished the sweepstakes processing and picked a cabin winner."

"Great. Who won?"

Kari grabbed a folder and flipped through the printouts contained inside, stopping on the fifth page. "A young couple from Plymouth. They're new checking customers, recently married."

"Normal people," Wil said. "That's good. Maybe it'll deflect some of the bad news we keep getting in the press."

Wil and Kari went on to discuss the next promotion: the opening of the Eagan branch planned for late November. It was the first new branch opening in more than two years, and Barney Jennings had asked Wil to make a big splash with it.

They didn't get far in their conversation when Mindy appeared at the door. "Security just called," she said through a panicky shortness of breath. "Bloomington's been hit with a robbery."

Kari let out a long sigh. Will looked at the date on his watch.

"That didn't take long," Wil said. "It's the second hit this week. Is it our cowboy?"

Mindy nodded, but then stood motionless in the doorway, her large carriage filling the frame. Wil could see by the look on her face that there was more bad news.

"Anyone hurt?"

"They aren't sure," she answered. "But Wil...there was a shooting."

Duke Slaytor was ticked. Lanny was used to his boss's tirades, and he usually just sat back and let him finish. Today, though, Lanny was in no mood to put up with the man's diatribes.

"You're not hearing me, Duke," Lanny shot back forcefully. "Our processing system is nearly out of capacity. When we're out of capacity, we can't service the growth."

"We are not going to spend another dime on this system," Mr. Slaytor said, his right fist pounding the table as he spoke.

"You were hired to figure this out. I suggest you start doing just that."

Lanny unbuttoned his shirt cuffs and rolled the sleeves halfway up his arms, an unconscious attempt to cool himself off. He leaned forward. "Our core system is not capable of withstanding more growth, and it's as simple as that," he said defiantly. "It certainly won't support any more cobbling. And if we don't strengthen the company's firewall, none of it will matter anyway, because the whole system will get infected." Lanny's cell phone started vibrating, and a quick glance at it showed him that his wife was calling. Normally he'd never take a call while talking to his boss, but the two men's foul moods compelled Lanny to hit the Talk button anyway.

"I'm in a meeting," he said, snapping at Jill. "Can I call you back?"

There was a pause, and then Jill's voice, low and hoarse, rattled through the phone. "You need to get down here right away," she said. "Something terrible has happened."

His mouth went dry. "What's the matter? Where are you?"

"At the Bloomington Police Department," she said. "Get down here right now. Please."

THIRTY-SIX

Rays from the warm New Mexico sun shone in through the massive windows of the great room at the Cramer ranch, illuminating the freshly treated timbers that pyramided to a peak above the huge space. The ladders were finally gone, and the disruptions of Mexican workmen were a memory as the CEO's wife sat alone on the long leather couch that faced the rebuilt thirty-foot-high stone fireplace in the center of the room. Her hair hung loosely and attractively about her shoulders, and her blouse was tightly cut, all in a more natural and relaxed look reserved exclusively for those private times when she didn't have to be Mrs. Richard Edmund Cramer.

Harriet had been blessed with a visit from her husband just twice during her month-long stay. Constant meetings, conferences with stock analysts, and other business interruptions were the usual excuses that she received from him on a regular basis. Of course, she knew the real story. Early in their marriage, she had always given her husband the benefit of the doubt. But it didn't take long before she became suspicious of his extracurricular activities, and it was three years ago this day when she decided it had gone on long enough. Ever since, she was fighting back.

"Maria," Harriet said while straightening the pillows on the new couch, "can you bring me the album?"

"Sí, señorita," Maria said. Maria was forty-six years old with a family of 10 children. She lived in Albuquerque for five years after emigrating from Mexico to the United States, and was Harriet's ranch helper since the couple bought the place in the mid-1990s. It was her first and only job in America.

Maria was short and of moderate build, walking with a slight limp, the result of knee surgery following a fall from a horse while riding with her oldest son. As instructed, Maria retrieved the blue photo album out of a locked safe and limped across the great room's rustic wooden floor. "Would you like anything from the kitchen, Miss Cramer?" Maria asked in her purposeful English, setting the album on the huge glass coffee table in front of Harriet. "Some hot tea?"

"That would be very nice, Maria," she answered. "Gracias." Harriet watched as the woman strode with her limp toward the kitchen. As Maria disappeared through the doorway, Harriet picked up the album, which was the kind that was sealed with a leather flap and could not be opened except with a key, which she produced from her pocket. She immediately opened the album to the first page of photos, and then flipped through the next six pages, which were filled from top to bottom with a variety of color and black-and-white photographs, all containing muddy images of her husband and snapped from hidden locations.

Six pages, she thought. *That's two pages a year.*

The envelope that contained the photos retrieved several weeks earlier from the corporate jet was shoved between two of the pages. She was so disappointed that the photos hadn't been found; she had taken great pains to ensure they could be easily seen.

"Crema y azúcar, señorita?" Maria called out from the kitchen.

"Sí, Maria. Cream and sugar would be appreciated." Harriet turned the album to page seven, the first blank page. One by one, she removed the grainy photos from the envelope and placed them into the clear sleeve of the album's page. She purposely held out one particular photo—one that was sharp, clear and captured a portion of her husband's face in mid-grimace, frozen in time in his momentary, climactic, unfaithful bliss.

"I check the phone," Maria said as she ambled back toward Harriet, carrying a silver tea tray. "No call yet from the Mister."

Harriet tore a small white sheet of paper from a notebook and retrieved a nearby pen. She put up her hand, facing her palm toward Maria. "Un momento," she said, causing Maria to obediently halt her approach, hot tea slopping over the sides of the cup and onto the tray.

Harriet began scrawling something onto the paper, and Maria noticed that whatever was being written, it wasn't lengthy. Harriet folded the paper into thirds, inserted the color photo into the folds, and placed the items into a blank cream-colored envelope. She turned the envelope over and scrawled an address on the front. She then licked the back of the flap and sealed it up.

"Ven aquí," she said, motioning Maria to come forward. Harriet was quick to grab the hot tea from the tray as soon as Maria got close. She handed the envelope to Maria with her free hand. "The company jet is making a delivery here today," Harriet said. "Make sure this gets on board, por favor. I want it delivered when they return north."

"Sí." Maria placed the silver tray near the edge of the massive coffee table. As she turned to leave, Maria glanced at the address on the front of the envelope. While her reading abilities in English were limited, she recognized one string of words that were scrawled in Harriet's handwriting, and she knew instantly that the letter was addressed to one Richard Edmund Cramer.

Lanny had taken considerable chances driving on the shoulder, weaving in and out of traffic lanes during rush hour. Finally arriving at his destination, he found the parking lot full at the Bloomington Police Department. In a fit of desperation, he parked his car in an empty stall marked *OFFICER OF THE MONTH*.

The air temperature was uncomfortably crisp as Lanny made his way across the lot and into the station. At the front desk, he was directed to a conference room that was located at the end of a long, stark hallway. He knocked softly on the closed door, and then opened it a crack. Inside he could see that most of his family—Jill, Jonathan and Zack—were all seated at the conference table.

As soon as Jill saw him, he opened the door the rest of the way and entered the stuffy room. She stood from her chair and gave him a somber hug. Lanny noticed that she had been crying, but what bothered him most was that she barely looked at him before returning to her seat.

At the end of the table was FBI agent Dean York, age 50, brown hair, with rimless glasses. He wore a tan suit with a white shirt and brown tie. His name and credentials were printed on a large clip-on name tag that dangled from the breast pocket of his suit coat.

He stood and approached Lanny, then shook his hand. "You must be Lanny Taylor," the agent said without expression. "I'm agent York, in charge of this investigation. Please have a seat."

Lanny gently patted the heads of Jonathan and Zack as he walked by them. Both kids were sitting motionless and sported looks of uneasiness. Lanny sat down next to Jill and watched the man as he wrote something in a manila file folder.

"Where's Kevin?" Lanny asked, leaning toward Jill.

"At hockey practice," she answered quietly.

Lanny waited for the agent to fill him in, but the man kept writing. "Can someone tell me what's going on?"

Jill put her head into her hands, her face red and swollen from sobbing. Mr. York finished his writing and looked up at Lanny.

"First of all, no one was hurt," he said evenly. "They were all quite fortunate. We are not going to file any charges against your son, Mister Taylor. No worries there."

"What?" Lanny asked, his eyes wide with surprise. "No charges? What are you talking about? What did he do?"

"There was a shooting," Jill said, fighting back the urge to cry again.

"A shooting? What shooting?"

"There was no malicious intent here," Mr. York said. "Your son was merely defending his mother." The agent spent the next several minutes going over the additional details of the incident. "What we're most concerned about is the gun," Mr. York said. "Can you explain where the gun came from?"

"The gun?" Lanny asked, withdrawing a few inches from the table. "What gun?"

Mr. York leaned to one side to retrieve the revolver that was in a box on the floor. He placed the gun on the table, a white evidence tag attached to it. "This gun...does it look familiar at all?"

Lanny blinked nervously. He could feel the color drain from his face. "Yes. It's my father's."

The agent leafed through several pages of notes in his file folder and stopped on one particular page. "Is that a Kenneth John Taylor of forty-seven-fourteen Ames Boulevard in San Francisco?"

"Yes."

"Mister Taylor, can you explain how this vintage firearm, which is registered in your father's name, came into your possession?"

Lanny looked at Jill as she finally moved her tear-filled eyes toward him. Lanny couldn't bear looking at her, so he immediately diverted his gaze. "I...I got it from him," he said tepidly, gazing into space.

"He gave it to you?" Mr. York asked skeptically.

Lanny looked down, but was silent.

Jill grabbed his arm. "He already talked to your dad," Jill said softly. "He said he didn't even know it was missing."

Lanny looked at his two boys. Their eyes were cast downward at the table, and the look of bewilderment on their faces broke his heart. He turned to the FBI agent and scooted up his chair closer to the table. "My dad's right," Lanny said, folding his hands in front of him. "I took it from him."

Jill let out a grief-filled sigh. "Why Lanny? Why would you leave a loaded gun unlocked for the kids to get to?" Jill's tone was increasingly angry, and more tears welled up in her eyes that ran down her cheeks.

"I didn't mean it to happen like this," Lanny said, his voice cracking. "I can't understand how the kids could have gotten to it. I had it locked up. I thought the chamber was empty before we even moved from California."

"Well it wasn't," Jill snapped, turning away from him and sobbing, her face lowering into her hands again.

Lanny turned to his youngest son and tried to refocus. "Jon, how did you get to it? Where did you find the gun?"

Jonathan's face was sad and pale, his hair disheveled and partially matted down. "Kevin found it," he said slowly, looking down dejectedly at the table. "In the basement."

The agent closed his file folder. "We're going to send someone to see Kevin, Mister Taylor," Mr. York said. "We have a few questions to ask him."

THIRTY-SEVEN

Wil fielded media inquiries from his home in Edina throughout the early evening. He was on the phone with a local TV station when someone banged loudly on his front door. "We have no comment," Wil repeated into the phone as he walked to the door, the handset pressed to the side of his head. "It's under investigation, but I can confirm that no one was hurt."

He hung up with the reporter just as Lanny stepped inside. The wind was gusting with a raw November chill, and a few dry leaves blew into his entryway, following Lanny onto the carpet.

"My God, Lanny. Are you okay?"

Lanny looked terrible, as though he had just run a marathon in business clothes. "I need a drink."

Wil poured his friend a Scotch, and they sat facing each other at Wil's dining room table.

"I should have returned it," Lanny said into the void, his eyes closed and his head shaking with regret. "Why didn't I just return it?" Lanny gulped nearly half his drink in one swig.

"Jonathan's okay, that's what's most important," Wil said, trying to deflect the conversation with a positive note of consolation. "Things could have been much worse."

Lanny emptied the remains of his drink into his mouth, leaving the ice cubes rattling at the bottom of the glass. "I just should've returned the gun. You've got to believe me, Wil. I knew that having it in my possession was a mistake. Why didn't I just give it back?" Lanny's eyes were red and moist. He stared absently into space.

Wil paused, studying his friend. "I have to ask this," Wil said quietly. "What were you doing with that gun in the first place?"

Lanny looked up and met his gaze. He nervously licked his lips. "You're my best friend, Wil. Can I put this on you?"

"Of course."

Lanny went on to tell his friend of his struggles during his time of unemployment, of his fractured marriage, and of his deepest, darkest despair that drove him to steal his father's revolver. Then, he told him of his abandoned plan for suicide.

He explained that it was Wil himself who had kept Lanny from committing such a despicable act.

Wil sat in silence, trying to process the overwhelming information he had just heard. "How did the kids find the gun?" Wil finally asked.

"With my life back on track, I had put it behind me. I had forgotten all about it. It ended up in a locked wooden box in the basement. Jill had unpacked the box when we moved to Minnesota, not knowing what was inside, and somehow the kids got into it. Then Kevin found it. You know how curious kids are."

Wil watched as Lanny's eyes again filled with tears. "Have you talked with Jill about how this all happened?"

"Yes," Lanny said. "But she just doesn't understand it. How could she? What I was contemplating to do with that gun was an awful, cowardly thing. How can she ever forgive me?"

Wil sat with him for a while, doing his best to comfort his friend. Shortly after 9 p.m., when Wil felt he could do no more, he decided it was best to personally drive Lanny home.

THIRTY-EIGHT

Over the next few days, the local TV stations in the Twin Cities were leading with the robbery story, despite a lack of details that were not revealed by Midwest Federated, the FBI or the local police. The media referenced the "young boy" who was "a relative of a bank employee" who "shot at" the now infamous Cowboy Bandit, causing the robber to flee. As Wil watched the replays of the news reports on the video player in his office, he marveled at how some of the TV reporters were making Jonathan Taylor out to be a kind of local hero. Thankfully, no names were released to the press, so reports were vague and largely sensationalized.

Wil's office phone rang. "Hi, Barney."

"Wil, we-we-we need to squash this thing. The press is having a field day with this."

"Pretty tough to squash this kind of story, Barney. I've stuck with the 'no comment' line all along. Unfortunately it's the kind of story that the press loves. They're going to report what they think they know."

"Yes, but Duke Slaytor is really breathing down my neck on this one," Mr. Jennings said in an emotionless tone. "Dick doesn't like seeing this press. It's a distraction. We-we-we need to ask the media to stop reporting on this."

Wil thought his boss's tone seemed to lack conviction. "I'm doing what I can," Wil answered. "Best if we just let it all blow over. It'll be the lead for a day or two. Then, they'll be onto something else."

Mr. Jennings finally let the whole thing drop, and Wil couldn't help but think that the man's backing-down came far too easily.

After hanging up, Wil tackled the growing pile of paper in his inbox. In it were more customer complaint letters, which he set aside to review later. Next up was an interoffice envelope that contained a memo to senior management, written by Barney Jennings. He opened it immediately.

Wil scanned the memo, and his blood pressure slowly rose as the rumor of a discontinued pension plan, pay freeze and suspended bonuses were confirmed on the page in front of him. He laughed out loud—a reaction of disgust, really—when he read the last sentence: *Find ways to gently discuss these issues with the rest of your staff.* He put the memo down, closed his eyes, and tried to rid himself of extreme frustration by executing a long, slow, deep exhale.

Lanny was trying his best to repair his marriage and salvage the relationship he cherished with Jill. He vowed not to let a stupid mistake from his past ruin his family, so he took extra time in the mornings to spend with his wife before heading off to his job downtown.

Most of the employees at the bank, including the staff in his department, supported Lanny and showed genuine concern for what had happened on that awful day at the Bloomington branch. Lanny's boss, however, was in no mood for sympathy.

"You've embarrassed this institution, Taylor," Duke Slaytor said, slamming Lanny's office door behind him. "You must know that Dick is not happy about this kind of ongoing publicity."

Lanny stood up from behind his desk, fidgeting with a pen in his hand. "I understand that," Lanny said. "But the main thing is that no one was hurt, don't you think?"

"No one was hurt, yes. However, our reputation as a bank—"

"Our reputation as a bank is one of robbery," Lanny interrupted, his own temper flaring. "If you've been paying any attention, that seems to be the only kind of press we get. At least it makes my six-year-old son look like he was trying to do something about it, and that's more than I can say about the execs around here." Lanny bit his lower lip and paused, knowing he had passed the point of no return deep inside dangerous territory.

Mr. Slaytor took a few steps closer to Lanny, and the man's voice got sterner. "I've been around here a lot longer than you, Taylor," Mr. Slaytor said, his artificial white hair taking on a yellowish hue under the department's ceiling lights. "Our reputation is built on integrity and the reputation of Richard Cramer. You need to respect that. Banks get robbed, and that's a simple fact. But there shouldn't be gunfire in our branches, especially when it comes from our employees' children."

Lanny could only clench his teeth and take it. Mr. Slaytor stopped his tirade long enough to retrieve an envelope from the inside pocket of his tacky tweed jacket. He handed it to Lanny.

"Here. Read this."

Lanny grabbed the letter as Mr. Slaytor turned and exited his office in a huff. Lanny's heart was beating a mile a minute.

Have I just been fired?

He took a deep breath and ripped opened the envelope, unfolding the memo inside. It was from Barney Jennings, which informed the troops of the impending budget cuts.

Anger slowly welled up inside Lanny. In a brief fit of rage, he ripped the memo into tiny shreds and threw the pieces into the air in a burst of confetti that covered the floor around him.

Letter after letter, Wil was reading the same things from customers: *Poor service, screwed up my statement, bad morale,* and *inconvenient hours* were the most common phrases he highlighted with his yellow marker.

Wil felt increasingly perturbed that his emails and conversations with Barney Jennings concerning the mounting customer complaints were being ignored. Wil knew all too well that the complaints were symptoms of the bigger problems that showed up in droves in his consumer research.

One final letter remained. It was addressed to Richard Edmund Cramer, and it was opened already, the result of the Mailroom strictly following a policy that required the CEO's correspondence to be screened for sales pitches, unusual substances, and customer complaints.

Wil extracted the cream-colored parchment from the envelope. He unfolded it to discover just four words written on it, done in beautiful handwriting and dark blue ink. He noticed it was signed *Harriet,* and neatly written beneath her signature were the letters *ENC.* Wil looked back in the envelope to see if he had missed something, but it was empty; he could find no enclosure.

He read the four words over and over, trying to grasp their meaning: *I know too much.*

He refolded the letter and replaced it in the envelope. Wil now realized that the letter was a personal one meant for Mr. Cramer—a cryptic note from the man's wife.

I know too much.

Wil looked down at the envelope, wondering what could have been inside that was now apparently missing. After a few moments of thought, he grabbed his phone and punched in the five-digit number to call the Midwest Federated Bank Mailroom.

THIRTY-NINE

Forty-eight-year-old Lynette "Trixie" Tanner hailed from Little Rock, Arkansas. She was tall, rail thin, but busty, with elbows and knees that were so sharp that they seemed nearly transparent through her skin. Her freckles had never completely gone away since childhood, although they had faded in intensity over the years. What stood out the most on Trixie Tanner, as she preferred to be called, was her flaming red hair, which barely covered her ears and was often disheveled in a wild, haphazard arrangement.

The meeting she attended several days prior with Barney Jennings was brief, and it was the first time in her career that she was hired for a job on the spot. She had flown in this day to get settled into her new executive office on the second floor of the Midwest Federated headquarters building in downtown Saint Paul.

"Trixie!" Mr. Cramer beamed, standing with his arms outstretched in her office doorway.

"Dick," she drawled, "it's soooo gewd ta see ya'll."

The two embraced for a time, his hands up on her bony shoulders, with Cramer finally easing back to get a good look at her. "You haven't changed a bit, Trixie," he said with an approving smile.

"Don't ah know et!"

Mr. Cramer knew that Ms. Tanner had spent most of her life in New Jersey, where they had first met while working in the steel industry. Like him, Trixie Tanner had jumped from steelwork into banking, relocating many times and finally settling in Little Rock. Since moving there eight years ago, she had worked for the mammoth Solar Financial Corporation. Mr. Cramer always suspected that her southern accent was artificially adopted, but he liked the sound of it. She knew he did, too.

"I'm so glad you were able to get up here so quickly," he said.

"Anythin' fer yew, ma dear Mista Crama."

Marci, the CEO's executive assistant, knocked lightly on the doorframe and entered with a broad smile, carrying a large bouquet of roses in a glass vase. She placed the arrangement on the small conference table in Ms. Tanner's office and adjusted it for the correct angle of display.

Ms. Tanner rushed over to the table and bent over to smell the mixture of red and yellow roses. "How bee-you-tee-full! Dick, are these from ya'll?"

Mr. Cramer grinned with the look of a proud father. "Just a little welcoming gift," he said. "I want you to feel right at home."

She brushed back the red-colored bangs that were strewn across her forehead. "Ah dew."

"Here." Mr. Cramer pulled out one of the four chairs that surrounded the table and motioned for her to sit. She obliged, and he hurriedly plopped down in another chair, letting out a relaxing sigh. "Now that you're here, we can get started."

"Great," she said in her overly exuberant, forced southern tone. "Let's git goin'."

Mr. Cramer clasped his hands together, put them behind his head and leaned back. "There's a lot of work to do around here, Trixie. A lot of work, indeed. We need your help. And I have a few things for you to work on right away."

"We don't have a record of that particular letter," Aretha Moss said from the Mailroom, her deep voice knifing through Wil's phone receiver, her gum chewing incessant.

"But it was opened, just like all the rest of them that I get on a daily basis," Wil said, holding the Harriet envelope, fidgeting with its loose back flap. "How can you be sure that you didn't process this one?"

"We log all our entries," Aretha said. "There's no record."

"It came with the same stack of other mail, and you processed those," Wil said pointedly.

"All right," Aretha said, smacking her gum. "Let me look again. You say it was signed by a Harriet something?"

"Yes. It was handwritten." Wil could hear papers shuffling on the other end of the phone.

"No. There is no Harriet anything on my sheet. What does the postmark say?"

Wil flipped the envelope over. *Wait a minute.* Wil sat motionless, staring at the empty upper-right-hand corner of the cream-colored envelope.

"Did I lose you, Wil?"

He gently rubbed his forehead. "Tell me something. Would you have processed a letter that had no postmark?"

"No postmark?"

"No stamp, either."

"No postmark and no stamp?" She chuckled. "Wouldn't come here, then. Sounds hand-delivered. Anything that gets delivered by hand from the outside hits the security desk in the lobby. They route it directly from there. We only process postage mail. My operation wouldn't even get access to something like that."

Interesting, Wil thought. *If this did come from Harriet Cramer, who delivered it, who opened it, and why did I get it instead of her husband?*

Wil thanked Aretha for the information and hung up the phone. He turned the envelope repeatedly from front to back, and back to front, thinking. *And what happened to the enclosure?*

FORTY

Lanny was relieved that the media attention on the robbery had died down, but things were still strained at home. He made it a personal priority to redouble his efforts to earn back Jill's trust and to get reengaged in his career. He hadn't seen his boss in several days, which had allowed him some rare, uninterrupted swaths of time to focus on work. Even the sight of Mr. Slaytor would have sent Lanny back into depression, a lethal combination with his overwhelming fear of being fired.

With problems at home and ornery members of his staff who recently learned of a freeze in pay, a dropped pension plan, and no year-end bonuses, Lanny was in desperate need of a distraction. He sat at his keyboard, expertly punching in codes and commands that gave him exclusive access to the bank's systems. At his staff meeting that morning, he had made it his top priority to bolster the Internet firewall to prevent what was predicted to be an unprecedented period of viruses and email spam in all corporate environments. He was particularly adept with such issues, learning much of his technical knowledge during his product management days at Continental-American Bank in L.A.

The text of numbers, letters and code filled his screen from top to bottom. Lanny took a swig from the can of diet cola that sat near his mouse pad, and then punched in a few sequences of numbers, eventually landing on a white screen with black text that was marked SYSTEM STATUS. He entered in a few more commands, which displayed a string of one-line updates that were coming in from every system throughout the enterprise. Near the bottom of the screen, a red-colored, blinking line of text caught his eye. He scrolled down and clicked on it, which produced another full screen of detail.

What's this? he wondered. It didn't take long for Lanny to realize that the very thing he was trying to prevent had infiltrated the flimsy firewall of Midwest Federated Bank. Lanny leaned closer to his computer monitor, examining the codes and numbers that were arranged in neat, vertical columns. He quickly deduced that this newfound virus carried some type of attachment, and it was primed to attack the bank's internal email system. Luckily, he had discovered it just in time before it populated itself to every email user in the company. If he didn't find a way to delete it now, he knew it was to be a very long day.

He punched in a few more commands onto his keyboard, which brought up the system's main prompt. He typed in a precise string of code that instructed the system to completely delete the virus. He then hit the Enter key and watched gleefully as the software obeyed—albeit sluggishly—by eliminating line after line of foreign code right before his eyes.

Lanny allowed himself a faint smile, watching with satisfaction as his commands created a virtual war of software, with the attacked now attacking the attacker. He happily observed the software battle for a few moments, and he swallowed another mouthful of diet cola as lines of text and code continued to disappear.

Lanny's smile quickly faded when he saw that something was amiss: A strange line of type was appearing after every fourth line of deleted code. He put his cola down and hit a few keys to view the line more closely.

The words he dreaded seeing sat idle on his screen, and they seared into his brain. His mouth went dry as the computer-generated words blinked incessantly in front of him. Lanny's eyes did not blink as he read them over and over to himself:

```
Program successfully executed and sent.
```

Lanny went limp. He now realized he had jumped the gun; he should have given the problem to his team to work on instead. But he wanted the distraction to keep his mind off of his personal problems. Unfortunately, his distraction had suddenly turned sour, blossoming into a full-scale technological emergency.

For Lanny, it was indeed going to be a very long day.

Wil sat in the comfy gray chair outside of Mr. Jennings' office on the fifteenth floor reading a months-old issue of *Bankers' Life* magazine when the door finally opened. Wil didn't know what his boss wanted to see him about, but he had decided not to say anything about the Harriet Cramer letter—or the rumored photos. Wil figured he'd try to deal with that later.

"Come in, Wil," Mr. Jennings said, standing in his office doorway.

Wil followed Mr. Jennings through the office door to find a tall, thin, redheaded woman standing in the middle of his boss's office.

"Wil, I'd-I'd-I'd like you to meet Miss Trixie Tanner," Mr. Jennings stammered.

She rushed up to him and extended a freckle-covered hand toward him. "Ha, nice ta meet ya'll."

Wil reached for her hand, but got distracted by the woman's wild red hair. This caused him to slightly miscalculate his grip, grabbing only the scrunched tips of her four outstretched fingers.

Mr. Jennings motioned for the two to sit down in the guest chairs while he sat behind his desk. Considering the situation, Wil thought the seating configuration was unusual: If Ms. Tanner was a vendor or consultant, Barney typically would want to meet at his round conference table. Wil figured that his boss was initiating a type of defensive shield for a reason that he did not yet comprehend.

Wil didn't wait to get the explanation for the meeting's purpose. "Where are you from, Miss Tanner?" Wil blurted out, trying to adjust his suit jacket from being pinned too tightly between his spine and the back of his chair.

"Ahm from Lil' Rock, Arkin-saaw," she said, forcing a long drawl.

The woman's twang didn't seem genuine, and it struck Wil funny. He squashed a chuckle, avoiding it by directing his reaction straight out of his nose.

Mr. Jennings leaned forward onto his desk, fidgeting with the silver wedding ring on his left hand. "Dick has-has-has made some great changes," he stammered. "You'll be glad to know you're finally getting some help."

Wil held his boss's gaze, but had trouble reading his expression. "Oh?" Wil asked quizzically. "Help with what?" Wil looked over at Ms. Tanner, who was completely immersed in her large white leather purse, digging for something.

Mr. Jennings fidgeted more with his wedding ring, spinning it around on his bony finger. "Trixie comes to us with a great marketing background, don't you, Trixie?"

She was looking into her massive purse, digging and digging. "Oooh, yes ah dew, Mista Jennin'," she said, keeping her eyes trained on her search mission. "Ah sure dew." She kept digging...and digging.

Wil felt his blood pressure increase, an automatic defense mechanism that made his face turn hot. He looked at Mr. Jennings and raised an eyebrow—a nonverbal attempt to gain the real story. But Mr. Jennings didn't bite, opting to keep his face expressionless.

"What exactly is it that she's going to help with, Barney?" Wil asked, trying to mask his irritation with faked enthusiasm.

Ms. Tanner finally stopped her excavation when she reached the bottom of her purse, hauling out a long silver canister. She twisted the bottom of it, which produced a pointy tube of red lipstick. "Ahm jist here ta help, that's ahl," she said, talking through the stiffening of her lips as she applied the bright red wax to them.

Mr. Jennings finally looked Wil straight in the eye. "We're-we're-we're going to make a few changes. It's-it's essential that we raise this bank to the next level. Trixie's going to do just that for us."

Wil's face got even hotter. He tried to keep his breathing measured, and fought hard not to look or sound ruffled. He crossed his arms tightly in front of him, as if trying to keep himself from exploding into a million bits of flesh that were sure to stain his boss's office walls.

"Really, Barney?" Wil asked, his tone leaking out some obvious irritation. "How so?"

"Itta ba fine, juss fine," Ms. Tanner interrupted, tossing the lipstick canister back into her open purse and setting the heavy bag onto the floor beside her. "Itta ba fun ta werk tagether."

Wil couldn't imagine what this woman was here to do. He glared at Mr. Jennings, hoping again to prompt him for a better, more logical explanation. All Mr. Jennings could do was to blink nervously.

"You'll-you'll enjoy working with her," Mr. Jennings said in a higher than normal pitch. "Trixie is in a brand new role as the company's Chief Marketing Officer. Dick created it just for her. She's-she's-she's your new boss."

Wil envisioned steam puffing from his own ears. *Chief Marketing Officer? New boss?*

It took everything in Wil's power to avoid sliding out of his chair and onto the carpet. Wil felt betrayed. He was hired as a change-agent nearly six months ago, yet many of his proposals to alter the bank's sales and marketing culture for the better were met with stiff resistance. What exactly this little woman from Little Rock could do any differently was beyond him.

He craned his neck to look at Ms. Tanner, whose body was turned toward him, her red hair flaring under the fluorescent lights. An enormous smile of white teeth was outlined on her face by a thick layer of red-covered lips, flashing garishly at him.

"We've lots ta dew. Dick wants us ta git started righ' away."

Wil was speechless. He turned back toward Mr. Jennings, who was now avoiding any eye contact with him, opting instead to shuffle through a stack of papers piled on his desk.

After an uncomfortable moment, Mr. Jennings looked up at Ms. Tanner. "Why don't-don't-don't you two go get acquainted?" he asked. "Wil, be sure to give her a copy of the research you did. That was good stuff." He raised his arm to look at his watch. "It's almost lunch. Lots of places to eat in the skyway." He looked back down at the papers on his desk.

"Oooh, the skah-waaay," Ms. Tanner droned. "I juss luv that name."

Wil rose slowly from his chair and felt nauseated. Thinking of nothing even remotely positive to say, he simply closed his eyes briefly and paused, trying to get the sickness in his stomach to subside. Part of him wanted to rip the head off of his former boss; the other part wanted to set fire to the carpet and run. Instead, after a few deep inhales of stale, recirculated air, he opened his eyes and glared down at Mr. Jennings, who was nervously flipping through his paper stack.

After more uncomfortable silence, Wil turned toward the door and signaled his new boss to follow, reluctantly leading the way toward what was sure to be a contentious lunch date with Ms. Trixie Tanner of Little Rock, Arkansas.

It was Cal Jennings who, as one of the lead technology experts in the company, was first to confirm that an email containing an executable virus had been sent to more than 5,000 email users in five Midwest Federated states. Cal was a product of what many long-time bank employees jokingly referred to as the "EKP," or Executive Kid Program. It seemed that the higher the income of Midwest Federate Bank executives, the less likely it was for their offspring to be able to find employment on their own. Such was the case with the only son of Barney Jennings. Cal was placed into Midwest Federated employment—the result of a well-placed phone call made by Mr. Jennings to Duke Slaytor—when it became certain that the freshly graduated kid couldn't possibly land anywhere else.

While the bank had employed more than its fair share of executives' relatives who didn't need or want a job, Cal turned out to be different. He liked his role, was smart, and understood the technical and archaic bank operating system better than most. Dressed in jeans and a dark shirt, the auburn-haired, 26-year-old kid stood in front of Lanny's desk, nervously rocking back and forth from heel to toe as he talked.

"Somehow the virus was configured to populate itself to every known user in the infected system's memory," Cal said, clicking his pen and shifting his weight between both feet. "It was developed to trigger upon the execution of one event, which was to occur only when someone tried to..." Cal's voice trailed off. Lanny wanted him to finish the sentence, but Cal apparently couldn't bring himself to do so, too nervous to break the news to his manager.

"Delete it?" Lanny offered.

"Yes. It was set to populate once it was deleted from the core system."

"No thanks to me, I'm afraid," Lanny said. "How come no one has reported receiving it yet?"

Cal nervously cleared his throat. "It had a fairly large attachment with it. When the program executed and five thousand people were emailed all at once, the bandwidth maxed out. It's clogging the entire system, so nothing's going out...or coming in."

"Any idea what the attachment is?"

"None. Could be anything."

Lanny bit his lower lip, thinking. "Can the entire thing be deleted from the system so that it never gets delivered?"

"Not without powering down and resetting the whole system," Cal said. "If we do that, we risk losing customer transactions coming in from our external website. The virus message is grinding its way out there, and it's just a matter of time before it hits everyone's computers in the whole company. No real way around it, I'm sorry to say."

Lanny shook his head in defeat. "Is it possible the attachment contains yet another virus?"

Cal shifted back and forth some more, and then firmly pressed the tip of his pen onto his bottom lip. "I'd say that's possible, given its size. However, it's probably just a file, like a joke, say a video, or something like that."

Lanny rubbed his face with his hands. He looked up at Cal with tired, bloodshot eyes. "Fax an emergency user bulletin out to every branch, every department, every nook and cranny of this place. Tell them to expect an email that contains a virus, and under no circumstances should they open it or the attachment it contains. Tell them to delete the message immediately upon receipt. I don't want this thing, whatever it is, to take on a life of its own."

"We'll need executive approval to do that," Cal said sheepishly.

Lanny looked down at his paper-strewn desk, realizing that he'd have to face Duke Slaytor with the issue. "I know," Lanny said hoarsely, resisting an urge to frown. "I'll get the approval."

Wil's head was pounding, and he realized the jabs of pain were in perfect sync with his footsteps as he and Trixie Tanner walked along in the Minneapolis skyway system. After stopping by his office to pick up a copy of his consumer research, he found himself walking several feet ahead of his new boss, wondering the whole time what restaurant could be both informal—and mercifully quick.

Within moments they were sitting at a small table inside Nick's American Kitchen, a bustling eatery that faced a busy corner of downtown Minneapolis. They had beaten the noontime rush, so they ended up sitting next to the bright, double-paned windows that somehow managed to keep out the blustery November weather.

After a waitress took the drink orders, Ms. Tanner was again digging into her purse. Wil watched in amazement as she dug into the depths of the massive bag, leading him to wonder if she was intending to freshen up her lipstick before eating lunch.

"I have a question for you," Wil said, loosening up the ice in his water glass with a spoon.

"That's juss fine," she said, continuing her dig. "What can ah help ya'll with?"

"Well, I guess I'm confused about something, and I thought that you could straighten me out on it."

"Ahl-rightee," she said, her tone indicating a gap in attention, her head nearly submerged inside of her purse.

"I was hired as the marketing guy earlier this year, and they kind of promised me that I was to become the main marketing director for the company...eventually."

"Oh-kaayyy." Her purse-digging, and the rattling noises that accompanied it, made it sound as though she held a bag full of rocks on her lap.

Wil couldn't be sure that she was paying any attention to him, so he took several shallow sips of water for effect. "I just thought that, perhaps, you could shed some light on this."

"Oh-kaayy." She dug.

Wil watched and waited for a more congruent response. But her focus was solely on whatever treasure it was that she sought deep inside her bag.

She finally stopped her excavation long enough to look up at Wil. "Oh, ahm so sorry," she said, realizing that she was being impolite. "Ah juss wanna make sure ma phone is still on." She hauled up her cell into the light of day. "Ah still dunno how ta work these thangs."

She fidgeted with the contraption for a moment and set it down on the table. Wil could see that the phone's green light was blinking, indicating that it was powered on.

"Trixie, here's my question," he said forcefully, his elbows on the table with his hands rubbing together. "What is it exactly that you were asked to do for Midwest Federated?"

Ms. Tanner plopped her purse onto the floor and slid her chair up closer to the table. "Weeell," she said, dragging her drawl out as far as she could, "Ah think that Dick, er, ah mean Mista Crama, wants ta centra-lize the marketin' fungshun. Ah think they juss wanna have one central place fer it, ya know?"

The waitress delivered Wil's coffee and Ms. Tanner's iced tea. She promptly took their food orders and returned to the kitchen.

"So...if I'm following you," Wil asked, "there won't be marketing directors in the other states? It'll all run through Minnesota?"

"Oooh, ah dunno. Mayba, or mayba not. Ah juss dunno. What're ya'll thinkin'?"

Wil caught himself before he executed a full rolling of the eyes, opting instead to watch his guest take a long swig of iced tea. Beads of condensation from the glass dripped onto Ms. Tanner's tan blouse, expanding across the fabric as they soaked in.

"I suspect you haven't yet met any of the other directors?" he asked. "There's one in every state."

"Oooh no," she said, shaking her head, a movement that vibrated the loose strands of red hair that were tightly curled and brushing her face. "Ah juss started, ya know? Ah won't have tahm fer meetin' folks fer a while."

Wil decided to really test her mettle. "Certainly, Miss Tanner, you've given the structure some thought. As the Chief Marketing Officer of Midwest Federated, what are you going to do to bring the bank to the next level?" Wil tried hard to restrain his sarcasm, but his delivery came out fully loaded.

"Ah really see us bein' the friend-la bank, ya know?" she said, pinning the red hair that barely covered her ears behind them with both hands. "We should juss be flat out friend-la. That's what the pee-poll want."

Wil needed to burn off his frustration, so he stirred creamer into his coffee until it whirled into a fine froth. He vowed to himself to work even harder to keep his tone from escalating out of control.

"Friendly is fine, as long as the service is there," Wil said, forcing a smile. "I think this bank has a ways to go before Mister Cramer's friendly mantra can become believable by consumers. I did some research earlier this year that proved we were—"

"Oooh, ah don't think Dick, er Mista Crama, really likes ra-search," she said, lifting her drink off the table, dripping more condensation onto her blouse. "He alwahs sed, 'if ya can't dew it on the back ova nap-ken, then it ain't worth dew-in.'"

Wil fought back a reactionary choke that threatened to spray his guest with hot coffee from his mouth. "Perhaps so," he said, pressing his napkin to his lips, "but we hired Cox Research, who is very reputable, and they found that most consumers want competence and accuracy first before any other kind of—"

"Ah juss think maybe we need a maz-kot, ya know?" she interrupted. "Ah luv maz-kots. We need somethin' that pee-poll can iden-tee-fy with. Like da-hogs, er somethin'. Pee-poll love cute da-hogs."

Wil felt another surge in his blood pressure. *Dogs as a bank mascot? What is she talking about?*

The food finally came, with a chicken-topped salad for Wil and a luncheon plate of messy barbequed ribs for Ms.

Tanner. Wil decided his line of questioning was going nowhere, so he changed the subject and got personal.

"Barney said Dick hired you," Wil said, looking down and aggressively cutting up his salad as he talked. "Did you know him...Dick, I mean?"

"Ah sure did," she twanged, her expression lighting up as she snagged a barbecued rib from her plate with her manicured fingernails. "Ah've known Dick fer years now."

"Were you in banking together?" he asked.

"Nooo," she said while taking a bite, the barbeque sauce smearing above her red-painted mouth, giving her the awkward appearance of having a fat upper lip. "We werked tagether in the steel in'stree." She talked even as she licked the edges of her mouth with the tip of her tongue.

Wil pursed his lips to avoid a smirk. "Really? You were a steel worker?"

"Ooooh, nooo," she chuckled, finally wiping away the sauce from her lips with a napkin. "Ah was juss a lowly typist in the office back then. That wuz the days ba-fore computers."

Wil looked at his salad. "So...you worked in the office, and he was working steel?" Wil took a bite of salad, doing everything possible to avoid chewing his lower lip in half.

"Yep, we've known each otha fer years an' years an' years," she said, bringing another sauce-covered rib to her ruby-red lips. "That's whah Barna hired me on the spot."

Wil felt his consciousness retreating, wanting to be anywhere else but at the table with Trixie Tanner of Little Rock, Arkansas. He had lost his appetite and had trouble getting even a quarter of the salad forced down his throat. The conversation eventually slowed to a trickle, and the waitress finally delivered the bill.

"Let ma git this," Ms. Tanner said. "Ma personal treat."

Wil feigned a grin. "I'm sure you know that you can expense this to the company, since you're now an employee. It was, after all, a business lunch."

"Ooooh, nooo, I jess don't dew that. Gotta save on 'spences, ya know?" After another series of additional dives into the big white purse, she located some cash and pinned it to the bill.

Wil stood quickly, convinced that his blood was draining from his brain and making a beeline down to his feet. He paused until he recovered slightly and, staggering a bit, he led her out of the restaurant.

"It was nice meeting with you," he managed, handing her the research report he had brought along.

Ms. Tanner smiled broadly, a small dot of barbecue sauce still clinging to her upper lip. "Pleasure's ahl mahn," she drawled.

FORTY-ONE

Felicia Cortez's tellers balanced their cash drawers without finding a single discrepancy after what turned out to be a long, difficult day at the Snelling Avenue branch. Felicia couldn't remember the last time she had encountered so many customer problems in a single day. She looked down on her complaint log and counted five instances of statement errors, three reports of inaccurate addresses on checks, and nine complaints about the ATM being out of service, the third outage that week. She took some solace in the fact that the errors were not a direct result of her actions or those of her staff, but they discouraged her nonetheless.

Sitting in her small office that was tucked in the corner of the branch, Felicia scanned the top of her desk, which was stacked with piles of loan applications, rate exceptions, and general correspondence, all neatly arranged, but seemingly insurmountable to process and file.

Felicia's operations supervisor, Desiree Landau, poked her head into the office. "You want me to help with anything before I get out of here?" the young woman asked.

Felicia was busily reorganizing the paper piles into priority order. "Maybe you can help with this one," Felicia said. She handed Desiree a stack of papers that was closest to her.

Desiree pulled up a chair to the corner of Felicia's desk and sat down. "This was one crazy day," Desiree said, shaking her head, flipping through the stack with efficiency.

"Never seen anything like it in a while," Felicia said glumly. "I don't know what's happening lately. Every day that goes by seems to get a little worse on the service side." Felicia turned around in her chair to face her small credenza, which contained her desktop computer. It, too, had acted finicky all day, but it seemed stable for the moment and didn't need another reboot. She logged into the system by punching in a password, dancing her long, well-manicured fingernails over the keys. She was promptly greeted with the MFB logo on her screen.

She immediately tried the email system again—her third attempt that day—but the computer's animated hourglass simply spun in a circle, a sure sign that the email server was still down. She then clicked on an icon that directed her into the Midwest Federated loan application system. Relieved that the loan system was responding, she decided to review the applications that awaited approval, and she would either grant the approval or ask for more information. She figured that she could review the more troublesome loan cases later, the ones that were represented by the hard copies stacked neatly on her desk.

After reviewing and approving the first three loans online, she started looking at the fourth, but got distracted by a flashing envelope icon at the bottom of her screen. Glad that the email system was finally up, she toggled out of the loan system and clicked on the flashing icon with her mouse, bringing up the email inbox. Once the messages loaded, she counted seven emails, with one marked URGENT. She clicked on it right away, but the screen went disconcertingly blank.

"Uh, oh," she said, moving the mouse around in a circle, trying to get an image—any image—to reappear on her screen.

"What happened?" Desiree asked, looking up from her stack of paper.

"I don't know. It just went dark." Felicia fussed with the mouse some more, but after getting no reaction, she resorted to punching the Escape key. She pressed it twice, and the screen flickered back to life, with the urgent email instantly reappearing. She noticed that it contained just two words:

CLICK HERE. She figured that she couldn't get out without sending the computer back into blackness, so with no other choice, she clicked on it.

In an instant, a photo appeared that set Felicia back in her chair. "Mary, Mother of..."

Desiree looked over at it and let out a scream of surprise. "Would you look at that!" she shouted.

The other bank staff members in the lobby were cleaning up their respective stations before locking up the branch for the day, and they all heard the commotion inside of Felicia's office. Felicia's doorway was soon filled with the heads of five curious people, each craning their necks to see what was going on.

Desiree stood and approached the monitor to get a better look. "Is that...? Oh my. Is that who I think it is?" Desiree asked.

"Who? What is it?" asked various overlapping voices from behind Felicia and Desiree.

Staring at the screen, Felicia covered her mouth with disgust and closed her eyes in repulsion. She didn't stop to think of any ramifications for showing the image to the curious throng that filled the doorway, so she grabbed the side of the monitor with her right hand, and with her eyes still closed, she turned it toward them.

Loud gasps rang out, then silence, then incessant laughter. As difficult and unpredictable a day it was for the branch, no one could have forecasted that the staff was to see their company CEO in all his glory—nude from the waist down, caught in an inappropriate act with someone who was definitely not his wife—displayed on a computer monitor in the branch manager's office.

The staff briskly entered and crushed in around Felicia's computer, each person trying to get a first-row look at the color image that filled the screen.

As the alternating laughter and disgust grew louder, Felicia could stand no more. She reached her hand toward the monitor, slowly at first. Then, using lightening quick dexterity with a single flick of her index finger, Felicia killed the power, sending the computer screen back into safe, blank, neutral blackness.

Wil went incognito right after his disastrous lunch with Ms. Tanner, spending the rest of the afternoon sulking in a skyway coffee shop located several blocks from his building. He sat nearly motionless at the table in the corner of the place, nursing a cup of coffee that got progressively colder and staler as the hours ticked by.

Who is that lady? Why did they hire someone like that as the CMO? Why didn't they offer that job to me instead?

He went over the conversations he had with her and Barney a dozen times, but he could not come up with any rational explanations to his mounting questions.

In the mood to drown his sorrows, he flirted with the idea of calling Jessica to have her meet him at a bar. He dismissed the thought when he realized how late in the day it was getting; she was undoubtedly readying herself for work. Wil decided to make his way back to the Midwest Federated building to retrieve his car keys to head home in defeat.

The force that pushed against his body during the elevator's fast ascent to the sixth floor felt double the normal gravimetric intensity. Wil's head pounded and his stomach fluttered as the perplexing luncheon conversation with Trixie Tanner repeated again and again, like a tape playing in his mind. As the electronic numbers above the elevator door increased, queasiness overwhelmed him just as the carriage stopped and the doors snapped open.

He placed his hand on one side of the opened elevator doors, holding himself up, trying to keep himself together. Recovering a bit, he slowly left the elevator and walked toward his department's entryway, his feet feeling like they were full of cement. He entered the department suite and passed Mindy's front desk without even looking at her.

"Where have you been?" she asked, noticing that he looked pale. "Are you okay?"

"No, not really," Wil said, keeping his eyes fixed on the floor in front of him as he lumbered toward his office door.

"I've been trying to reach you all afternoon. Don't you have your cell with you?"

Wil stopped in his tracks and reached for his pocket, suddenly realizing that his cell was powered off. He turned toward her. "I was...in a meeting. What is it?"

"Duke Slaytor has been frantically calling you. He needs to talk to you right away."

That was the last thing he needed to hear. Wil managed a nod and headed toward his desk. He took off his suit coat to cool himself down, and flopped into his chair, feeling his cheeks with his hands and rubbing his eyes. After a few minutes, he felt good enough to look up Mr. Slaytor's direct extension. He picked up the phone and punched in the numbers.

"Hold for Mister Slaytor," the female assistant's voice said.

Wil waited a few moments listening to the on-hold music. The tune had a Texas strum to it, and the memory of Trixie Tanner's twang came flooding back to his brain. It gave him the shivers as the music on the phone got drowned out by the memory of her drawling voice. The incessant playback of his new boss's intonations reminded Wil of something he once read about slow, methodical torture. It all stopped abruptly when Duke Slaytor came on.

"Fischer, we had an agreement."

Wil stayed silent a moment, assessing Mr. Slaytor's irritated tone. "Excuse me?" Wil asked in a gravelly voice.

"You were to keep this thing silent, yet you had to go and do this," Mr. Slaytor said.

Wil tried to straighten up in his leather chair, but he found himself slipping back into a slumped position. "Duke, I've had a rotten day. Can you please be more specific so that I know exactly what you're saying?" Wil's tone was deflated, and despite clearing his throat, he could not rid it of the gravelly sound he was producing.

"Are you denying involvement in this?" Mr. Slaytor asked. "You told me that you'd owe me one. This is not what I had in mind."

Wil paused again to shake his head rapidly back and forth, trying to become more alert. He looked out of his office door and could see Mindy from her desk, staring at him with a funny look on her face. "Involvement in what?" Wil asked.

"We're going to get to the bottom of this," Mr. Slaytor said. "I'm watching you, Fischer. In the meantime, you will say nothing about this or what you know. Do you understand me?"

Wil was trying to convince himself that he was part of a huge practical joke. But Mr. Slaytor's tone was one of genuine anger and irritation, so Wil knew he was being implicated for something about which he had no knowledge.

"Duke, I've got to tell you, I really don't know what you're—"

The phone went silent as Mr. Slaytor disconnected the call. Wil sat stunned in disbelief and hung up the receiver. He watched as Mindy got up from her desk and appeared in his doorway.

"I take it you haven't seen it?" she asked flatly.

"Seen what?" Wil put the forefingers from each hand up to his temples and rubbed hard. "Why in the world is everyone talking in code around here?" he asked. "Can you please tell me what's going on?"

Mindy waddled to his credenza and moved the computer's mouse, bringing up his email box on the monitor. She clicked on a message, which promptly filled the screen with the photo that was making the internal rounds.

Mindy took a few steps back to let Wil get a good look at the voyeuristic image of Mr. Cramer. Wil stared at the assembly of pixels before him, his eyes growing wider as his brain slowly constructed a web of paranoia. He looked away from the monitor and reached for Harriet's envelope, which was still on his desk. He picked it up and toggled the opened flap with his fingers.

The enclosure! "Oh no," he said, looking up at Mindy.

"What?" she asked, wondering why the envelope in Wil's hands seemed so intriguing to him.

"Call Lanny Taylor," he commanded. "Tell him I want to see him right away."

FORTY-TWO

The Pacific Resort Hotel in San Diego was a sprawling complex, and from Andy's and Ron's vantage points in the parking lot, they could easily see all the comings and goings of their CEO through a visible side door. Ron was in the passenger seat of the rented sedan, but sleepiness got the best of him and his snoring filled the vehicle's interior.

Andy noticed that the shadows outside the car were getting longer and sharper as sunset approached, which made it difficult for him to keep his eyes open, too. A pleasant breeze blew through Andy's open driver-side window, filling the car with the mild sea air. Andy turned the radio down and leaned back. Within moments he lost consciousness, quickly descending into a bliss that he had not experienced in quite some time.

The men awoke with a start when Andy's cell phone rang. Andy hit his knee against the bottom of the steering wheel, which shot an acute pain down to his ankle. He tried to tamp out the ache by stretching out his leg, but that only made it worse.

The phone kept ringing, and Ron was first to fish it out of the small storage compartment that was situated under the car's radio. "Yes, he's here. Let me get him for you." Ron was blinking his eyes violently, trying to feel and sound more awake. He handed the phone to Andy, who was now caressing his knee.

"Hello?"

"Andy, we're sorry to bother you. It's Wil Fischer and Lanny Taylor at Midwest Fed. Remember us?"

Andy could tell immediately that the voices on the other end were transmitting to him via a speakerphone. He rubbed his leg some more and remembered the night in the bar when he met the two men, having spent most of the evening talking to Wil. "Hello gentlemen," he said, straightening himself in his seat and still wincing from his leg pain. "What can I do for you?"

"We're wondering if you can confirm something for us."

Static crackled over the line and then quieted. "Confirm what?" Andy asked.

"Have you heard what's happened?" Wil asked.

Andy looked over at Ron, hoping he might be able to hear the voices rattling through the phone in the quiet car. But Ron was too busy yawning and rubbing his eyes and face, trying to get awake.

"No," Andy replied. "I haven't heard anything. What's up?"

Wil went on to explain the email virus that was moving quickly through the company and contained the incriminating photo.

"You've got to be kidding," Andy said with alarm.

"We're not," Wil answered. "The virus is one thing, but how the photo got scanned and attached to it is another. We remembered that you had knowledge of the photos, so we were hoping you might be able to shed some light on this whole thing." Wil's voice was calm; he was trying not to sound accusatory. With his own butt on the line, he wanted answers as much as anyone.

"I knew of these photos," Andy said softly. "That's certainly true. But I never had full possession of them. I only saw them briefly. Then they were stolen."

"Stolen?" Lanny asked. "By whom?"

Andy looked over at Ron, who was now paying attention to the one-sided conversation. The mention of the photos had piqued his interest.

"I think I might know," Andy said.

Andy started feeling queasy. He realized that his knowledge of the photos, and his close proximity to the subject on the night they were snapped, were problematic for him. But he also knew that Wil Fischer had expressed deep disappointments about the company and his dealings with the CEO, which were somewhat comforting and affirming to his own plight. After all, misery loves company. Yet, the quizzing from Fischer and Taylor was unusual to the say the least, and getting more uncomfortable by the moment.

"Can you think of anyone who might have had access to these photos who could have done this?" Wil asked.

Andy paused a moment to carefully generate an answer. His mind was reeling from the growing realization that he was being swept up into a controversy for which he had no good alibi. Without warning, the rear passenger door of the car noisily opened, shattering the relative quiet of the car's interior. In the rearview mirror, Andy caught a glimpse of the body that wore the canary-yellow shirt as it climbed clumsily into the back seat. Andy knew immediately that he was in trouble.

"Where the hell have you guys been?" Mr. Cramer bellowed. "You have ten seconds to tell me."

Andy snapped the phone shut and turned to his backseat passenger. "I'm sorry, Mister Cramer. We both must have fallen asleep."

"You're paid to pay attention to me," Mr. Cramer snapped. "Not to sleep. Understand?"

Andy and Ron shot each other a look of embarrassment. Andy grabbed the keys that hung in the ignition slot and twisted it forward, firing up the vehicle with a brief rev of the engine. Through the long shadows of a late California afternoon, they headed back to the airport in complete, discomforting silence.

"I think he just hung up." Lanny hit the power button of the speaker phone, silencing the fast busy signal that was echoing through his office.

"What do we do now?" Wil asked.

Lanny looked at his watch. "It's after six, so everyone's gone. We're both in Dutch over this one, Wil. I got chewed out so badly by Slaytor when he found out about this virus, it's a wonder I wasn't fired on the spot. I'm already in big enough trouble because of the gun incident."

Wil nodded. "I got a similar kind of chewing."

Lanny studied his friend's face. "From whom? Slaytor?"

"Yes." Wil looked down at the table, remembering the lunch he had months before with Mr. Slaytor when the Miami debacle was still fresh on executive's minds. "He thinks that I knew about this Miami thing all along. But of course, I had no idea. It was my first day of work when this whole thing started. I just tried to keep whatever it was from hitting the newspaper pages."

Lanny stared at Wil. "That doesn't explain why he called you. What was his beef?"

Wil didn't want to admit that he had maneuvered Slaytor into hiring Lanny with the implication that Wil would keep quiet about Cramer's indiscretions. Even though Wil didn't know any of the details, he was an adept poker player and knew when to bluff, which is exactly what he did with Mr. Slaytor when his friend was in need.

"He's just fishing, that's all." Wil raised his arm to glimpse his watch. "I've had enough for today," he said, forcing a yawn. "Let's get some rest and approach this with a fresh brain tomorrow."

FORTY-THREE

To those who knew her well, Trixie Tanner was not known for being punctual. She often ran as much as 30 minutes late to meetings and almost never made it to work before 8:30 in the morning. The one exception to her usual tardiness was scheduled meetings with upper echelons, and only an Act of God could make her late for this morning's appointment with Dick Cramer.

In her rented condo, she briskly applied some makeup and reddened her lips. Jumping into her freshly delivered, company-leased sedan, she floored the accelerator to propel the vehicle through the morning rush of the eastern metro, squealing her way into the parking stall of the Midwest Federated headquarters building in Saint Paul. It was a little before 8 a.m.

Hurrying to the executive floor, Ms. Tanner hustled down the hallway and past the entrance of Mr. Cramer's massive office. "Lights er still out," she mumbled aloud, relieved that she had beaten him into work.

She turned the corner and walked down the spacious hallway to her office. Once inside, she clicked on the overhead lights and found a memo from Duke Slaytor placed on her chair. She dropped her keys onto the desk, and then set down her heavy white purse. She picked up the memo and read it quickly.

> To: All MFB employees
> From: Duke Slaytor, EVP, MFB Corp. I.T.
> Subject: Urgent: Email scam – virus alert
> Do not open any emails that are from recipients unknown to you. Delete any emails that come from an unidentified source immediately.
>
> Being in possession of the 'doctored photo' that is being distributed without authorization is a violation of the code of ethics and the email policy. Employees who do not destroy it immediately are subject to dismissal.

Ms. Tanner read again, but still had no idea what it was about. She quickly dismissed it as something that must have occurred prior to her employment—and therefore none of her concern—so she didn't give it another thought.

Ms. Tanner took one look at her desk and sighed. She was never the organized one in her family. She had always suspected that her lack of an orderly demeanor was why no man could ever marry her, but coming to terms with such reasons was not her current priority.

Her desk was covered with spreadsheets, memos, papers, files, and other reading materials, so she tried to organize the mess into neat little piles. She didn't get very far when her office phone rang.

"Ah'll ba right there!" she said cheerily into the handset. Moments later, she was sitting in one of the guest chairs in Mr. Cramer's office. She wore a low-cut black blouse, fully aware that points were to be scored if Mr. Cramer received an occasional flash of skin from her.

The CEO was seated comfortably in his high-backed leather chair. He was wearing his trademark canary-yellow shirt, which was framed by a jet-black Armani suit coat. He leaned forward to catch more than a glimpse of what Trixie Tanner so graciously offered.

As if on cue, Ms. Tanner brought one foot up onto her knee, bending forward enough to be able to fidget with her high-heeled shoe. Her intention was to lean in even more, giving Mr. Cramer a full and tantalizing view of a major portion of her cleavage.

"Ya know," she said, pulling off her shoe and shaking it in the air, as though trying to dislodge a stone the size of Texas, "Ah've bin thinkin.' Ya'll hired me ta git some buzz goin' here, ya know? I think we need a maz-kot."

Mr. Cramer's eyes were locked on Ms. Tanner's chest. "What kind of mascot?" he managed.

"Oooh, ah dunno. Somethin' colorful, ya know? Somethin' that pops. Has some sizzle." She could fidget with her shoe no more, so she put it back on her foot and returned to a more upright and ladylike position.

Mr. Cramer looked into her eyes. "That's a great idea. We need to be the Midwest's friendliest bank. We've got to get the word out about that, and it's just not getting done. I need you to do that, Trixie."

"Ah know, Dick," she drawled. "Ah've also bin thinkin' that we should spend more money trainin' folks, ya know? Ah think pee-poll want betta service. We should alsa go with longa hours, ya know? Pee-poll want longa hours so they kin bank when they're shoppin' an' all."

Cramer shot up from his chair and headed toward his wall of windows. He picked up his binoculars and tracked a lone bird above Saint Paul's buildings as it was being buffeted by the November Minnesota winds. "What kind of hours are you talking?" he asked, slowly panning the binoculars from left to right as he tracked the bird.

"Ah dunno," Ms. Tanner replied, turning her body to face him in case he wanted another sneak peak at her chest. "Maybe we stay open lata at night, ya know? Saturdays we need ta ba open inta the afternoon. Mayba we should c'nsider Sundays, tew. Sundays'll be a big hit 'round here, ya know?"

Mr. Cramer removed the binoculars from his face and slowly lowered them to his side. "Trixie, that's the kind of thinking we need around here. Out of the box. Fresh. That's a great idea."

"We gotta attract some attention in otha ways, tew," she continued. "That's why ah juss luv maz-kots. Mayba like a da-hog or somethin' like that as a maz-kot, ya know? Whaddya think?"

Mr. Cramer smiled appreciatively and sauntered over to the spare guest chair next to Ms. Tanner. He sat down and leaned back comfortably, his hands resting behind his head. "I remember when I was a kid," he said, gazing up at the vaulted ceiling above his massive office, "and I used to go to the circus. That was years and years ago, but it seems like yesterday. My dad was a big fan of the circus back then. I think we went every single weekend."

"What're ya'll thinkin'? An elee-fent er somethin'?"

He shook his head, and continued gazing dreamily at the ceiling. "No, no. You had the idea before. Something more lively...more colorful."

She paused a moment, and then she lit up. "A cla-hown!"

"Bingo!" he shouted, a broad smile erupting on his face. If a cigar could be produced and lit on the spot, he would have made it so.

"Ah like it!" Ms. Tanner screamed, rapidly jotting notes on a small pad of paper she had brought in with her.

"Let's get it all tested in Minnesota first," he barked, suddenly at the top of his game. "Coordinate the extended hours with Duke Slaytor. Sit down with Barney Jennings and figure out a way to give everyone a round of training. Then issue a press release. I want us to be known as the Midwest's friendliest bank!"

Ms. Tanner scribbled as fast as he talked. "Ah'm sure we will be, once ah'm dun with et, Dick."

"If we do longer hours, we need to do it with minimal increases to staff. We've got to cut expenses, Trixie. I don't want us getting too fat out there. We must hit those numbers this year."

Her pen flew over the note page at lightning speed. "Ah'm sure et won't be a problem," she said. "We can git craytive with staffin.' And ah bet I kin git someone right here in town who'll be a cla-hown fer us, on the cheap."

Mr. Cramer moved his feet across the divide of the two chairs, pressing the soles of his shoes onto one of her armrests. He leaned back even farther against his chair, making his body nearly horizontal.

"Clowns for the Midwest friendliest bank," he mused, staring dreamily into the vast airspace above his head. "That's all right, Trixie. That's all right!"

FORTY-FOUR

Wil was running late and didn't make it to downtown Minneapolis until 8:30 that morning. He dashed into his office and checked his voicemail and email, hoping that Lanny had left him a message with more information about the email virus. But no such message was sent, so he turned his attention to the snail mail that was piled on top of his desk.

First on the stack was the memo about the virus from Duke Slaytor. Wil laughed as he read the last part aloud: "Employees who do not destroy it immediately are subject to dismissal." He crumpled it up and threw it in the trash. *Violators will be shot on sight,* he sighed.

His mind was jarred with a sudden knock at the door, followed by the appearance of Mindy filling his doorframe. "There's a guy here to see you."

"Who?" Wil got annoyed whenever his admin didn't provide vital information up front, something he thought could be accomplished with little extra effort. "Who is it?"

"An Andy-something," she said.

Wil was pleasantly surprised at the announcement. He only knew one Andy, and he was pleased that the corporate pilot had finally come to see him. "Show Andy-something in."

Andy didn't wait for Mindy's invitation and strolled in. He wore dark blue jeans and a brown leather bomber jacket. His hand was immediately extended.

"Well, I'll be," Wil said, standing to shake his hand. "I figured that I ticked you off on the phone for good yesterday."

"Sorry about that," Andy said. "I was interrupted. Mind if I sit?"

Wil gestured for him to take a seat at the round table, and Andy took a chair without removing his jacket.

"I was thinking about those photos," Andy said.

"Haven't we all," Wil answered, sitting down beside him. "There's been a lot of action on that front over the past twenty-four hours. From what you said over the phone, have you thought more about who might have snapped them?"

"Yes. There are only two people who I know for certain who were initially in possession of those photos."

"Who?"

Andy extended his forefinger. "Ron, my copilot."

Wil's eyes narrowed. "You think Ron Mayville did this?"

Andy shook his head. "I know he couldn't have taken the pictures himself. He was never in the bathroom. I asked him a lot of other questions, and now I'm certain he wasn't involved in any way. That leaves only one other possibility."

Wil crossed his arms. "I'm listening."

Andy extended a second finger. "Harriet Cramer."

"Excuse me?"

"The photos were on the company jet for a while, but I didn't know it until a recent trip to New Mexico, when Harriet was on board. I went to retrieve the photos after she left, but they were missing. I'm certain that she took possession of them."

Wil went wide-eyed as Andy talked. He rose from his chair to grab the Harriet envelope from his desk. "Does this look familiar at all?" Wil handed it to Andy.

Andy examined it, turning it over from front to back. "Yes, it does," he said. "I delivered this to the Saint Paul office myself a while ago. We shuttle a lot of things between the ranch and the corporate office. This particular envelope was in one such package. I remember it because I was going to drop it off personally at the security desk on my way home that day. But on the way in, I ran into Mr. Jennings. He was headed into the headquarters building from the parking ramp, so I asked him if he'd take it to Mister Cramer."

Wil studied him for a moment. "Apparently it never made it. I got it instead."

Andy raised an eyebrow. "You? Why?"

"Believe it or not, it's bank policy," Wil said with a smirk. "All communication to Mister Cramer has to be screened first. The policy has been in place so long that the originators of the procedure no longer work here, and with mail coming in from a lot of different areas, it means the system works about half right. This piece didn't come through the regular mail. So I suppose it's possible that once Barney delivered it, someone at the Saint Paul headquarters mistook it for complaint mail, and then sent it back to me."

"To the marketing guy?"

Wil shrugged. "Leave it to the Marketing Department to screen the mail. They must have thought it was a complaint letter. I get tons of those." He pointed to a cardboard box in the corner of his office, filled to the top with customer mail.

Andy looked at the envelope again. "So...was it a complaint letter after all?" he asked, grinning.

Wil took the envelope back and removed the letter from inside, unfolding it. "This is all it said: 'I know too much.'"

Andy grabbed the note from him and examined it. "That's her signature, all right." Andy looked at the bottom of the letter. "It says E-N-C. What was the enclosure?"

Wil leaned back and shrugged. "That's the real mystery. There wasn't anything else with it. Just the letter."

Andy paused, and blinked. "The photo."

"Yes," Wil nodded. "It's the only explanation."

"She must have been trying to call his bluff, a wife calling out in desperation to stop her husband's exploits. Too bad he never received it. But who would've stolen it?"

Wil shrugged again. "Could've been anyone along the way. And how it ended up getting attached to an email virus is a most interesting question. But believe me, there's nothing in this world that I want to know more than who did this."

Candy Luther was fighting a 4 p.m. copy deadline. Her gossip column in the *Minneapolis Daily Post* was unusually light in subject matter, due largely to the time of year. She knew that famous people tended to be on their best behavior before the start of the holidays, and she would have to wait for the next primetime gossip season to hunt for more meat, a season that began closer to spring and extended into mid-September.

Wendell Reid was her cubicle neighbor for the past four years and shared the distinction of having as many paper piles on his desk as she had on hers. There the similarities ended, as the 54-year-old former New Yorker fashioned himself a serious journalist. His job was to pursue corruption and political intrigue, and he had very little time or respect for unverifiable gossip. But he liked Candy Luther just the same, as she was one of the few people in the newsroom who didn't make fun of his receding hairline.

"What's in the big column today?" Wendell asked from the other side of the cube wall, pushing his thick glasses over the small hump on his nose.

"A little less quantity than I'd like today," she answered.

"Let's hear it," he said wryly, clacking the keys of his outdated computer.

"All right," she said. She picked up the freshly printed proof of her column from her desk and stood to look over the four-foot-high cube wall that separated them. "If you must know, I've got the Mayor being seen with that young intern again. The head of Strident Telecomm was apparently fired and didn't just quit like everyone thought. And Gavin McCabe is not going to renew his contract as anchor of the ten o'clock news on channel eleven."

Wendell let out a chuckle as his fingers tapped on the keyboard. "All the news that's fit to be tied. Is that all you got?"

Candy playfully tossed a paperclip at him. "I suppose you're writing some tripe about Thanksgiving travel plans or the results of a school referendum somewhere."

"Nothing that clever." He stopped typing and looked up at her face as she peered at him from the ledge of the cube wall. "However, I might have something that's made just for you."

"Oooh, how tantalizing," she said, rolling her eyes. She sat back down at her desk where she knew the conversation could continue through the thin cube walls.

"Seriously," he continued, stroking his goatee with his right hand. "I think this time you'll be thanking me."

Candy forced a chuckle. "Like the time you claimed my husband was seeing someone half his age?"

"I was right about that one."

"That person you were speculating about was *me*. If you were right about that one, it would have made my husband-to-be some eighty years old back then," she laughed.

"Well, he does look older than you."

Candy picked up a pink eraser from her desk and tossed it over the cube wall, expertly hitting him square on the head like she had done a hundred times before.

"Okay," he said in singsong, "if you don't want to know what I know, that's not my problem. You have no idea what you're missing."

Candy stood again and rested her arm on the top of the short wall, propping her chin up with her hand. "At this point, I'll even take a tip from you," she sighed. "What have you got?"

Wendell hit a few keystrokes on his computer and turned his monitor toward her. It took a few moments for the pixels to generate an image, but when they did, a ghastly color photo filled the screen.

"What in the world?"

Wendell removed his glasses. "Candy, allow me to present to you, in all his greatness, Mister Richard Edmund Cramer, the Chief Executive Officer of Midwest Federated Bank."

Duke Slaytor had let it go on long enough. Controversies that had erupted over the years surrounding Mr. Cramer often died under their own weight or were snuffed out by the people closest to him. Mr. Slaytor knew that the photo fiasco was different, and it was escalating out of control. He had no choice but to break the news to his CEO.

"Then get it shut down, damn you!" Mr. Cramer yelled, spraying a mist of saliva into the air as he held a printout of the photo in his hands.

Mr. Slaytor stood motionless while his boss flew off the handle. Like all of those who were inside the inner circle, Mr. Slaytor knew from experience to stay still and calm, no matter how bad the beating got. "We did what we could do, but some email users refuse to follow directions," Slaytor said. "We know that at least a few of them opened the email and the attachment. It got out of hand from there."

"I want anyone who opened that thing to be fired, period!" Mr. Cramer crumpled up the printout and threw it toward Mr. Slaytor. The ball of paper hit Mr. Slaytor's leg and rolled across the carpet.

"We can't do that, Dick. The email was already out there for a good fifteen minutes or so before the recall bulletin went out. We can't fire someone for clicking on an email that looked legit."

Mr. Cramer's face was growing more and more red, contrasting sharply against the blinding yellow of his shirt. "You need to fix this right now. If anyone in this company forwards that email or prints it, I want them hunted down and dismissed. Do you read me?"

Mr. Slaytor handed him a copy of the internal memo that was distributed to all employees. "They've all been informed," Mr. Slaytor explained. "I also threw in language about the photo being doctored. That should slow things down and cast some doubt on it."

"It had better," Cramer yelled. "How in the hell could this happen? And who took that picture?"

Mr. Slaytor shook his head. "I have a few theories. And we're trying to track down the origins of the virus. Whoever put that worm together knew exactly what they were doing. It was very much intended to embarrass us."

"Embarrass US?" Mr. Cramer shouted. "This could ruin me! If Harriet sees this, then the party's over." Mr. Cramer stood up and paced back and forth between his desk and his wall of windows. "If my wife gets one glimpse at this thing, I'm out two-hundred-and-fifty-million bucks. You have got to keep this from going too far. Whoever in this company does not follow instructions needs to be terminated. CLEAR?"

Mr. Slaytor had never been in the Marines, but his boss had, and that made Mr. Slaytor occasionally feel drafted when the going got tough.

"Crystal clear, sir," Slaytor said, snapping his feet together in a subconscious salute.

FORTY-FIVE

Wil could not find Lanny Taylor. He called his office several times, but no one had seen him on his floor for hours. He didn't answer his cell either, and that made Wil even more nervous.

Wil had no choice but to go on with his day, finishing a long meeting in Kari Bender's office to discuss the promotion planned around the launch of the new Eagan branch. He looked out of Kari's office window toward the late afternoon traffic that was snarled on the streets six stories below. "I just can't believe what's going on around here," he said.

Kari picked up the Duke Slaytor virus memo from her desk and reread it. "I've got to admit that it's pretty underhanded," she said. "Who do you think would've done this...snapping these photos, creating viruses and all?"

Wil shrugged. "Someone with a vendetta against Dick Cramer. I talked to Andy Gerhardt earlier, the corporate pilot. He thinks Cramer's wife is somehow involved."

Kari's eyes widened. "Interesting. But what does she have to gain? She's ungodly rich as it is."

Wil turned to her. "One thing's for sure. We need to comply with that memo. Let's make certain that no one has copies of that photo in this department."

Kari snorted a quick laugh. "Have you seen what's hanging on people's cubes?" She nodded toward her open door.

Wil followed her gaze toward the three cubicle offices that lined the other side of the department suite. Each of the cubicle occupants had tacked up the now famous photo of Mr. Cramer—finely laser-printed onto copy paper—with the most offensive portions blacked out. Wil could also see that someone had scrawled words in black marker below the picture, which read:

THE MIDWEST'S FRIENDLIEST BANKER.

Wil couldn't help but to let out a chuckle himself and roll his eyes. He sighed heavily, and forced a serious expression. "Get those things down," he said. "Right away."

"They have pictures of me."

Wendell slowly raised himself from his desk and stood at the cube wall to be level with Candy Luther's face. "What do you mean?" he asked.

"I caught wind of this whole Midwest Fed story about five months ago," Candy explained, holding a printed copy of the Cramer picture. "This photo of Cramer was allegedly taken in Miami at a meeting the bank was holding. While I never saw the photos until now, I had an anonymous tip that the party was quite out of control. To keep me quiet, the bank threatened to disclose some pictures that were taken of me. They were snapped at Dick Cramer's house during a political fundraising event held a few years back," Candy confessed.

Wendell paused. "What were those pictures of?"

Candy's expression changed to one of embarrassment. "Dick was getting flirty with me. In my job, sometimes flirting leads to good inside information, if I play my cards right."

"I understand. What happened?"

"I remember that they were all drinking some awful beer that he raved about—Maynards or Maylards, or something like that. It packed a wild punch. Never had anything like it."

A huge grin came across Wendell's face. "Candy Luther! You didn't get wild, did you?"

"No. I didn't, but Cramer did. He kept trying to kiss me and hug me, and I remember whispering in his ear, asking him to stop. I didn't want to embarrass him in his own home. I remember someone snapped a picture at just the wrong moment, so it makes me look guilty as ever."

"Have you seen this photo?"

"Yes," Candy said. "A copy was delivered to me a few months ago, apparently to prevent me from going deeper into the Miami story." She dug it out of a drawer and gave it to him.

Wendell examined it and stroked the hair that covered his chin. "You've got to hand it to them. They know what they're doing."

She nodded. "You know that old saying? Keep your friends close, and your enemies closer."

Wendell pushed his glasses up. "But it's out of context, right? There was really nothing to any of it?"

She shook her head. "Dick Cramer is just a pig, and you can believe me, I'd have nothing to do with him if he were the last CEO on earth. But if they used those shots against me, my Abbott would be livid and his career would be wrecked. He's already taken enough grief for marrying a gossip columnist. Pictures would send him over the edge."

Wendell leaned his right elbow on top of the cube wall. "There are three ways to handle this."

"And they are?"

"First, let's get this photo of Cramer legitimized. Forward the electronic version to the photo lab guys downstairs and have it examined to eliminate the possibility of any tampering, digital enhancements, and the like."

"Good idea. Second?"

"When you run with the story, be sure to also use the photo of Cramer flirting with you to lend more credence to his philandering. Just give the whole background of how it came to be."

"You mean, go on the offense?"

"Precisely," Wendell said. "It will make for a great story, showing the big, tough champion of the little guy trying to eliminate his enemies."

"What's third?"

"Let's find out who snapped that picture of you at that fundraiser."

Candy frowned. "That was a long time ago. Why will that help now?"

"I have a hunch that whoever took that picture of you and the CEO wasn't really after you. If I'm correct, there's bound to be even more pictures of our beloved Dick Cramer."

FORTY-SIX

The middle-aged man was out of breath as he climbed the steps to the second floor of the Midwest Federated headquarters building. The tire of flab that hung around his midsection slowed him down significantly, but he was confident that his costume made him look slimmer than he really was.

He walked slowly and methodically down the wide corridor, and the toes of his huge floppy yellow shoes thudded against the Persian rugs as he strode along. When various administrative assistants caught sight of him, they burst into laughter. He could only hope that his appearance was generating joy—not sympathy.

He turned the corner and lumbered through the door at the end of the hall. The woman with the bright red hair who occupied the office shot up from her desk.

"Wha, that's juss fine! Ya'll look great," Ms. Tanner said, quickly rounding her desk and approaching the sad-looking clown who stood before her.

She examined the man from all angles, slowly walking a counterclockwise circle around him, scanning his oversized, baggy business suit, the fat green tie, the long yellow shoes, his garish white makeup and bright orange wig. Ms. Tanner eventually stopped in front of him again to look straight into his eyes.

The man coughed, his chest rattling from years of smoking. "Pardon me," the clown muttered apologetically.

"That's okay," Ms. Tanner said, her hands on her hips, a look of pride swelling on her face. "Ah'm juss glad ya'll could git here sew quick."

"It's been a while since I put the full makeup on," he croaked. "But the agency said you needed a clown in a hurry."

"It's real good," she said. "Ah'm vera proud of ya'll gittin' the look juss right. Ya'll bein' a former actor n' all, ya know yer stuff."

The man coughed again, forcing a cork of phlegm loose from deep inside his chest. "Thanks," he managed through a mucus-riddled gurgle.

Ms. Tanner took another full lap around him. "Can ya'll juggle?"

He cleared his throat. "Juggle?" The man's bloodshot eyes got wide with concern.

"Yeah. Ya know, throw some balls er plastic bowlin' pins in the air? Can ya'll dew that?"

"I'm...I'm sure I could try," he answered hesitantly, nervously licking his painted lips.

Ms. Tanner's smile widened, her ruby-red lipstick creating a kind of clown face of her own. "Good. Now let's git ya'll scheduled up fer some branch visits. Yer now the 'ficial cla-hown of the Midwest Federated Bank!"

Wil left the parking garage just after 6 p.m. and was turning onto Marquette Avenue in Minneapolis when his cell phone rang. Jill Taylor's voice was shaky and upset.

"I haven't heard from him all day," she said. "It's unusual for me not to get at least one call."

"I tried him several times today myself," Wil said, sharing her concern. "But with everything that's happening at work, he might be sequestered somewhere." He hoped to calm her with his assuring tone.

"Wil, I'm very scared about this, considering..." She couldn't bear to continue.

Wil decided to turn his vehicle sharply left to take him around the block in the opposite direction. "I've got an idea," he said. "I'm going to check something out and I'll call you back."

Parking was always abundant in the early evening at the North Country Bar, so Wil pulled his car into a space right next to the back door. He quickly scanned the lot for Lanny's car, but it was dark and he couldn't see much of anything. He opted to check out the bar anyway and bounded through the rear entrance.

Country music was blasting from the jukebox, and with the space virtually deserted, one look at the empty tables and dance floor reminded him of a college party he once attended when nobody showed up. He counted only three people sitting at the long bar, and after allowing his eyes to adjust, he recognized Lanny as one of the patrons, sitting alone on the last stool at the far end. Wil quietly walked up and sat down next to him.

Lanny didn't even look up; he knew Wil was there. "I got fired."

Wil was silent, letting Lanny's words dangle. He had suspected as much, but Wil thought that anything he said to comfort his friend would only sound foolish and empty. "Jill's worried about you," Wil finally said, barely loud enough to hear above the music. A male bartender walked up, and Wil ordered a beer.

"I know she's worried and upset," Lanny said hoarsely as the bartender walked away. "How can I face her now?"

"She's come this far with you. Just tell her the truth."

Lanny's eyes were locked on the bar's counter in front of him. He didn't respond.

Wil fidgeted. "The gun, Lanny," Wil said tepidly. "What about the gun?"

Lanny sat motionless. "I can't believe they put this whole thing on me," he said, ignoring the question. "It wasn't my fault. I was just trying to do my job."

Wil looked at Lanny's puffy face. "What do you mean?"

"Slaytor had the virus traced back to my workstation. I was the one who was in the system and initiated the virus to spread. It was all unintentional, but it had guilt written all over it."

"They can't blame you for that," Wil said. "You're right. You were just trying to help."

Lanny slowly shook his head. "They needed a scapegoat. I was convenient for them."

Wil stared at the beer glass in front of him. "This isn't right," he said. "We need to get to the bottom of it."

The two men sat silently for a time. Lanny finally looked over at Wil, his grim expression replaced with a look of reassurance.

"Hey," Lanny said with some confidence. "Don't worry about the gun." He put his hand on Wil's shoulder and managed a strong grip. "It's right back where it belongs."

FORTY-SEVEN

Dick Cramer was anxious to start his weekly conference call. He gave each of the presidents the usual two-minute limit to deliver their regional updates. The call was to be all business; no one dared bring up the brewing photo debacle.

As usual, Barney Jennings listened from his Minneapolis office, wondering how he was going to broach the subject of low employee morale. Jane Duprey had delivered the bad news from Human Resources that morning that the vacancy rate of branch personnel was now at an all-time high. Judging by the attrition rate of his employees, he was fully aware that the pay freezes, pension cuts and bonus suspensions had gone over like a lead balloon. And there was no telling what the ramifications of incriminating photos of the CEO might do to morale.

When it came to be his turn, Mr. Jennings decided to cover only the vacancy rate topic. He did so quite eloquently, just seconds shy of his two-minute window.

"Barney," the CEO's voice said, crackling over the speakerphone, "we need to do a lot more with less. I'm of the opinion that we're overstaffed as it is. I don't want anyone, repeat, *anyone* to fully replace vacant positions. You can rehire for the critical ones, but let's reduce our overall platform staff."

Mr. Jennings was stunned. He knew by the latest financial reports that the prospect of the company hitting its financial targets—thus freeing up millions of shares of stock and cash bonuses for the executives at year's end—was to be close at best. But he also realized that cutting staff during the critical holiday season meant big service problems in the longer term. "I-I-I think we should reconsider, Dick," Mr. Jennings said forcefully. "If-if-if we want to stay open longer hours, we'll need more staff, not less."

Mr. Cramer's voice got increasingly louder and more forceful. "We're not only going to stay open longer, we're going to be open more! Gentlemen, this is a diverse country. If we're going to look out for the little guy, we need to stay open every day of the year."

Mr. Jennings slowly slumped at his desk as he listened to his boss's pontifications. While Mr. Cramer was renowned for his liberal political views, it grated him whenever a whiff of politics was interjected into the daily business setting.

"No one cares about Christmas or Easter or even the Fourth of July anymore," Mr. Cramer bellowed. "Holidays are a thing of the past—just another day when it comes to a retail operation. Therefore, I've made a bold decision. Beginning this Thanksgiving Day, we will be open on every single holiday. That means Christmas, Memorial Day, Labor Day...the whole calendar of holidays."

The regional presidents who were parked at speaker phones in the other states remained awkwardly silent. But the void was quickly filled by the voice of Trixie Tanner.

"Ah think it's a great idea, Dick," she drawled. "We've gotta be the Midwest's friendliest bank!"

Mr. Jennings couldn't help but wonder if this latest idea was Dick Cramer's way of getting back at employees who found good humor with the infamous email photo. Finally he could take no more of it. He pushed the mute button and sat back, the ocean waves crashing and the bright sun baking in his mind, his thoughts turning exclusively to the southern coast of Georgia.

FORTY-EIGHT

Wendell Reid scoured the three long file drawers of photos that the newspaper's political reporter kept neatly stored. Normally Wendell asked for permission before searching through someone else's files, but the reporter in question had taken some time off following the recent elections. Wendell had no trouble dispensing with such formalities, feeling that this exploration was his best shot at uncovering an essential lead.

Wendell hit pay dirt. It was in the last manila file folder in the bottom drawer, and from what Candy had described, it was full of pictures that fit the fundraising event's description. He walked over to Candy's desk and dropped the thick folder in front of her. "Do these look familiar?" he asked.

Candy noticed that the folder was labeled *DEMOCRATIC FUNDRAISER 1997* and she thumbed through the first few photos, immediately recognizing the venue.

"Yes," she said smiling, "this is definitely the right event. See right here?" she pointed to one photo that showed a large group of people. "This was taken inside of Dick Cramer's foyer where the receiving line had formed." She picked up several other photos that included well-known Minnesota senators and representatives, all snapped as they entered Mr. Cramer's mansion that night.

"Do you think you'd be able to remember who took the picture of you and Cramer?" Wendell asked.

"I know it was a very young woman, possibly even a teenager. I recall she was nicely dressed considering her young age—more like an adult. But as soon as she snapped the picture, she left the room. I do remember thinking at the time that there was something unusual about her, but it happened so fast, and it's been years now. Frankly, I don't remember what it was that caught my eye."

Wendell watched as Candy went through each photo, calling out the names of certain individuals she recognized. Near the middle of the pile, she stopped on one particular photo and swiftly inhaled with surprise.

"Something?" Wendell asked, hovering over her.

"This woman," Candy said, pointing to a beautiful young woman who could not have been more than 18 years old. "It's too bad it's not a clearer shot. Help me find more pictures with her in it."

Candy divided the remainder of the photo stack in half and handed one pile to Wendell. After both of them reviewed their halves, four pictures were set aside containing various angles of the young woman in question.

Candy opened a desk drawer and removed a loop, a small magnifying device that resembled an upside-down shot glass that was used for close examination of photos and negatives. She grabbed the clearest photo she could find and bent her head down to her desk, putting one eye through the loop's eyepiece, with the lens side pressing onto the photo itself. After a moment of studying the image, she stopped what she was doing and looked up at Wendell, smiling. "This is her."

"How do you know?"

"Look at her neck."

Wendell took the glass loop from Candy and examined the image of the young woman in the photo. "That looks very much like a tattoo."

"Yes, and that's the thing I had forgotten until now. She had this red mark on her neck. Back then, I thought it was big birthmark or something. Now that I can see her more clearly, it's obviously a tattooed rose."

Wendell looked at the photo again with the loop. "Any idea who this woman is?"

"Are you kidding?" Candy asked with a laugh. "Cramer's place was wall-to-wall people that night. I had presumed she belonged to one of the politicos who attended the party."

"Know anyone who could identify her?"

"Right," she said sarcastically, folding her arms in front of her. "On the day before Thanksgiving."

"Come now," Wendell chided. "With your vast network, you must know someone."

Candy bounced her pen off the tip of her nose, thinking. After a long pause, she grabbed her leather-bound book of contacts and allowed a wide grin to overtake her face.

"What is it?"

"Bobbie Berg," she exclaimed, holding her index finger in the air, and then using it to flip to the correct page in her book. "The best event planner in the cities."

FORTY-NINE

Thanksgiving Day, 2000

Felicia Cortez had to move mountains among her large, extended family to rearrange the day's holiday dinner schedule. Felicia was no cook, but her mother definitely was, and there was no way she was going to miss this year's Thanksgiving celebration. The traditional 1 p.m. serving time had to be scrubbed and delayed until later in the day, when Felicia was finally done at the bank.

The skeleton crew manning the branch was grumpy, forced to work on a weekday holiday due to Dick Cramer's latest brainstorm. Branch employees across the company questioned the wisdom of management's decision to stay open on such holidays, given that most people were known to spend time with families or enjoy time at home, especially on

Thanksgiving. With the infamous Cramer photo still fresh in employees' minds, coupled with the pain caused by pay freezes and pension cuts, it made it even more difficult for people to stay motivated for the sake of corporate profit.

Felicia brought in a pumpkin pie for her staff that she had purchased from a local bakery the previous day. She thought the few dollars of investment would go a long way toward picking up everyone's spirits. She also reasoned there would be light customer traffic, creating plenty of time for eating.

Her four female employees gathered around the teller line where Felicia had placed the pie. After a few jokes were lobbed at her about her well-known lack of cooking skills, Desiree suddenly interrupted the banter with a loud gasp.

"That's him!"

Desiree pointed toward the windows on the far side of the branch.

Everyone grew silent and turned to follow her panicky gesture. A man was following the sidewalk that rimmed the branch, and he was heading to the lobby door at a rapid pace. His speed of approach gave them little time to react.

"GET DOWN," the Cowboy Bandit yelled as soon as he sprang through the lobby's entryway. "Don't no one move."

Each of the employees complied and hit the floor. By happenstance, Felicia Cortez was the only person behind the teller counter, so she instinctively remained standing, waiting for his next command. She knew what he wanted next, and by obliging him as efficiently as possible, she could end the ordeal all the more quickly.

"You, pretty lady," the man said, glaring at Felicia. "I want all your money. Right now." He raised a tan-colored pillowcase above the counter and opened it with both hands.

Felicia noticed the man wasn't carrying a gun, nor was he implying he had one. All the news and FBI bulletins she had read regarding the Cowboy Bandit had indicated he was probably armed, though no one had actually seen the purported gun in any of the previous robbery incidents.

He's getting sloppy, she thought.

The man's eyes narrowed and his speech slurred. His cowboy hat was dirty, and he reeked of alcohol. "You give me that dye pack, and I come back to kill you."

Whimpering came from the employees who hugged the carpet, gripped with fear. Felicia stayed calm, remembering her training, efficiently emptying the contents of the teller drawer into the pillowcase. She then slowly moved her hands up with palms out, facing the man. "That's all there is."

The man looked over at the empty teller stations beside her. "Those too," he slurred, nodding toward the other teller drawers.

Felicia followed his gaze and hesitated. "There's nothing in those." She was not very convincing.

"Listen, chick," he said, leaning toward her over the counter, his acne scars appearing deep and rutted under the teller line's counter lights, "I said those, too."

Felicia studied the robber's pitted face and took several steps to her right to get behind the next teller station. As she slowly moved over, more whimpers from her employees emanated from the floor below. The man's head snapped around to look down at them.

"Shut up!" he yelled. "I don't like no crying!"

His intimidating tone made Felicia furious. Her branch had been robbed before, but the perpetrators in those crimes just wanted the cash—not a fight.

There was another burst of sobbing from his victims, and that made the Cowboy Bandit even more hostile. "I...SAID...SHUT...UP." His words slurred as his voice grew louder and angrier.

With the robber's attention focused on his sobbing captives, Felicia opened the second teller drawer a crack, hesitating to open it any wider. A strange feeling overwhelmed her senses as overlapping thoughts culminated into a massive buildup inside of her. She angrily thought of the fear created by this man's repeated holdups, then of the apathy of Midwest Federated management to prevent such robberies from happening. She seethed at the thought of law enforcement's inability to catch the guy.

With this fresh anger coursing through her system, Felicia instinctively shut her teller drawer and reached for an object on the counter in front of her. With both hands around it, she waited patiently until the whimpering from the floor subsided, something that she knew would force the man to turn his head toward her again. The whining eventually quieted, and as if on cue, the man looked up from the floor and into Felicia's eyes.

It was then that the Cowboy Bandit was introduced to a face full of store-bought pumpkin pie.

The impact was so forceful that it sent him reeling backward, the pillowcase full of money thudding to the floor, his arms flailing and rotating in an effort to counterbalance his rapidly tilting body. The sight reminded Felicia of an old western movie, when the bad guy takes a gun blast to the chest, and he falls backward in slow motion to the ground.

As the robber recoiled with limbs pin wheeling at his sides to regain his balance, Felicia hit the silent alarm button under the counter.

Desiree saw the whole thing from her horizontal position on the floor. She noticed the robber had become temporarily blinded, the pie filling completely covering his face and eyes, his cowboy hat tilting downward, stuck to his forehead. The bag full of money was in a crumpled ball next to her, so Desiree grabbed one end of it and swung it around her body in a sweeping arc, sliding the heavy pillowcase along the carpet, propelling it with all her might toward the far end of the teller line, and out of reach.

The robber had finally regained his balance and brought both hands to his face. He attempted several times to clear away the gooey filling from both eyes with his forefingers. He simultaneously spit out several gobs of the creamy pie from his mouth.

Felicia stood watching calmly as the man struggled to regain his composure. At the same time, she realized that she had just taken a big gamble. Worse yet, she had done the exact opposite of what she was trained to do, which was to never, under any circumstances, try to be a hero.

The Cowboy Bandit could only stand there stunned, spitting out more of the pie filling. He blinked wildly, his green eyes peering through the thick application of brown goop that coated his zit-stained face.

A long moment of indecision ensued as he stood facing his pie attacker. The distant sound of police could be heard, their droning sirens growing ever louder as the precious seconds ticked by.

As the man's window of opportunity slowly closed upon him, he pivoted toward the branch's front door. With catlike reflexes that didn't match his body style, he quickly bolted from the building, his face still coated with thick streaks of pumpkin dessert.

"That's Eliza Updike," Bobbie Berg said with confidence through Candy Luther's cell phone. "I do all of the Cramer events, and she's always present, without fail."

"She's an Updike?" Candy asked. "An Updike with a rose-shaped tattoo?"

"Hard to believe, isn't it, dear?" the event planner said. "It has been quite the family controversy ever since she got it. She was just a teenager backpacking across Europe. Word has it that she's been drummed out of the family for a variety of other reasons, perhaps even cut out of the money. Now that I think of it, dear, that rose is probably a symbol of protest."

Candy was getting evil stares from her husband Abbott, who was forced to entertain their Thanksgiving Day guests in the couple's dining room while she chatted on the phone. The would-be Minnesota Attorney General was not much for small talk, and he definitely didn't want things to progress to a point where he'd actually have to serve the food. The dinner hour was upon them, and he made his impatience known to her through his steely glare from the dining room table.

"Dick Cramer's most recent wife is an Updike, isn't she?" Candy asked, lowering her voice into the phone and turning her back, disappearing through the kitchen door.

"Oh yes, dear," Bobbie said. "That's Harriet Updike Cramer. She is Randall Updike's older daughter."

Candy picked up two large wooden spoons and tossed the lettuce salad in a bowl that was sitting on the kitchen island. "This Eliza person...is she Harriet Cramer's daughter?" she asked, the phone pinned under her chin as she repeatedly tossed the lettuce and vegetables.

"No, honey," Bobbie said. "Eliza is her niece. She belongs to Harriet's younger sister. But Harriet sort of adopted her. You see, her sister had Eliza out of wedlock, and I think Harriet was an influence over Eliza from the moment she was born—more so than her own mother."

Candy tossed the salad aggressively, losing track of how many times she had flung the lettuce concoction into the air and back into the bowl. "So Eliza and Harriet are close?"

"Yes, my dear, but I think it is Eliza and Dick who are even closer."

Candy realized that she was in danger of turning the salad into mush, so she put down the two wooden spoons. "They're close, too? What could those two people possibly have in common? They're miles apart in age."

There was a pause. "Well, you didn't hear this from me, dear, but there's something irregular going on with them. I've noticed that they seem a little...too familiar with one another. They're together a lot, if you know what I mean, but in kind of a strange way."

Candy started to respond with a question, but she halted in mid-breath as Abbott burst into the kitchen. The man in the Cardigan sweater was in no mood to continue being stuck in a holding pattern. With all his nervous energy, Abbott impatiently hovered around his wife.

Candy raised her forefinger at him, a signal that she was wrapping up. "Bobbie, I don't know how to thank you for the information, especially on Thanksgiving Day. As always, I owe you."

"Don't give it a second thought, dear," Bobbie answered gleefully. "It's always my pleasure."

Candy then wished her confidential source a happy Thanksgiving and snapped the cell phone shut. She grabbed the salad bowl with both hands and forced a smile, rushing past her impatient husband and out to her hungry, waiting guests.

FIFTY

It was the Saturday of a long holiday weekend, and Wil was driving east in a pesky snow squall on Interstate 90 after spending Thanksgiving with his mom in Sioux Falls when Kari Bender called. Kari often served as the secondary media contact when Wil was out of town, and she called to give Wil the latest information on the Saint Paul branch robbery.

Wil couldn't stop laughing and nearly swerved off the road when she told him the story of Felicia Cortez tossing a pie into the face of the Cowboy Bandit.

"Wanna hear the best part?" Kari asked.

"You mean there's more?" he asked, chuckling.

"As of an hour ago, the guy's been caught."

"They got the Cowboy Bandit? How?"

"Get this," she said, laughing through her explanation. "Turns out he had a severe allergic reaction to the ingredients in the pie. His face and head swelled up to the size of a watermelon, and he ended up in an emergency room somewhere. An alert medic recognized him from the police descriptions, and he put two and two together."

Wil was now laughing so hard that he was forced to slow his car to ensure he didn't cause a wreck. "Now that's a fitting end to our Cowboy Bandit," he said, "and all because of Felicia."

Wil then asked Kari for an update about the upcoming promotional campaign that was set to start the next week, scheduled to kick off as part of the opening of the new Eagan branch on Pilot Knob Road. Kari assured him that the ads were done and the media contracts were in place, and he was looking forward to the distraction of something positive happening for a change.

If all went well, Wil figured the year would end on a relatively high note, with a record number of new checking accounts being generated. The thought made him proud.

Wil got back into town early that evening and arranged to meet Jessica, Lanny and Jill at their favorite Minneapolis hangout. The three were already seated at a table when Wil walked through the doors of the North Country Bar. He also noticed that Felicia Cortez was working that night. He waved at his friends across the room, happy to see Lanny and Jill sitting together, apparently having a good time. He opted to stop by the bar first to order a drink and congratulate Felicia for her recent stunt.

He nudged his way through a thick layer of patrons who crowded around the bar. After a short wait, he finally caught her attention. "I hear congratulations are in order," he shouted over the loud music.

"Depends," Felicia said without looking up, frantically mixing several drinks in front of her.

"Seriously," Wil said, leaning on the bar as he stood. "That was incredible what you did at the branch. Somebody had to take charge and get that guy. I heard all about it."

She grabbed a bottle of vodka and tipped it upside down, nimbly filling a shot glass several times and repeatedly dumping its contents into a glass. "Too bad management didn't think so."

"What do you mean?" Wil thought he had misunderstood her due to the loud music and commotion. "They weren't happy about what you did?" he asked loudly.

She placed drinks in front of two nearby patrons and then filled a mug of beer for Wil. "I got fired," she snapped, setting the mug on the counter in front of him.

"What?"

"You heard me right," she said, her eyes showing a hint of moisture. "I didn't follow procedures. They wanted to make an example of me."

Wil was so stunned that he ignored the overweight man who was trying to ram his way toward the bar. "But the guy was captured," Wil said, his voice's pitch raising an octave. "Just today."

"So I heard. It won't mean a thing. What's done...is done."

Wil squinted as though in pain. "How can that be? They can't just fire you for trying to do the right thing."

"They can do anything they want, Wil. Besides, it's my own fault. I took the risk. Desiree thinks I was let go partially because I opened the file of Cramer's photo on my computer."

Wil raised an eyebrow. "Do you believe that?"

She shook her head, filling a beer glass and setting it in front of the fat man who had wedged himself next to Wil. "All I know for sure is that I shouldn't have interfered with the robbery."

"But you showed bravery. No one else in the company was willing to take control."

Several more thirsty customers got Felicia's attention, and she was off to the other end of the bar to fill their orders. Wil watched as she continued to smile and act professionally, a trait that he doubted he could muster under similar circumstances. *Another good one gone,* he thought.

Wil's expression was melancholy as he approached the table that was surrounded by his friends, touching Jessica's shoulder as he sat.

"Rough weekend with mom?" Jessica asked with a giggle, trying to shake his glumness.

He shook his head solemnly and looked over at Lanny. "Felicia was fired."

Lanny turned toward the bar where Felicia was serving more customers. "Felicia Cortez?"

Wil told his friends the whole story of the robbery, the capture, and her dismissal.

"Seems to me they're firing all the wrong people for all the wrong reasons," Jessica said. "What's going on over there, anyway?"

As he thought of his answer, Wil was distracted by the appearance of a male figure entering through the back door: It was Andy Gerhardt, bomber jacket and all. Wil immediately raised his hand, luring the corporate pilot to their table.

"You may not want my company tonight," Andy said with forewarning, dragging an empty chair over from another table.

"We're not celebrating here, either," Wil said, raising his hand again, this time to capture the attention of the roving waitress.

"Then I'm probably at the right table after all. What's so bad here?"

"Let's see," Wil said, holding out his right hand to count on his fingers for effect, "Lanny lost his job this week, and our friend Felicia over there had her branch robbed on Thanksgiving Day, then took steps that caused the guy's capture, and she was subsequently fired for it."

The waitress stopped by the table and Andy ordered a mixed drink: a double. His expression changed to match the mood around the table. "I guess I am in good company."

Wil, Lanny, Jill and Jessica exchanged glances, and then looked quizzically at Andy.

"Don't tell me..." Wil said, his tone lowering.

"Yep. Me too. Fired."

Everyone at the table sat back in their chairs as though they'd been hit in the chest.

"You're not joking?" Lanny asked flatly.

Andy slowly shook his head.

"What the hell?"

Andy managed a smirk. "Seems your CEO thinks I was taking inappropriate pictures of him."

"Cramer is blaming you for that photo?" Wil asked.

"I guess so," Andy said. "That's the implication, at least. Slaytor did the actual firing. Officially, it's a job reduction."

Lanny leaned in. "Slaytor fired you too? You mean Cramer didn't even have the nerve to do it himself?"

The waitress returned with Andy's drink, and he took a quick swallow from it. "I've been working at that bank a long time. Slaytor always does the dirty work for Cramer."

"I hope you try to fight this," Jill said.

"How? They have very deep pockets over there, and lawyers are stacked on top of lawyers."

Wil stared blankly at the tabletop. "If you got fired, then I'm sure to be next."

Andy gestured dismissively. "You'll be fine."

"No, listen...Slaytor thinks I'm involved somehow. Only he doesn't have anything concrete on me, because there is nothing. But I'm sure to be his next victim if he can wriggle it."

"You really think so?" Jessica asked.

Wil looked down at the table for a moment, and then looked up at Andy. "Who really shot that photo?"

"Cramer runs with a gaggle of young women," Andy said. "Whenever he gets the urge, we jet off to Vegas, or San Diego, or Miami where he meets up with them and has his way. I won't miss that at all. But I've noticed one of the women with him always seems a little distant, and she's never very affectionate. Not like the others."

"You think it's this particular woman?" Wil asked.

"I was in the bathroom in Miami the night the photo was taken. I've been over and over the details of that event in my mind, yet I keep coming up with the same answer. That one woman is the only person who could have taken that shot. In fact, I saw her remove what could've been a camera from her purse. At the time, I just thought it was a makeup case or something. They make cameras pretty small these days."

Lanny chimed in. "Any idea who she is?"

"No," he said, raising an eyebrow. "But she has one very identifiable characteristic."

In a welcomed moment of levity, Lanny and Wil looked at each other with a silly grin, eyebrows raised, intrigued.

"Oh?" Wil asked.

"First of all guys, yes, she is gorgeous. Second, she has a rose, tattooed right here, on her neck." Andy traced the approximate location of the mark on his own neck, pointing to an area just above the shoulder blade.

Jessica adjusted her long hair by grabbing it with one hand and layering it onto her back and shoulders. "Wil, like it or not, you're the only survivor as of right now. You owe it to your comrades to do something."

"Like what?" he shrugged. "I'm all ears."

"Well," she said, grabbing a handful of stale popcorn from the paper basket on the table, "I have this idea, as devious an idea as I've ever had."

Lanny leaned in. "We're listening," he said.

Jessica paused as she chewed a few kernels of popcorn, carefully framing her idea. "There's a technique that I learned while working for this guy at a restaurant chain in Chicago a few years ago."

"And?" Wil asked, interested.

She carefully wiped her lips with a square bar napkin. "This is almost the same exact situation. What I did then was quite effective. And I guarantee that it'll work just as well on the boys at Midwest Federated Bank."

FIFTY-ONE

Candy Luther's repeated calls to Eliza Updike remained unreturned over the weekend. Candy hoped that with the holiday weekend finally over, life for a 22-year-old woman might return to normal—and that she'd eventually call.

As Candy sat at her desk working on more mundane leads for her next column, she got the news that she was waiting for. The *Minneapolis Daily Post's* photo lab had given her a 98-percent probability that the Cramer photo was untouched—and legitimate.

"I hope you realize that you're going to have a tough time convincing management to run with this," Wendell said from the other side of the cube wall, his fingers clacking away on the keyboard as he talked.

"I'm a gossip columnist," she said. "I've got a better shot at this than anyone else around here."

Wendell stood to look over the cube wall, cinching up his tacky blue necktie. "You don't understand. Cramer's got friends here. He writes op-ed pieces for this newspaper to support the editorial board's stance on everything from abortion to gay rights. Plus, his bank is an advertiser."

"Cramer claims he runs a clean shop, the champion of the little guy," she said, looking up at him. "He's said it over and over very publicly. That theme is even in the Midwest Federated annual report, right on the front cover. Yet, I've got leads that tell me he's really into excess, that he uses the company's jet in pursuit of his sexual trysts. Now we've got the photographic evidence to prove it. That alone is worth more than page five of the Entertainment Section, but I guess my column will have to do."

Wendell tapped his short fingernails on top of the cube wall as he thought. "Maybe you can get some confirmation from the bank itself," he said. "It'll give this thing more legs."

She nodded. "I have a contact there who I talked to last spring when this all started to bubble up."

"So...what are you waiting for?" Wendell asked. "Call him, already."

"Done," she said. "I just hope Mister Fischer returns my call before deadline."

"I don't know what you're talking about," Wil said.

"Come now, Mister Fischer," Candy said in her best condescending phone voice. "I know for a fact that this photograph was blasted out to nearly every employee in your company. Surely you weren't the only one who didn't see it."

Wil squirmed in his chair. He secretly wanted to just tell her to run with it, but he was still employed, and he had a job to do. "Miss Luther, I appreciate that you're a so-called columnist, but there are so many other stories out there. Surely the governor must be having an affair, or there's a local celebrity with a cat up a tree somewhere."

Candy didn't appreciate the loftiness, but she did admire Wil's tenacity. She decided to go for the jugular. "My sources say the CEO of Midwest Federated is using the company jet improperly. The photo seems to justify it."

"Really," Wil said with forced sarcasm. "How does one grainy and obviously faked photo justify that kind of claim?"

"So you have seen it for yourself," Candy said. "Then you should know that our lab guys enlarged the photo, and they were able to pick out the 'Miami Beachside Resort' stitching on one of the towels hanging behind Mister Cramer."

Wil was taken aback. She was either a good bluffer, or she was telling the truth.

"Those things can be faked too," he said in a denouncing tone.

Candy threw out more bait and hoped the fish would strike. "Mister Fischer, do you have any idea why a relative of Mister Cramer's wife would be taking incriminating photos of him?"

Wil stopped breathing as he remembered the conversations about the young woman who Andy spoke about. "A relative?"

"Yes," Candy answered. "A young woman in her twenties. It's the one other thing my lab guys found when they enlarged the photo. Part of her face is reflected in a mirror that's in the background, and she's holding onto what looks to be a camera. She's also the same young woman who snapped the picture of me with your CEO several years ago."

Wil was suddenly nervous. "You and...Mister Cramer?"

"You don't have to play dumb with me anymore," Candy said angrily. "That was dirty pool, threatening me with that picture."

Suddenly the conversations Wil had had with Gene Danielson, and the earlier run-in with Ms. Luther at the *Daily Post,* all made perfect sense. His company must have shut down the Miami story originally with a threat of an incriminating photo of their own, one that involved Candy Luther and Dick Cramer. The thought of such shenanigans from his employer made him feel uneasy—and ashamed.

"This young photographer that you speak of," Wil asked hesitantly. "Would she happen to have any distinguishing characteristics?"

"Oh," Candy said enthusiastically. "Do you want to play now?"

"Just answer the question, Miss Luther."

"Turns out she just might have a distinguishing characteristic. It might even be, say, a rose on her neck," Candy said.

Wil moved the handset away from his mouth to prevent her from hearing his gasp. "And you say that this is Harriet Cramer's relative?" he asked after a pause.

"Harriet's niece, named Eliza. She travels with Mister Cramer quite often, doesn't she, Mister Fischer?"

Wil knew Harriet was an Updike, but he wasn't familiar with anyone named Eliza. "Listen, Miss Luther, I'm going to ask you to hold on this story until I can formulate an official response for you."

Candy sighed, sensing a stall tactic. "Are you the company spokesman or aren't you?"

"Yes," Wil answered swiftly. "But now, you must trust me. I may have even more for you to chew on in a little while."

Wil immediately called his new boss out of respect for corporate protocol, but he only reached Ms. Tanner's drawling voicemail message. He tried Barney Jennings too, but he was unavailable. He had no choice but to call Mr. Cramer's office to let him know that the *Minneapolis Daily Post* was about to run a damaging story about the CEO.

He reached Dick Cramer's assistant immediately and learned that he was out of town. Wil explained to Marci what he knew in vague terms. She dutifully took down the information, promising a return call from Mr. Cramer himself.

By the end of the day, no such call came.

FIFTY-TWO

Wil did not sleep a wink that night, and he dragged himself into the office with the morning newspaper tucked under his arm, too nervous while at home to check whether or not the Luther story had actually published. Part of him hoped it had run on page one, but he knew it meant the official end of his career if such a thing did happen.

After sitting at his desk and rubbing his eyes to fight for lucidity, he finally built up enough courage to leaf through the paper. Relief overcame him when he turned through every page, ending on the benign Sports Section. *She listened to me after all,* he thought.

His feeling of accomplishment didn't last long. Marci called his phone from the CEO's office, and she was frantic.

"All advertising at the Post needs to be pulled," she said curtly.

Wil's blood pressure went through the roof. "But you don't understand," he said, teetering on the edge of being disrespectful. "Our ad campaign starts tomorrow for the new branch opening. It's too late for this."

Marci's tone was apologetic, but firm. "I'm just conveying what Mister Cramer has told me to tell you," she said. "Pull the ads. He wants no more advertising in that newspaper anymore, period."

Wil figured he had no choice but to comply, so he promised he'd get back to her with a confirmation and hung up the phone. *We'll have to resort to shouting in bullhorns to promote this bank,* Wil thought.

"That account is worth millions over the next five years, Candy!" Gene Danielson's voice could be heard in every corner of the newsroom.

Candy stood with her arms crossed, so close to Gene's face that she could smell the stale coffee on his breath. "Are we going to report the news or not?"

"You're a gossip columnist, Luther, not Woodward and Burnstein," Gene said. "Get back to writing about who-is-wearing-what to parties, and stop intimidating my clients." He turned and stormed off through the newsroom.

Candy felt dozens of eyes on her as she raised a hand to her face, wiping off the dots of saliva that had pelted her during the exchange.

"A mighty fine mess you've gotten yourself into," Wendell said, his hands dancing across the keyboard, the keys clacking away.

FIFTY-THREE

The late November day was unusually mild in the Twin Cities, with temperatures approaching 45 degrees by late morning. A good crowd of dignitaries and guests had gathered for the ribbon-cutting ceremony of Midwest Federated Bank's newest, most modern branch. Eagan was a bustling community about 10 miles south of Saint Paul, and its incredible growth was attracting many new businesses to the area. Wil felt that the branch location was a good move for the bank, and he was particularly proud of the advertising campaign he and Kari had created—that is, until the ads were pulled from the area's dominant newspaper.

Wil and Kari had scrambled to rearrange what advertising they could at the last minute, but they both knew that any positive impact from their late-year promotion was to be muted. Wil's concern of the moment, though, was the branch's christening ceremony, which was to be attended by many dignitaries, including Richard Cramer himself.

"The band's here," Kari said, pointing to the Eagan High School bus that had just arrived.

"Great," he said. "Get them arranged and strike it up."

With the help of the marketing staff, the branch was beautifully decorated for the occasion, with balloon arches arranged above the entryways, bouquets of flowers adorning desks and the teller line, and complimentary food neatly positioned on a table nearby. When the band was finally in place, it wasn't long before they were playing *America the Beautiful* in the parking lot.

The Eagan mayor, representatives of the City Council and Chamber of Commerce, Barney Jennings, Duke Slaytor, bank officers and several members of the bank's board all congregated in the lobby. Curious onlookers from the nearby shopping complex also stopped by and joined the crowd.

Through the front windows, Kari saw the cherry-red sports car zoom into the parking lot just after 10 a.m., and the car quickly occupied the handicapped parking stall right next to the front door. "His highness is here," Kari said, whispering to Wil as he turned on the power supply to the portable sound system they had rented.

Mr. Cramer breezed in through the doors, his canary-yellow shirt shining brightly between the lapels of his dark black suit coat. Wil watched as the man shook hands with various people in the crowd. He waited nervously for the right opportunity to hand Mr. Cramer four index cards, which contained the key bullet points of the welcoming speech he was to give.

As the mingling continued and Mr. Cramer shook more hands, Wil stood patiently nearby, marveling about how he was able to hear the drawl of Trixie Tanner from the far side of the cavernous lobby—heard even over the increasing din. He couldn't see her, as the mass of people attending the event had grown to insurmountable proportions.

As he awaited the right moment to interrupt the CEO, Wil was puzzled by the sudden sound of cackling from the crowd. Something was obviously disrupting the proceedings, but his sightline was obstructed by a wall of suited executives.

Kari instantly appeared from the crowd and rushed up with a panicked look on her face. "Did you see that?" she asked, her voice revealing dread.

"What's going on over there?" Wil asked in a hushed tone.

Kari grabbed Wil's arm and pulled him to the center of the lobby, getting him closer to the disruption that he was hearing, but not seeing.

"Oh no," he said, catching a glimpse of the sorry-looking clown who was attempting to juggle.

The plastic orange bowling pins spun dangerously in the air, falling and bouncing on the carpeted floor near the man's long, flat clown shoes.

"Isn't he gr-rreat?" Ms. Tanner drawled as she walked up to Wil.

The clown bent down to retrieve the fallen pins, but his big gut prevented stability, and he nearly lost his orange wig and striped hat when gravity took over. The clown paused to adjust his headgear, and then spread his legs outward to keep himself more balanced.

"Who in the hell is that?" Wil asked, his eyes wide with alarm.

"That," Ms. Tanner said, "is whah we're fren'ly. He's our new maz-kot."

A heavily congested cough erupted from the clown as he stood up again, the bowling pins freshly reloaded in his hands. The portion of the crowd that surrounded him giggled mostly from embarrassment, but then fell silent as the man attempted to juggle some more. Another deep cough threw off his concentration, and the pins thudded again to the carpet below.

It was a confusing spectacle, and Wil couldn't believe it was happening. He could not bear to watch anymore, so he looked at Ms. Tanner, whose smile and wide eyes reminded him of a proud parent at a piano recital.

Kari tapped him on the shoulder and pointed to her watch. Wil nervously nodded to her in acknowledgement, and he took the opportunity to lose himself in the bigger crowd to reacquire Dick Cramer.

It was show time, so when Wil found the CEO talking to Barney Jennings, he immediately walked up to the men, his hand extended. Mr. Cramer, though, barely looked at Wil and did not return the handshake. Wil's shoulders slumped, and he simply handed Cramer the four index cards.

"I wing these events," Mr. Cramer huffed, pushing the cards aside while still in Wil's hand. The man then headed directly to the podium that was set up near the teller line.

Mr. Cramer tapped the microphone, causing a sharp and brief squeal of feedback. "Welcome, everyone. Welcome!" His voice belted out of the speakers, quickly quieting the throng. As the noise subsided, the only remaining perceptible sound came from the bank's new mascot—the middle-aged clown who was coughing up a lung.

"I'm very proud to be here opening our newest branch," Mr. Cramer bellowed. "Midwest Federated Bank is all about progress. We are the most progressive bank in the whole state, the friendliest bank!"

A smattering of applause erupted, but Wil noticed that the dozen or so lower-level bank employees in attendance did not respond.

"You all know me as the champion of the little man, the hero for the guy who can't catch a break. We're in business for him as a what-you-see-is-what-you-get bank. We have no secrets. We don't waste money like the other banks. Our resources go into our service, our people. We're all about progress and employees."

More meek applause came from the crowd. Wil winced when he heard the clown unsuccessfully muffle a phlegm-filled cough.

Wil listened as Mr. Cramer winged his speech with stale sentences from countless previous events. Wil's stomach felt tight, so to avoid spilling his insides in front of a hundred people, he withdrew to the back of the assembly.

Mr. Cramer's voice continued its echo through the crammed lobby. "This is a great company, and it wouldn't be so without our employees..."

As Wil slowly eased himself dejectedly to an unoccupied space near the branch's back wall, he noticed a tall brunette standing at the entry doors. She was stunningly beautiful, and out of place. Most of the crowd was dressed in business attire, and most were middle-aged. This woman, though, was young, tanned, and trying hard to be innocuous as Cramer blubbered away.

"...they are our number one resource..." he continued.

Wil took several sidesteps toward her, getting as close as he dared without looking like a stalker. Locking his eyes on Mr. Cramer, Wil slowly turned his head to get a better look. He then adjusted his eyes on his new target.

It's her.

The rose was impossible to ignore, its delicately drawn petals gently curving up the side of her neck. He noticed something else: She was rolling her eyes in disgust as the CEO talked.

Wil could feel his heart beating in overdrive. He knew he needed to strike, even if it was only based on a hunch. He eased his hand into the inside pocket of his suit jacket and removed a business card and pen.

"...and now open on all holidays, because we're a country of diversity, and we're a company that does not distinguish holidays separate from our business..."

Wil scrawled four words on the card:

I KNOW TOO MUCH.

He perched the card between his fingertips and eased it toward her. He turned his head away from her in a veined attempt to make the rest of his body invisible.

"...we will be the number-one bank in the markets we serve..."

Wil kept looking straight ahead. The droning voice of Dick Cramer seemed to get louder and louder, and everything around him seemed to be moving in slow motion. The business card hung in his extended hand for an eternity, until suddenly, it was snatched away.

"...and that's why we're the Midwest's friendliest bank!"

As Mr. Cramer finished his remarks, the crowd meekly applauded. Cramer clasped his hands together and raised them above his head, pumping them up and down, undoubtedly hearing the deafening ovation of a winning prizefight in his head.

As the lobby quieted, the band outside was cued to start playing, the clown automatically started to juggle, and Wil turned to finally face Eliza.

But she was already gone.

FIFTY-FOUR

By the time Wil got back to Minneapolis it was late afternoon, and the sun was already low in the sky as he pulled into the bank's parking garage. He was dead on his feet; event management always took the life out of him.

He walked into the Marketing Department past Mindy's empty desk. She had taken the day off, something she could do at a moment's notice while working for a temp agency. He flipped on his office lights and saw a package sitting on his chair. It was a large manila envelope, his name typewritten on a white label. He grabbed a letter opener and sliced through the top. He carefully inserted his fingers and pulled out a thick wad of cards that were banded together inside.

He slowly pulled the stack clear of the envelope. Once he was able to look closely at them, it became apparent that Eliza had understood his request: The cards were the actual color photographs he so desperately wanted.

Wil sat down with the stack of photos, removed the rubber band and flipped through the pictures. Each one featured Cramer in incriminating situations in exotic locations and surrounded by young, often naked women. It was damning evidence of Mr. Cramer's infidelity. It was also a smoking indictment of the man's abuse of company resources, namely the company jet.

Wil felt sorry for the man's wife and family. And he felt even sorrier for Andy Gerhardt, Felicia Cortez, and Lanny Taylor, all of whom lost their positions at the bank for no reason other than for simply doing their jobs.

He turned to his computer and fired off an email to three people. It read:

Lanny, Andy, Felicia:
Operation Blue Christmas shall commence.
Make your calls.

"You may now consider me a source," Wil said.

"Excuse me, Mister Fischer?" Candy Luther asked from the other end of the phone, astonished.

"I am now a source for your story, as I am in possession of more evidence regarding the Chief Executive Officer of

Midwest Federated," Wil said glumly. "It's more than you've ever dreamed."

"I'm afraid you're too late, Mister Fischer," she said candidly. "This story's dead. Management won't let me run with it."

Wil looked down at the stack of photos, still amazed at what he now possessed. "Your management won't be able to ignore this story after they've seen the photos now in my hands."

Candy paused. She was intrigued. "What are your conditions?"

"First, I remain anonymous."

"Of course."

"Two, you must wait for three weeks before breaking this."

"Three weeks? That's Christmastime. Why three weeks?"

"You have to work with this timeframe, Miss Luther, or I don't cooperate."

She sighed. "What else?"

"Call your sources. Get the filed flight plans of the Midwest Fed corporate jet out of Holman Field in Saint Paul for the past few years. Trust me. You won't be disappointed."

By noon the next day, Andy, Lanny and Felicia had called every bank employee that they knew and trusted. The "method" that Jessica had shared over drinks during the Thanksgiving weekend was mobilizing into a full-fledged, highly orchestrated event, and it was to be only three short weeks until Operation Blue Christmas became a reality.

FIFTY-FIVE

Christmas Day, 2000

The cherry-red sports car squealed around the corner, racing to the rear of the Snelling Avenue branch in Saint Paul where the drive-through lanes were situated. Mr. Cramer was in need of cash, and he was in a hurry. Just a few miles away, the Gulfstream jet was sitting on the tarmac, gassed up and waiting for him, but he wasn't worried. His new holidays-open edict was firmly in place, and no matter what holiday it happened to be, his errand to get wads of cash couldn't be more convenient for him.

He rounded the corner and pulled into the inside drive-through lane. He lowered his driver's side window, hit the call button on the kiosk, and began to write out a check for cash.

As he scrawled the information with a ballpoint pen onto his check, he became annoyed that the teller hadn't yet responded. He grimaced as he reached over to hit the call button again and again—an action that many people performed on elevator buttons when impatient, for all the good it would do.

He finished writing out the check, but still no response came from the branch. The low Christmas Day sun was glaring off the windows of the drive-through station, so he couldn't see anything inside. "Damn it all!" he shouted as he sped off in his car toward the front of the branch.

From the front parking lot, he leapt out of the vehicle and marched with fury to the main door. A sign affixed to the window read: THIS BRANCH WILL BE OPEN CHRISTMAS DAY. He looked at his watch—it was 11:15 a.m.—and he tugged on the door. It was locked.

Mr. Cramer was boiling mad. He cupped his hands and pressed his face to the tinted windows, leaving a grease mark on the glass, trying desperately to get a glimpse inside of his branch. He couldn't see any activity in the lobby, so he pounded on the door with his fists. No response. He cupped his hands again to get a better look inside, and then pounded his fists even harder until he realized he might set off the master alarm.

His face was red with fury. He reached into his pocket for his cell and quickly punched in Duke Slaytor's home number.

"NOBODY showed up to work in Saint Paul today," he yelled as soon as Mr. Slaytor answered. "They're supposed to be open, don't they know that? Get Barney on the phone and get somebody down here right away. You have ten minutes!" He slammed his phone shut and noted the time on his watch, a man full of rage on Christmas Day.

He stormed fitfully back and forth in front of the locked door, pacing like a caged animal at the zoo. After deciding that he could wait no longer, he returned to his red sports car in a huff, fired it up, and raced it down the road to the nearest branch in Inver Grove Heights.

In the spring of 1996, Jessica Tolkin had landed a job as a waitress for the defunct Zindel restaurant chain, which once operated a dozen restaurants throughout Chicago. Business was brisk and the money was good, allowing Jessica to save the lion's share of her tips for a rainy day.

But within a few short months, the shine on the new job had worn off. The general manager was an egomaniac and a manic depressive. It wasn't long before Jessica heard that the man was pressuring workers for sex in exchange for job security. Many of her coworkers succumbed to his demands; but if confronted, she would have nothing of it. She started documenting everything she heard and saw, and then began to formulate a master plan.

Mr. Cramer gritted his teeth as he circled his car around the Midwest Federated Bank in Inver Grove Heights to approach the two drive-through lanes in the rear. He was doubly irritated for wasting precious time while his Gulfstream jet sat waiting for him, engines idling at Holman Field.

He impatiently shot another look at his watch as soon as he noticed cars occupying each lane. He brought the sports car to a halt behind a rusty station wagon, whose driver appeared to be having trouble with the kiosk. A minute or so went by, and Mr. Cramer had no choice but to hop out and assist his customer.

"The call button's right here," Mr. Cramer snapped, pointing impatiently to the lit button in the middle panel of the silver-colored kiosk.

"I know," the young man in the stocking cap said, leaning out of the rusty car's window. "I've been hitting it for the past minute or two. She just don't answer."

Mr. Cramer looked over at the black truck that occupied the other lane. The older driver was apparently having the same difficulty.

With his blood approaching a boiling point, he glanced over at the drive-through window to see who was manning the lanes, but those windows were also too darkly tinted and afforded no clear view.

He marched up to the windows and cupped his hands on the glass. This time, he could see inside quite clearly. There was no one inside.

As young as Jessica was back in 1996, her smarts made her an invaluable asset to those around her. Customers loved her, and her coworkers respected her pragmatism and sense of humor. But when the Zindel's general manager turned into an ogre, she knew she had to take charge and do something.

Illinois law enforcement could get nothing on the man. None of the affected employees dared to talk. Knowing that she needed the safety of bigger numbers, she and several other employees made repeated phone calls to those who had been approached—or were otherwise affected—by the manager's infuriating behavior. Eventually a date was set, and the word was spread: Action to end the nightmare was to come from the hands of the man's own employees.

With unity among 150 restaurant workers, Jessica's plan had finally come together. The timing could not have been better.

But when the date arrived, Jessica's luck had evaporated. Her worst nightmare had come true when she found herself being groped by the manager in a back room. Young and feisty, she was able to fight him off successfully, and she escaped.

Then, at 6 o'clock that evening, on the busiest day of the week, more than 100 workers of the Zindel's Restaurant chain all showed their solidarity—and walked off the job.

The coordinated event brought the entire chain to its knees. The restaurant walkout lasted for three days. The manager of Zindel's was subsequently indicted on a variety of charges, including molestation, money laundering and fraud.

The new branch in Eagan was also dark and locked up tight. The situation was the same, Mr. Cramer found, at the bank's branches in Cottage Grove and Oakdale.

"What the hell is going on here?" Mr. Cramer shouted into his phone.

"Not one of the employees on the call list answers their phone," Mr. Slaytor said from his living room in Woodbury. "It's as though they all just...left."

"Left?" Mr. Cramer barked. "What? Where's Jennings?"

"Can't reach him. It's Christmas Day, Dick."

"I don't care what day it is!" he screamed. "It's a work day! What the hell is going on here?"

Mr. Slaytor was silent for a long time, and Mr. Cramer could hear nothing over the phone except for Christmas music playing softly in the background.

"You have ten seconds to explain this to me, Slaytor!"

Mr. Slaytor could hold out no longer. "Dick," he began softly, "have you seen the paper this morning?"

"The paper?" Cramer asked. "What paper?"

"The Minneapolis Daily Post. The story. It ran."

FIFTY-SIX

February 2001

Randall Updike sat silent in his wheelchair, his lap covered by a thick plaid blanket, his face warming in the Florida sun. His aged hearing could barely make out voices, especially in an outdoor setting such as this. But it was no matter. What he was about to witness with his own eyes was most important.

The wedding was extremely private, with only a few of the couple's closest friends and relatives in attendance. The view of the Gulf of Mexico was breathtaking as the waves washed against the beach some 20 feet below the Florida coastal site where the enclave was assembled.

The minister who presided over the ceremony was also elderly, but he had a loud enough voice to compete with the sounds of the churning waves below and the seagulls that sang and circled above. He closed his Bible and held it in front of him with both hands.

"Do you, Cal Jennings, take this woman, Eliza Updike, to be your lawfully wedded wife, and do you promise before these witnesses, to love her, to comfort her, honor and keep her, in sickness and in health, and forsaking all others, keep thee only unto her so long as you both shall live?"

"I do," Cal said loudly.

"And do you, Eliza Updike, take this man, Cal Jennings, to be your lawfully wedded husband?"

Eliza's beautiful white dress was flowing away from her body, caught in the slipstream of wind that coursed across the Updike's Florida estate. "I do."

As the young couple kissed, Barney Jennings looked to his left to see a smile emerging on old man Updike's face. Barney craned his neck a bit more and could see a similar expression on Harriet Updike, as she now preferred to be called, with her long dress flitting dramatically against the southern breeze, its delicate material curving around the white wooden chair in which she sat.

With only 20 guests in attendance, the normal receiving line was not necessary, so the entire gathering was soon huddled in a circle beneath the noontime sun to congratulate the new bride and groom. Barney's wife, Samantha, beamed with pride as Cal gently shook the shriveled, fragile hand of

Randall Updike, the man who was now firmly back in control of Midwest Federated Bank.

Harriet Updike walked up to Barney and touched him on the elbow, leading him away from the crowd. After they retreated to a safe distance, she pecked him on the cheek.

"What's-what's that for?" he asked, trying to squash an uncomfortable grimace on his face.

"For everything. You helped me get my life back."

Humbled, he shook his head. "My son loves your niece, Harriet. And that means he loves you, too. He-he would do anything to ensure your happiness."

The two richly dressed people stood facing each other, the breeze gently swirling around them, each privately thinking of the events that led up to this moment.

Harriet remembered the day she asked her niece to follow her husband like a private detective, an activity that ultimately led to damning documentation, with photos that would end their marriage—and Dick Cramer's career.

Barney thought of his conversation with Randall Updike, who would do anything, pay any amount, to protect his institution, and his daughter. He thought of the photo of Cramer, and the handoff he made to Cal, who created the perfect computer virus, bringing Midwest Federated Bank to a screeching halt. Then there was the employee-contrived walkout, which lasted three days. It was an event so perfect that even Mr. Updike and Mr. Jennings could not have conceived of such a plot.

The bank was in turmoil ever since. With federal regulators now in the final throes of their investigation, it wouldn't be long for Barney Jennings to officially become what he had always desired, and what Randall Updike had always promised his protégé: the CEO position at Midwest Federated Bank.

Randall Updike bumped along in his wheelchair across the uneven grass, coming closer to Barney and Harriet, ably pushed by a paid nurse who took care of the old man's every need. His blanket fluttered on top of his lap as the nurse positioned the chair away from the sun and out of the breeze. Squinting against the bright sky, he looked up at Barney Jennings, his confidant.

"You'll be happy to know the money was transferred," the old man said softly, his voice strained and weak from being outside too long.

Harriet bent down, getting closer to her father's face. "All fifty million?" she asked.

"Yes, my love, I pay all debts," he said in a painfully slow cadence. "Remember, the newlyweds get a portion now, and greater amounts in three and five years. They must remain married for it to be so." Randall Updike's breathing was becoming labored, a sign that he was overtaxed.

"Come," the nurse said from behind his wheelchair. "You must rest." She spun the chair around and pushed the old man up the wooden ramp of the grand home. Harriet patted her father on the arm as his chair rolled by.

"He doesn't have long," she said, watching as the nurse and her father ascended the shallow incline.

Barney turned toward Harriet, the lapels of his suit fluttering in the variable breeze. "And this will all be yours?"

She nodded. "The bank too," she said. She allowed herself a grin. "Of his two daughters, he liked me best." Harriet looked him straight in the eye, and despite their similar ages, she did it in a way that a mother might do when scolding a son. "And you, sir. Take care of my bank. You will find that I do not have the patience of my father."

She held his gaze for some time, and then sharply turned away, gingerly walking across the uneven landscape in high-heeled shoes, back toward the guests in the distance that huddled tightly around the newlyweds.

Barney watched her as she strode away, his thoughts turning to his new elite position and to his next obvious steps, his preoccupation of retirement along the Georgia coast becoming ever more distant in his calculating, over-stimulated mind.

The bumps in the Interstate highway thumped rhythmically underneath the vehicle as it moved quickly westward across the flatlands of southern Minnesota, racing toward the tabletop landscape of South Dakota. Even though the February winter had a firm grip, Wil felt it was superbly refreshing to have the car's window down just far enough to chill him into sobriety.

During the previous night, he had said his farewell to Lanny and Jill, who finally sold their house and were moving back to California. It was difficult to see them go, but he knew that Lanny believed the job opportunities were better in California than in the Midwest. He looked at his watch and figured they were headed to the airport by now, and that they would await the arrival of their belongings that would traverse cross-country over the next few days.

As for Wil, he didn't know what he'd do. For now, he was going to stay with his mother in Sioux Falls and probably sell his house in Edina. He had his eye on a sales job at a Sioux Falls network TV affiliate, but he wasn't looking forward to the cut in pay.

As the road thumped beneath him, he thought in amazement how quickly things had changed. He thought of the headlines that burned up the front pages of the Twin Cities' papers over the past months, all reporting the scandal that had taken place at Midwest Federated Bank.

He thought of Candy Luther, the woman who broke the story of Mr. Cramer's misdeeds on the same day that Operation Blue Christmas went into effect.

He thought of Trixie Tanner, and wondered if she had returned to Arkansas. He thought of the clown...

He thought of his friends—Lanny, Andy, Felicia—whose careers had gone sour at the height of the fiasco.

And then he thought of his own predicament. He hung on at the bank throughout the investigation and then left abruptly, feeling painfully hollow in an organization that had spun so completely out of control.

The methodical rhythm that came from the uneven highway beneath the car's floorboards was interrupted by the sharp shrill of Wil's cell phone, slicing through the droning wind that howled into the driver's side window. He glanced down to see who was calling, but he didn't recognize the number. He was in no mood for more reporters' questions, so he thought he'd let it ring. But something compelled him to raise his window and take the call.

"W-Wil, is that you?"

Wil couldn't believe his own ears. "Yes," Wil answered. "Barney? Is that you?"

"Yes-yes, Wil," Barney Jennings said. "Listen, we have some things to talk about."

Wil jerked his head back in disbelief. *Now what?* "We do, Barney?"

"I've got a great new job for you," he said. "A-a-a really big job...the one you should have had."

The border of South Dakota was quickly approaching, the mileage markers getting lower in number, the snow softly falling...

Wil pulled his car over to the shoulder and brought it to a stop. He lowered his driver's side window again, letting a blast of icy air sting his face. With the phone still pinned to his ear, he shut off the car's ignition and stared at the western horizon, all the while listening...and wondering.

Made in the USA
Monee, IL
08 June 2024

59473943R00246